The Lovers OF Amherst

Also by William Nicholson

The Trial of True Love
The Society of Others
The Secret Intensity of Everyday Life
All the Hopeful Lovers
The Golden Hour
Motherland
Reckless

BOOKS FOR CHILDREN

The Wind Singer
Slaves of the Mastery
Firesong
Seeker
Jango
Noman

WILLIAM NICHOLSON

The Lovers OF Amherst

Quercus

First published in Great Britain in 2015 by Quercus Editions Ltd

Quercus
55 Baker Street
7th Floor, South Block
London W1U 8EW

A CIP catalogue record for this book is available
from the British Library.

HB ISBN 978 1 84866 647 4
TPB ISBN 978 1 84866 648 1
EBOOK ISBN 978 1 84866 649 8

10 9 8 7 6 5 4 3 2 1

Printed and bound in Great Britain by Clays Ltd, St Ives plc

Typeset in Bembo by CC Book Production

This is my letter to the World
That never wrote to Me –
The simple News that Nature told –
With tender Majesty –

Her Message is committed
To Hands I cannot see –
For love of Her – Sweet – countrymen –
Judge tenderly – of Me

Emily Dickinson, 1862

1

The screen is black. The sound of a pen nib scratching on paper, the sound amplified, echoing in the dark room. A soft light flickers, revealing ink tracking over paper. Follow the forming letters to read:

I've none to tell me to but thee

The area of light expands. A small maplewood desk, on which the paper lies. A hand holding the pen.

My hand, my pen, my words. My gift of love, ungiven.

Lay down the pen and cross the room. The light in the room grows. There's a window on the far side. Outside it's daylight.

Now the window frames the view. A road, a hedge, a strip of land planted with trees and shrubs. A path runs between the trees to the neighbouring house, The Evergreens. A middle-aged man is coming down the path, his head a little bowed.

I know him well, I love him dearly. He is my brother.

Moving faster now, across the bedroom, out onto the

landing. To the right is a bright window, to the left, a flight of stairs. Down the stairs, the hem of a white dress brushing the banisters, to come to a stop in the hall. The door to the parlour is ajar.

Pause before the almost closed door. Through the crack a thin slice of the room is visible within: a fire burning in the grate, a wing chair by the fire, the middle-aged man settling himself down with a sigh into the chair.

I know that sigh. I know that he's unhappy. I know that he leaves his home and comes to my house because he finds no joy in his marriage. I am his refuge.

Open the door, and enter. He raises his bowed head. He has a heavy lined face, a sweep of thick hair above a high forehead, bushy whiskers. He smiles.

'Here I am again,' he says.

Sit down before him, not speaking, waiting for him to speak. After a little while he rises to his feet, paces up and down before the fire. He talks in fits and starts, as if to himself.

'I've been remembering Mattie, Mattie Gilbert, Sue's sister. You liked her, I know. She was the quiet one. She was fond of me, I think. I wrote her a letter, after Sue and I became engaged, but she never answered. Now I wake in the night and think, What if I'd married Mattie?'

He paces in silence for a few moments. Then he comes to a stop and stands before the fire, his eyes cast down.

'I had such great hopes. And what have I left? I have nothing.'

Reach out a hand and touch his arm.

'I call it very unkind of you, brother.'

He smiles at that.

2

'Am I the unkind one?'

'You think only of yourself. Remember, you're living for me too.'

'What am I to do?'

'There's joy to be had in the world,' I say. 'You're to find us joy.'

2

'You must have read Emily Dickinson,' says Alice, 'when you were at Cambridge.'

'Maybe one poem, once,' says Jack.

She can't get over how much the same he is: the same tousled haircut, the same gentle brown eyes. He's a teacher now, in his mid-twenties, as she is. How long since they last met? It must be almost three years.

'So Emily Dickinson had a brother,' she goes on. 'A brother who was trapped in an unhappy marriage. In late nineteenth-century Puritan New England, when trapped meant trapped.'

She's opening a bottle of wine as she talks, both of them frayed by their day's work, in need of a drink. Good of Jack to come in person, all things considered. This could have been done in a couple of texts. But perhaps he too is curious to see her again.

'The brother falls in love with the wife of a colleague. He's in his fifties, she's in her twenties. They have a passionate affair. And guess where they make love?'

So here they are in the kitchen of Alice's shared flat in Hackney talking about sex. Megan, her flatmate, has as usual left a pan soaking in the sink which she won't clean until she reuses it in the morning. This should not send Alice wild with rage, but does. Scrambled egg has to soak, says Megan. What do you want me to do, take a saucepan of cold water into my bedroom? Alice does want this, but is it reasonable? Is it neurotic?

'No motels in those days,' says Jack.

'They make love in Emily Dickinson's dining room.'

'In the dining room!'

'With Emily Dickinson listening outside the door.'

Jack looks suitably startled. This is always the line that sells the story. Not that she's told it to many, the enterprise is still fragile. And odd that she should be telling it to Jack of all people, given that it's a story of illicit passion. This after all was the first boy ever to desire her. He trembled when he took her in his arms. A good way to start a love life, new to each other, inexperienced, amazed.

'And that,' says Alice, 'is what I'm going to write my screenplay about.'

A film by Alice Dickinson, featuring Emily Dickinson, no relation. But the shared last name is where her love for the poems began. And after that, the dream. With a mother a journalist and a stepfather a screenwriter, she's grown up in a world of stories. Her own writing began in secret, but it was a secret she had no desire to keep. Her stepfather Alan read the few pages of a short story, and admitted to amazement and envy. Envy, the purest form of praise.

'You really are a writer,' he said.

He showed the pages to his producer. His producer asked Alice if she had any ideas for a screenplay.

'Adultery in Amherst,' Alice replied. 'Sex and poetry.'

No promises, but worth a first, and of course unpaid, draft.

'And that's why I have to go to Amherst, Massachusetts,' she tells Jack, 'to do the research where it all happened.'

It's so strange that Emily Dickinson should have brought Jack back into her life. Their last meeting, or rather their last parting, had been at Victoria station, a private moment buffeted by hurrying crowds. He was hurt and angry. She had no good reason for ending their relationship, or none that she could make him understand. Their parting, unresolved, had rendered him proud and distant. He had not looked back as he had walked away across the busy concourse.

Now all it takes is a general message on Facebook to all her friends, asking if anyone has a connection to Amherst, Massachusetts, and Jack turns out to be the one.

'His name's Nick Crocker,' he says, pulling out a scrap of paper, an email address, a phone number. 'He teaches at Amherst College. He was Mum's first boyfriend, a million years ago.'

'English or American?'

'English, married to an American. Mum says he may turn out to be useless. They've not been in touch for years.'

Alice taps the address and number into her phone.

'This is great, Jack.'

She gives him a glass of wine. He raises his glass to her.

'Here's to your screenplay.'

'I expect it'll all come to nothing. But a girl can dream.'

She likes the way he looks at her, as if he's not sure it's really her. In the time since they last met she's got a new job, a new look, a new haircut. Jack has gone on being Jack, but that's not so bad.

'Are you packing in the job?' he says.

'Christ, no! I'm just taking two weeks off. It's a great job.'

'I've no idea what it is you do.'

'I'm a copywriter,' she says. 'And don't say, "Oh, so you copy writers."'

'Is that what people say?'

'People like you, who disapprove of advertising.'

'You mean people who earn less than you.'

She relaxes after that. It comes as a surprise to find that she wants Jack to approve of her, but it also touches her. Like finding she's not left all her past behind after all.

'So what sort of copy do you write?' says Jack.

'You really want to know this?'

'Yes.'

It's not in his appearance, but it's there in his voice: he's more comfortable with himself than he used to be. He's become surer. He's not handsome, never has been, but he has a loveable face. At first you think he's too soft, too unformed, but then you start to see the self-awareness, in the wrinkling of his brow, the twitching of his lips. Alice feels his gaze on her, and realises she wants him to admire her.

'My biggest account,' she says, 'is a hair products company. Which means I'm marketing bottles of hair product to hair-dressers.'

'Hairdressers.'

'There's more to the psychology of hairdressers than you think.'

'They see themselves as artists?'

He offers it as a random shot, but it's right on the money.

'How did you know that?'

'If I was a hairdresser, that's how I'd be.'

The power of empathy. Good for Jack.

'They see themselves as sculptors with scissors,' she says. 'Henry Moores. Rodins.'

'And you're there to help them.'

'Now you are laughing at me.'

He shakes his head, smiling at her, saying nothing. Alice feels confused. Where did Jack get his new manner? It's like he's learned how not to speak, how to create the expectant silence that fills a room. She guesses it must be a teacher's trick.

'Is this what you do in the classroom?'

'What?'

'Just stare at the kids until they start making fools of themselves.'

'Not at all,' he says. 'I'm very encouraging.'

'Lucky them.'

'I think your screenplay idea sounds terrific.'

'You don't have to encourage me, Jack.'

Which is wildly false. Alice is in constant need of encouragement, for all Alan's kind words. This research trip, for which she is sacrificing two precious weeks of her annual leave, is driven solely by hopes and dreams. She doesn't yet know how to shape the story. In particular, she doesn't see a way to bring it to a satisfactory conclusion.

She wants to tell Jack all about it. She wants Jack to believe in her dream.

'The love affair was tremendously passionate,' she says. 'It's all on paper, they both kept journals, they wrote each other streams of love letters. And all the time it was going on there was Emily, the spinster, the recluse, writing these sexually charged poems.'

She pulls a book off the shelf and finds a poem to read to Jack.

'You must know this one.'

She reads, but because she knows the poem by heart, she's able to watch Jack at the same time.

> *Wild nights – wild nights!*
> *Were I with thee*
> *Wild nights should be*
> *Our luxury!*
>
> *Futile the winds*
> *To a heart in port –*
> *Done with the compass –*
> *Done with the chart!*
>
> *Rowing in Eden –*
> *Ah, the sea!*
> *Might I but moor tonight*
> *In thee!*

Jack gazes back at her in silence. The poem always has this effect. The look on people's faces that says: why isn't my life like that?

'Is Emily Dickinson supposed to have ever had sex?' says Jack.

'No one knows. Most likely not. But her brother sure as hell did.'

'In the dining room.'

They drink the wine sitting side by side on the sagging sofa, and she shows him pictures of the main characters in her story. Mabel Loomis Todd, twenty-four years old, wife of the newly appointed assistant professor of astronomy at Amherst College. She looks sly-faced, a little pop-eyed.

'She was tremendously attractive, apparently. She wrote in her journal, "I have simply felt as if I could attract any man to any amount."'

'When did all this happen?'

'The Todds came to Amherst in 1881. This is David, her husband.'

A neat little man with a close-trimmed beard and a pointed moustache.

'And this is Austin Dickinson, Emily's older brother.'

Austin is taller, with a heavy lined face, a sweep of thick hair above a high forehead, bushy whiskers down either cheek.

She reads him extracts from the letters and journals. Austin writes of '*the white heat which engulfs my being.*' Mabel writes, '*What else could have made heaven to us but each other?*'

'David didn't mind?'

'Apparently not.'

'So Mabel had sex with both of them.'

'Sometimes on the same day.'

'My God!'

'She was in love with Austin, but she went on being very good friends with David.'

'Very good friends who had sex.'

'It has been known, Jack.'

He's watching her, and she feels herself actually blushing.

And then, because her own reaction says more than she means, she takes up the book again and turns its pages, as if looking for some new extract.

How complicated it all is. There are no rules any more, no agreed limits. Friends become lovers, lovers drift back into friendship. We owe each other nothing, but we still hurt each other.

Her gaze falls on a photograph of Mabel Todd taken in 1885, at the height of her affair. The collar of her dress is decorated with flowers, painted by her own hand. She wears long gloves, wrinkled at the wrists.

This long-ago story, this adulterous affair that touched the life of a poet, means more to Alice than the sum of its parts. It has become for her a meditation on the nature of passion. This is how she hopes to incorporate the poems. The lovers act, the poet reflects. And behind Emily Dickinson stands herself, a latter-day Dickinson, staring into the mysteries of love.

Did I miss it? she asks herself. Did I open the package and somehow mislay the instruction manual? Somewhere there has to be this cache of essential information on how men and women manage their emotional transactions. External facts don't correspond with internal feelings. Why is it so hard to be intimate with men? It's not physical prudery. She has no objection to sleeping with a man when the occasion seems to require it. But the men of her own age, her friends from university, her colleagues, rarely arouse passion in her. Brotherly love has replaced sexual desire.

So what is it I want? A tall dark stranger? Maybe just once, even if it all ends badly. Someone who'll sweep me off my feet.

I want to be seduced.

That's not about to happen with Jack. And yet, to her surprise, she finds she remains possessive. She has no right to such a feeling, but it's there. She'd like to get him into smarter clothes. She'd like to change the way he does his hair.

'So tell me about you. Is there a girlfriend on the scene?'

'Not right now,' says Jack.

'Not easy, is it?'

'The disease of our time,' says Jack. 'Everything's possible, so nothing seems enough.'

He gives a rueful grin. The comfort of old lovers.

'Oh, Jack.'

She's remembering him sitting beside her on a bench looking out over the bleak expanse of Seaford beach. She's remembering their first kiss.

'As it happens,' says Jack, 'I have an insight of my own on this. You know I'm teaching in the East End?'

Alice has only a hazy notion of Jack's recent career. She associates teaching in the East End with missionary work, which gives her guilt cramps.

'Is it very rough?'

'No, not at all. It's a brand-new Sixth Form Academy in Stratford, right by the Olympic park. The idea is to get local kids into Oxbridge, which means selecting the most highly motivated, which turns out to be mostly kids from the Bangladeshi community. So I'm teaching seventeen-year-old girls wearing hijabs.'

He stops, and puts his head on one side. He's looking at her quizzically.

'I've never actually told anyone this.'

'Please don't say you're turned on by veiled women.'

'It's not a veil. It's a headscarf that covers the hair and frames the face and goes round the neck. Once you get used to it, it can be very attractive.'

'I think you mean sexy.'

'On the right girl, yes.'

'You really think that?'

'It's this whole thing about forbidden fruit, isn't it? Put something just out of reach and you start wanting it.'

'That is so depressing.'

But it's true. Isn't that exactly what went wrong with her and Jack? He was too much within reach. She tries to recall her feelings back then, through the intervening layers of guilt. When they parted she told Jack it was because she needed space, but there was something else too, something more like fear. Jack's need for her frightened her. It felt bottomless. He made her feel tired.

He's looking at her now, half smiling, and she gets the sudden disconcerting sensation that he's reading her thoughts.

'This love affair you're writing about,' he says. 'That's forbidden fruit, isn't it?'

'And the rest. They were breaking every rule in the book.'

'Not so easy for us.'

'Everything's possible, so nothing seems enough.'

Oh God, now I'm quoting Jack.

'You just said that, didn't you?'

'Even so,' he says, 'I don't want to go back to the old days. At least we can now actually talk to each other. Men and women, I mean. Men and women never used to tell each other the truth.'

'You think we do now?'

'We try.'

Here we are, trying. Everything we say has two meanings: one for the world and one for just us. He really has changed, but it's hard to say exactly how, because he looks so much the same.

But of course it's staring her in the face: he's no longer in love with her. She can no longer presume that he wants to please her.

'When I read Mabel's letters,' she says, 'I almost envy her. Her love was so passionate.'

'You think her passion was real?'

'Why wouldn't it be?'

Jack takes his phone out of his pocket.

'See this? This is an iPhone Five. There was so much demand for it I had to wait six days to get it. Over those six days I was sick with excitement, I wanted it so much. Then I got it, and I was in heaven. Undoing the box, taking it out, peeling off the protective film, touching it with my fingertips, arousing it to life – it was all a sort of ecstasy. Then by the next day it was just a phone again.'

Alice laughs.

'Jack has phone sex.'

'But you get the point. You can have passion or you can have gratification, but you can't have both.'

He's telling me this is how he's come to terms with the past. We were too available to each other, and so the passion died.

'So what are we supposed to do about it?' she says, answering both levels of their conversation.

'Don't ask me.' He gives his sweet rueful grin. 'I do diagnosis. I don't do cure.'

There is one way to go. She thinks of Mabel and David, good friends who had sex. But she can't do it. What would be the point? You can't reduce sex to comfort.

'You're not planning on running away with one of your sexy students?'

'No way,' says Jack. 'Strictly off limits. I'm just there to teach them Unit One, Aspects of Narrative.'

'Aspects of narrative? That's what I need. Maybe you should teach me.'

He looks at her, saying nothing, smiling. That damn teacher trick.

'What I mean,' she says, 'is I need to know how to tell a good story.'

'You're the copywriter.'

'You're the teacher.'

This is safer ground. Enough about real love. Stay with fiction.

'Well,' says Jack, 'I can tell you what I tell my students. All stories are defined by their endings. The ending is the story's destination, and the point after which the story can't continue.'

Alice thinks about that. Is it self-evident to the point of banality, or is it rather original? She's inclined to be struck by the fact that Jack has gone straight to the heart of her problem: she has no ending.

'So do you think,' she says, 'that you have to know the ending before you start?'

'Start what? A story without an ending isn't a story.'

'Isn't it?' says Alice humbly. 'I was rather hoping I could just write the screenplay and find the ending when I got there.'

'That's how they made *Casablanca*. But it's also how they made ten thousand really rubbish films.'

'Maybe I'll find an ending in Amherst. That's what research is for, after all.'

But she's more insecure on this point than she cares to admit. How much should she plan her screenplay, and how much should she rely on the inspiration of the moment and let it grow all by itself? She prefers the organic method, having already written some pages of strange, almost hallucinatory prose, without any clear notion where they might belong in any greater structure.

'Maybe I should show you my first draft when it's done. You can do your lit crit on it.'

Jack puts on a mock teacher voice.

'Structure, voice, language, setting, time sequence, character,' he says. 'I can do you the full service.'

The bottle of wine is finished. Alice hears herself say, 'Do you want to stay and have something to eat?'

'No,' says Jack. 'I have a pile of essays waiting to be marked back at my place.'

She only fully understands that she wants him to stay when he tells her he's going to go.

'It's good to see you again, Jack. It's been too long.'

He nods and smiles. They're still side by side on the old sofa, with the books open before them. Might as well try what Jack calls men and women telling each other the truth.

'So have you forgiven me?' she says.

Silence. Maybe that was a mistake. Maybe it's all so long in the past for him that he can barely remember what he felt. But when he speaks at last it's as if it all happened yesterday.

'Nothing to forgive,' he says.

'I think I made you very angry. I'm sorry, I really am.'

He closes his eyes, sitting there beside her, and says nothing. She can hear his slow breaths. She shouldn't be doing this, but she can't stop herself. She's reeling him in from the past.

'You never called,' she says. 'You hated me. I don't blame you.'

'I didn't hate you,' he says. 'I was heartbroken.'

So he's back. The soft sound of his voice tells her so. Now she starts to be fearful again. *If you break it, you own it.* Am I ready for that?

Footsteps on the stairs, a key in the lock. Megan to the rescue.

Alice's flatmate enters in a rush, shedding bags, coats, shoes, complaining of the rain, her lateness, the failure of her phone.

'Can you believe, the fucking battery's dead! I feel like I've died and been buried! Is there anything in that bottle? I need a drink. Actually, what I need most in the world is a pee.'

And she's gone into the bathroom.

Jack stands.

'When are you off on this trip?'

'Soon. October the fifth.'

'Let's get together when you're back. You can tell me all about it.'

'I'd like that,' she says.

She sees him down the stairs and out onto the street. They kiss goodbye, holding each other for a wordless moment in the doorway. Then she watches him lope away through the drizzle towards the tube station. Returning to her room she experiences a wave of sadness.

What's wrong with me? Maybe I'm like Emily Dickinson. Maybe I know too much, and will never fall in love.

3

Mabel Todd did not like Amherst at all. After the busy social life of Washington DC, where she had been something of a star, the little town in the valley of the Connecticut River seemed to be plunged in a perpetual twilight. There was the college, of course, but most of the faculty was made up of old men; David, her husband, was by far the youngest at twenty-six. The faculty wives dressed in dark colours, ate their suppers at six o'clock, and did not care for playing cards or dancing.

David too was disappointed. He had accepted the position at the college on the understanding that a wealthy benefactor was to endow a new observatory. President Seelye told him on arrival that this was no longer a likely prospect. Also it turned out that David was expected to teach three beginning divisions of mathematics, as well as astronomy.

'Then they must pay you more,' said Mabel.

'I'm afraid that's not possible,' said David.

'Oh, really, David! You should stand up for yourself.'

David was a little man, not given to standing up for himself, but the truth was this quite suited Mabel. He adored her and he indulged her, and most important of all, he gave her absolute freedom.

Sitting together by the light of a kerosene lamp in a room in the Amherst House on Pleasant Street, she allowed him to pet her. He fondled her and stroked her hair as if she were a favourite cat.

'I should have thought you would be bored with me by now,' she said.

'I'll never be bored with my beautiful puss,' said David. 'You know I can't stop looking at you.'

'That young Ned did some looking of his own.'

'Why wouldn't he? Amherst has never seen anyone like you.'

'You don't mind, do you? I think you rather like it.'

'I like everyone to look at you,' said David, taking her in his arms. 'Aren't you my blue sky? You know I kiss the floorboards where you've trod.'

'Wouldn't you rather kiss me?'

So he kissed her, and then became eager, and she had to push him gently away.

'It's not the right time of the month. Not for at least a week.'

'I'm counting the days.'

Mabel counted the days too. She limited their lovemaking strictly to the fourteen days in the month when she would not get pregnant, and this had been successful, but for one failed experiment. She had got the idea that she was only fertile at what she called 'the climax moment of my sensation'. This turned out not to be so. The result was a daughter, Millicent, now eighteen months old, left behind with Mabel's parents in Washington DC.

Mabel was not made by nature to be a mother. There had been a time when this had dismayed her. She was aware that motherhood was a woman's crowning achievement, but silently she believed that this did not apply to her. She was, she told David, too much of a child herself. Also they were new to Amherst, and living in lodgings. Once they were settled in a home of their own Millicent would join them.

In the meantime, unpromising though it appeared, Mabel intended to make her mark on Amherst. She was given to what she called 'presentiments'. She was filled with a presentiment that there was a great adventure about to unfold.

'I shall do things that will be heard of,' she told David. 'There's so much in me, waiting to come out.'

David believed her. Neither of them were quite clear what form the coming glory would take. Mabel had a talent for playing the piano, for singing, for painting, for theatricals.

While she waited for her adventure, there were lesser goals to achieve. Mabel's family background was modest, and she longed to rise in the world. She dearly wished for her own carriage. And she wished for her husband to be successful in his profession.

'You must discover a new moon of Mars, and this time it shall not be stolen from you.'

David had been at the telescope in the Washington Observatory when he had observed an inner moon of Mars that Professor Hall had mistaken for a tiny star. It was David who identified it as a moon, later named Phobos. But because Professor Hall had already measured it, the new moon was credited to him.

'No more moons for me,' said David. 'I shall make my name next year, with the Transit of Venus.'

David's teaching duties occupied him most of the day. Alone and restless, Mabel took to walking the lanes in the surrounding countryside, admiring the colours of the fall, and here and there plucking leaves to bring back to adorn their rented room.

One day, while ambling along the Leverett road, she paused beside the neighbouring stream to explore a copse of black alder. Hearing a carriage come to a stop behind her, she turned and saw a two-horse gig driven by a grave-faced older gentleman staring towards her. In the moment before he looked away, embarrassed to be discovered, she took in the frank admiration in his keen blue eyes. The gig then moved on up the road.

Mabel was accustomed to admiration in men's eyes, and thought little of the incident. However, a week or so later, at a gathering of faculty and their wives, she recognised the grave-faced gentleman again. He reminded her a little of her father, not so much in his appearance as in the impression he created. She thought she saw in him her father's patience and wisdom. From the posture of those round him, Mabel understood him to be a man of some distinction.

'Who is that?' she whispered to David.

'Why, that's the treasurer, Mr Dickinson. He's the one who hands out the money round here.'

'Would it help you if I were nice to him?'

'It certainly would.'

David introduced his wife to the grave-faced gentleman, who bowed and showed no sign that they had met before. Mabel was not so delicate.

'I think you like to ride about the countryside in your carriage, Mr Dickinson,' she said.

'The affairs of the college are wide-ranging,' he replied.

'I envy you. I have no affairs. My wanderings are without purpose. Unless you can call a love of nature a purpose.'

'I can indeed,' said Mr Dickinson.

'Oh, you've hit the right note there,' cried a professor's wife who had joined their group. 'Mr Dickinson is famous for his botanising.'

'I don't think of it as botanising,' said Mr Dickinson, his eyes still fixed on Mabel. 'I think of it as beautification. My ambition is to turn the town common from a swamp into a park. For that I need a great number of new young trees.'

'And what species of tree do you favour, Mr Dickinson?' said Mabel.

'Our own native American species,' he replied. 'Oak and maple, elm and laurel. Why look to foreign lands for beauty, when we can find it here at home?'

Mabel smiled prettily, accepting this as an elegant compliment.

'I like your treasurer,' she said to David later.

'He's a bit of a dry old stick,' said David. 'But in this town, his word is law. They say in Amherst you can't be born, married, buy a house, or die without a Dickinson in attendance.'

Mabel made it her business to find out more. There was no shortage of gossip. The word was that Austin Dickinson and his wife Sue did not get on, and lived virtually separate lives. Then there was the mysterious sister Emily, who lived as a recluse, and was known as the Myth.

'Why does she hide herself away?' asked Mabel, intrigued.

Some said she was mad. Others that her heart had been broken. Others still that it was all a pose, and typical of the Dickinsons, who thought themselves better than everyone else. The story was that Emily never left the house or received visitors, wore only white, and arranged her hair in the fashion of fifteen years ago, which was when she went into retirement.

All this touched a secret part of Mabel's heart. The more she learned about the Myth, the more interested she became. Here was a woman who lived not as society expected, but as she herself chose. Mabel too felt herself to be a rebel. Had she not named her daughter after the famous champion of women's rights, Millicent Fawcett? The Myth was said to write strange poems, unlike any other. Mabel longed to read them, and to reveal herself as the only one to understand their meaning. And surely the Myth, alone in her silent room, was unhappy, as Mabel was unhappy.

This was the deepest secret of all. To David, to all the world, she presented a cheerful front; going so far as to claim a particular talent for happiness. She would take trouble to find four-leaf clovers wherever she went, and press them in the pages of her journal.

'There, you see,' she would say. 'I have a right to be happy.'

My perpetual blue sky, David called her. *My sun and moon and stars.*

But when alone, Mabel told herself the truth. All was not well in her life. David adored her, but David was given to adoring young women. He had made her a full confession before their marriage. It had been a shock to learn that men could love more than one woman at once, and a further shock to learn that men had a taste for what she thought of as 'animal coupling', sex without love. But she was by nature a practical person, and she had learned fast. David had shared his sexual experience with her. It had pleased her to learn how to please him, and after a while she began to find pleasure in it herself. He was honest, and he was a skilled and devoted lover. This was much. But it wasn't enough.

Her father had taught her to love poetry, and was himself a poet, though only in an amateur way. Through him and with him she had found a spiritual home in the works of the great poets, from Shakespeare to Walt Whitman. On long rambles in the countryside her father had confided in her, telling her of the higher realm in which men and women found their lasting reward. Mabel was sensitive enough to understand that her father was a disappointed man. By profession he was a clerk at the Nautical Almanac Office in Washington DC. His job was to prepare the tables of moon, star and planet culminations, and to proofread the American Ephemeris and Nautical Almanac. He did his work dutifully, but he felt himself to be so much more than a clerk. He was not a vain man: he was proud. Mabel drank in his pride in her childhood, and swore to herself that she would not be crushed, as her father had been crushed, by the demands of a family. She would not be caught in the little cage prepared for her by the little world.

Somewhere, she knew, there was a finer love than David's waiting for her. There was a life waiting to be lived that was all-embracing in its intensity, that would satisfy all of her, body, mind and soul. Somewhere there was a secret garden behind a locked door, if only she could find the key.

'I would like to meet this Miss Emily Dickinson,' she told David. 'I feel we could become friends.'

'She sees no one,' said David. 'That's why she's such a mystery.'

'Why would she want to see people like the Conkeys and the Cutlers? She knew them once and found them to be without vitality, and chose to keep her own company. I have, I hope, some vitality left in me.'

The Todds were invited to The Evergreens, the home of Mr and Mrs Austin Dickinson, but not to the Homestead, the house next door, where Emily lived with her sister Lavinia. For now, The Evergreens sufficed. It was a handsome house, built in the style of an Italian villa, designed by the same architect as Mr Hills' house on nearby Triangle Street. Mrs Austin Dickinson maintained it in style, giving evening tea parties almost every week. She was enchanted by Mabel.

'You must call me Sue. You're going to be such a favourite here, I can promise. Everyone's talking about you. I do hope you won't find us too dull.'

'And I hope you won't find me too shallow,' said Mabel, settling down at the piano. 'I'm very young and ignorant.'

She then proceeded to play, and the company went into raptures. Most enraptured of all was the Dickinsons' son Ned, a sophomore at Amherst College. He declared himself to be Mrs Todd's admirer, and offered himself as an escort whenever David was unavailable. His mother smiled on the association. It could do her callow young son nothing but good to come under the influence of a sophisticated married woman.

Sue was sharp-tongued, and funny, and in her company Mabel began for the first time to think that she might find life in Amherst bearable. Sue's husband was more of a puzzle.

Austin Dickinson took very little part in his wife's gatherings, which he called 'Sue's sprees'. He was in his office in town, or visiting his sisters in the house next door, and only appeared at parties to look grave, and pay his respects to the guests, and take himself off again. Each time, when Mabel was present, she believed that his eyes turned in her direction, and lingered there.

Then one day he actually deigned to address her.

'I recall that you claim a love of nature, Mrs Todd.'

'I do indeed,' said Mabel. 'It's a sad day for me that doesn't include time spent under an open sky.'

'Ah, an open sky. Sadly, my concerns lock me too much in rooms. I must catch my glimpses of the sky through closed windows.'

'You're not a prisoner, Mr Dickinson,' said Mabel, greatly daring. 'You can leave your rooms any time you wish.'

'Am I not a prisoner?' he replied. 'There are times when it seems to me I am.'

As he spoke, the gaze he fixed on her told her that he admired her. This gave her courage.

'You should join in our little entertainments more,' she told him. 'It would lift your spirits.'

'To what purpose?' he replied. 'Am I to be taunted with joys I cannot taste?'

Mabel was astonished. It was as if he had drawn back a curtain and revealed to her the truth of his heart.

'Forgive me, Mrs Todd,' he said. 'I'm poor company for youth and beauty.'

Sue now came to Mabel's side, and was loud with mock astonishment.

'What, Austin still here! What have you done to him, Mabel? Have you nailed his boots to the floor?'

'I'm telling him he should be more sociable,' said Mabel.

'More is a relative term,' said Austin. 'Given that I have indeed spent *more* time among you than is my usual habit, I will now return to my desk.'

He gave a small formal bow, and left.

'I frightened him away, didn't I?' said Sue, taking Mabel's arm. 'What am I to do with him? He's such a long-face. Why must he always go about in a gloom?'

'I suppose he has business on his mind a great deal.'

'Business! A man can say no, can't he? Is he the only man in Amherst can do anything? No, the truth is he's become comfortable with this melancholy. I think he believes it makes him appear distinguished. Well, I can't be doing with it. A man should show some spirit once in a while.'

One day in the July after the Todds had come to Amherst, Sue Dickinson invited Mabel and David to join a group of family and friends on a picnic. The destination was Shutesbury, a good eight miles away, and they would go in two carriages. To Mabel's secret gratification, Austin turned out to be one of the party. Ned Dickinson escorted the carriages on horseback, along with two friends, William Clark and Brad Hitchcock. Ned's siblings, fifteen-year-old Mattie and eight-year-old Gib, rode in the carriage with their mother.

Sue had already chosen the site for the picnic, on a well-grazed hillside meadow that commanded a famous view. Here they laid out rugs and spread themselves round the wicker hamper and pointed out to each other the hills in the distance, disagreeing over which was Mount Tom and which was Mount Toby.

Austin stood about for a while, looking as if he meant to take himself off somewhere on his own. But then quite suddenly he sat himself down, legs crossed, on the far side of the hamper from Mabel and David Todd.

'Mr Dickinson,' Mabel said, smiling at him from beneath the brim of her wide straw hat, 'you don't have the air of a man who's accustomed to sitting on the ground.'

'I'm afraid you're right,' Austin said. 'I much prefer to stand. But if I were to stand, how would I talk to you?'

'You would talk down, of course, as is proper. And I would look up to you, in awe and admiration.'

'Not awe, I hope.'

'But you don't object to the admiration?'

'I'm grateful for any attention you're kind enough to bestow on me, Mrs Todd.'

Mabel dimpled prettily.

'Then I shall dare to ask you to do me a favour,' she said. 'I would like to be introduced to your sister, the poetess.'

Austin looked grave.

'Emily does not receive visitors,' he said.

'She would receive me,' said Mabel, 'if she knew me.'

She trembled a little as she spoke, all too aware of her presumption. But how else was he to know that she was not like the others?

Austin gazed at her in silence, clearly taken aback. Mabel caught Sue's eyes on her, her curiosity finally aroused. She retreated into light chatter.

'What nonsense I'm talking,' she said. 'Ned, give me some of that lemonade. Is someone going to cut up the bread, or are we to tear it, like lions? Except I suppose lions don't care for bread. Animals don't go in for baking, or cooking of any kind, don't you envy them that? How much simpler our lives would be if we ate everything raw.'

'I have some eggs here,' said Sue, 'but I'm afraid we like them hard-boiled.'

Later, restless, Mabel began to stroll up and down the meadow. Shortly she found Austin by her side.

'You like to walk, Mrs Todd.'

'I walk a great deal. Having no carriage of my own.'

'I would always choose to walk, if I had the time.'

'Surely a carriage is more comfortable?'

'Yes, perhaps,' he said. 'But the noise of the carriage wheels and the horses' hooves is all about you. I like to be able to hear the sounds of the countryside.'

'So do I,' said Mabel warmly. 'I listen out for the birdsong every morning.'

'And the song of the crickets in the evening.'

Mabel too loved the sound of crickets, though she was unable to say why. There was no music to it, but she had always found it soothing.

'I thought I was the only one who liked to hear the crickets,' she said.

'There is at least one other in the world.'

They stood in silence, listening. They heard Sue's sharp tones chiding the other picnickers on the rugs, and the whistle of a train steaming towards Belchertown. They heard the wind in the trees. And finally they heard the sound that formed so constant a backdrop to the day that the ear forgot to distinguish it: the bleating song of the crickets. It throbbed about them like the pulse of the land.

'What do you think they're saying?' said Austin.

'They're saying, "I want to live, I want to live."'

'Yes,' said Austin, nodding his head. 'I believe you're right.'

They began to walk again.

'If I had my way I would introduce you to my sister Emily,' he said. 'But I know she'd run away and hide.'

'Why does she hide?'

'She feels things more intensely than you and I. She thrives on solitude.'

'I admire her for that.'

'I would have thought your liking was for company.'

'I admit I like to be among friends,' said Mabel. 'When I feel something, I like to share it. But too much bustle and shout, no.'

'So how big is the company to be, to suit you best?'

'Just one other,' said Mabel, 'if that one feels as I feel.'

They walked on for a few moments.

'You speak of one who feels as you feel,' Austin said at last. 'That's a rare blessing, I think. There are many who are bound together in the eyes of the law, but are strangers to each other.'

'So I have heard,' said Mabel.

'Such a person, living such a life, might prefer solitude. But that choice is not given him.'

'What then does he do?'

'He does his duty. He lives as he has been taught to live.'

'Without joy?' Her voice low. 'Without love?'

'Yes,' he said.

'How can he bear it?'

'So long as he has no hope, his life can go on as it has these last thirty years. But give him just the smallest glimpse of how it might be – of another way of being – of a sympathy he's never known – how can he bear that?'

He fell silent, avoiding her gaze. Mabel felt a rush of tenderness for him, for the clumsiness of his confession, for the gift he made her of his unhappiness.

'I've been given so much of the good things in life,' he said. 'I have no reason to expect more.'

'Austin!' his wife called from across the meadow. She was standing up, shaking out the rug. 'We want to go!'

They returned to the group. Ned scowled sulkily at Mabel.

'You're not to bore Mrs Todd,' said Sue to her husband. 'You're not to make her think Amherst is all long faces. We need her for our theatricals. You will join us, Mabel, won't you?'

'If you have a part for me,' said Mabel, at once making herself useful, clearing up the picnic. 'I could be the prompter, or help make the scenery. Ned, will you be the leading man? I'm sure you will.'

Austin Dickinson did not take part in the packing of the hamper. He stood to one side, in an attitude of one who has more important things to think about. But all the while he was watching Mrs Todd.

On the journey back Mabel was silent, deep in thought.

'I saw you having a good chinwag with the old man,' said David. 'I think you've become quite a favourite of his.'

'I like him,' said Mabel. 'He's not nearly as formidable as I thought at first.'

She said no more, hardly able to explain her feelings even to herself. It had begun as no more than the usual minor gratification to her vanity, this making yet another conquest. But today something had changed. It was as if his soul had cried out to her soul, saying: save me. She felt that she held his fate in her hands. The sensation of power was thrilling; but it was more than power, it was a glimpse of a greater purpose.

There's so much I could give him, she said to herself.

At once, as if in a flash of illumination, she saw how she had mistaken the cause of the restless dissatisfaction she felt with her life. It was not that she wanted more to be given her: she wanted more to give. She wanted to give all, to spend herself to the limits of her being. All she had been waiting for was a worthy recipient. She loved David, but his needs were simple. He barely skimmed the surface of the deep pool of love within her.

Great love demanded a great lover.

As the carriage rolled down Main Street and lurched into the drive of The Evergreens, Mabel said to David, 'I think I shall like Amherst after all.'

4

On the plane to Boston Alice watches an American TV series called *Girls*. Two girls share an apartment, a thin pretty one and a fat plain one. The thin pretty one has sex with her boyfriend to stop him breaking up with her. In mid-sex he says, 'Say you love me,' and she can't, so they break up after all.

This matches nothing at all in Alice's own life, but she does recognise the general air of brisk dissatisfaction. Loving has become an extension of shopping. You want something and you get it and it turns out not to satisfy you and you discard it.

She thinks back over her own limited experience of love affairs. After Jack there was a holiday romance with a Greek boy called Socrates, whose name and body had charmed her, but they had been entirely unable to communicate. Then there was Charlie, a graduate student she met at the film club, who had just emerged from a four-year relationship. That had been exciting in the beginning, but the excitement faded. And most recently there was Adam, her boss at work. His attentions had flattered her, but neither of them were fully serious. For a few weeks they played the game of hiding their affair from everyone in the office. Then he was promoted and moved to a different department, and they stopped seeing each other. This was true in both senses of the word: once no longer in the same office, in daily sight of each other, they slipped out of each other's lives. Later she discovered the others in the office had known of the affair all along.

You can have passion or you can have gratification, but you can't have both. Jack's theory of love. Is it true? Is reciprocated love by its very nature unexciting? If so, it's a bad lookout.

She remembers then, all in a rush, how he sat on the sofa beside her and said with such simplicity, such vulnerability, 'I was heartbroken.' Time has passed. They've both grown up a little. Why not try again?

Because I want an adventure. Love should be an adventure, shouldn't it? Mabel Todd travelled to Amherst and got herself an adventure.

It's raining in Boston. The rental car smells of air freshener, like a public convenience. She drives out of town on I90, wipers snapping, America a blur of red tail lights. The rain eases as she leaves the interstate to enter a land of toy houses. Each one sits neat and white and porched on its own plot, without fences, like children in a playground not playing with each other. A tidy lonely world, set among trees.

By the time she pulls into Amherst the American day has ended and it's midnight in her body and all she wants is to sleep. She's booked a room in the Amherst Inn, a Victorian bed-and-breakfast across the street from the Emily Dickinson Museum. She goes to bed almost at once, and wakes early, and pads about the shadowy kitchen making herself coffee, and waits for the town to rise. As dawn approaches she texts the number she has for Jack's mother's friend Nick Crocker. A little to her surprise he answers within minutes. There follows a brisk terse exchange of texts, and they agree to meet for breakfast at a coffee shop called Rao's.

The café is almost full, even at this early hour. Silent students sit with their coffees bent over MacBooks at plain wood tables. Alice stands just inside the doorway, looking round. There are two older men at a corner table, deep in conversation. The one facing her is small and bald and wears a comical handlebar moustache. Surely it can't be him? The other has his back to her.

She weaves her way between the tables towards them. The man with the moustache sees her coming, and taps his companion on the arm. The other man turns, and Alice recognises him at once. This is impossible, since she's never seen him before, but he must be the one, even though she's been expecting someone in his late fifties, and he looks barely forty. But so English, the best of English, full head of dark blond hair, wide brown eyes, disconcertingly handsome, face creased with irony.

He rises to his feet and gives her a friendly smile.

'You must be Alice.'

'Yes,' she says.

He's tall, slim, wearing a casual navy-blue suit with a black T-shirt. His eyes are fixed on her with a degree of focused attention that catches her unawares.

'My friend Luis,' he says. A nod towards the man with the moustache. 'A colleague.'

The little man has risen. He holds out his hand.

'Luis Silva,' he says.

'Alice,' says Nick, 'is a Dickinson.' This being Dickinson country.

'No relation,' says Alice.

'What can we get you? They pride themselves on their coffee here. They have their own roasting operation in Hadley, down the road.'

Alice has already drunk a pint of coffee in the small hours, in the kitchen of the Amherst Inn.

'I'll have a cappuccino,' she says. 'And something to eat, if that's OK.'

It's lunchtime for her body.

'How about a blueberry muffin?'

He goes to the counter to order and Alice sits at the table. Luis Silva sits down with her. There's a fat book lying there, between the coffee mugs. Silva gazes at her with mournful eyes.

'This your first time in Amherst?'

'Yes,' says Alice.

'Abominable place. Nick's lucky to be getting away.'

'Getting away?'

'His course hasn't been renewed.'

'Oh. I didn't know.'

'Don't feel sorry for him. He has a rich wife.' He leans across the table to add in a confidential undertone, 'Also, too much pussy.'

Alice isn't sure she's heard this correctly. Silva is glancing over his shoulder towards the counter, where a line has formed.

'If this fucked-up country had had halfway decent abortion access twenty years ago,' he says, 'we'd be able to get some service round here.'

'Right,' says Alice.

Her eyes fall on the book lying on the table. It's *Don Quixote*. The marker in the pages is close to the end. Silva sees her looking at the book and pushes it away from him.

'Not mine. Nick's.' Another glance back towards the counter. 'You want my advice? Don't.'

'Don't what?' says Alice.

'Don't fuck him.'

'Oh.' Then, as she realises what he's just said, 'I wasn't planning to.'

'He's a narcissist. With depressive tendencies.'

'Are you a shrink?'

'I teach Latin American literature. Maybe that does qualify me as a therapist. I should be charging more for my services.'

Nick rejoins them with Alice's coffee and muffin. Silva rises.

'Some of us poor wage slaves have a class to prepare.'

'Off you go, Luis,' says Nick. 'Shine the light of your soul upon them.'

Silva makes Alice a small old-fashioned bow, and goes on his way.

'Fine teacher,' says Nick.

He settles down facing Alice. He studies her as she drinks her coffee, his gaze lingering on her hands, her froth-stained lips, her eyes. She hasn't expected this level of interest, and doesn't know how to respond. When he smiles his whole face wrinkles. His smile says: I'm happy to be here with you.

'Your friend says your course hasn't been renewed,' says Alice.

He nods. 'I'm a visiting professor whose visit has now come to an end.'

'What was the course?'

'Paradise on Earth: the Changing Image of Arcadia in Literature and Art.' He gives a little roll of his eyes, as if to mock his own pretensions. 'Now referred to by Luis as Paradise Lost. Luis has never really got irony.'

She wants to say, Your friend also warned me not to fuck you. There seem to be no rules here. She's feeling dizzy.

'So what will you do now?' she says.

'Early retirement?' He speaks the words with his head on one side, as if trying them out for the first time. 'I'm fifty-five.'

'You don't look it.' Then, embarrassed, she adds quickly, 'I'm twenty-four.'

This is ridiculous.

'That looks about right,' he says.

Alice drinks the coffee she doesn't really want, staring at the book on the table without seeing it.

Nick says, 'So you know Laura Kinross?'

It takes Alice a moment to realise he means Jack's mother.

'Yes,' she says. 'I used to go out with her son.'

'How is she?'

'Fine, as far as I know.'

Jack's mother is settled in life, part of the unchanging background. It doesn't occur to Alice to ask herself how she is.

'She was my first love,' says Nick. 'The one that got away.'

'Everyone has to have one of those.' She has no idea what she's saying.

'Jet-lagged?'

'Very.'

She attacks her muffin.

'So you're doing something on Emily Dickinson?'

She gives him the short version of her project. Nick listens attentively.

'I've heard of the Mabel–Austin affair,' he says, 'but I know very little about it. I've met the people who live in what used to be the Todd house. And of course the Dickinson houses are open to the public now.'

'I'm going on the tour at eleven,' says Alice.

'We live just down the road from the Homestead,' says Nick. 'On Triangle Street. Emily's buried in the cemetery half a mile up our road.'

Then, sitting back, watching her sip her coffee, 'So where are you staying?'

'I'm at the Amherst Inn.'

'How long are you here?'

'Two weeks.'

She catches a passing scent of the aftershave he uses, but fails to identify it. Together with the fragrance comes a sense of his physical presence: comfortable, assured, interested in her, but not troubled by what she might think of him.

'Might you really retire?' she says.

'Why not? Become a gentleman of leisure. All the great achievements of civilisation – art, music, literature – have been created for the amusement of gentlemen of leisure. I would take it as a solemn duty.'

'A solemn duty to be amused?'

'Oh, you mustn't think amusement is trivial. It's the polar opposite of boredom. Boredom is the loss of interest, the loss of appetite, the loss of desire. When we become bored, we begin to die. When we're amused, we're alive.'

Alice is silenced.

'Forgive me,' he says. 'I see I'm being too serious for break-fast time. Tell me about yourself. What do you do when you're not researching screenplays?'

She tells him about her job, and her flat in Hackney. Her life sounds trivial in the telling.

'And there's a boyfriend?'

'Not right now.'

'What happened to Laura's son?'

'Jack. He's fine. We're still good friends. I don't know what happened. It just didn't work out, I suppose.'

'Who left who?'

'It was mutual.'

'Who cried?'

'No one cried. Does someone have to cry?' It might have been easier if Jack had cried. 'You can't just go on drifting along, can you?'

'It's all about timing,' Nick says. 'You can meet someone too early. And you can leave things too late.'

A student who's just entered the café stops by their table. She points one finger at Nick while with her other hand she brushes back a mane of blond hair.

'You douche-bag,' she says. 'Why do you never get back to me?'

Her voice is soft, almost pleading, in contrast to her words. Nick raises his arms in a silent eloquent shrug. The girl tosses her mane.

'Why do I even ask?' she says, and sweeps away.

Nick meets Alice's eyes with a rueful smile.

'You disapprove?'

'None of my business,' says Alice.

44

Before they part Nick says, 'You must come over and visit us before you leave.'

'Thank you,' says Alice. 'I'd like that.'

'My wife's away in Boston at present. But I expect her back any day.'

He draws her a map on a napkin to show where he lives: 35 Triangle Street.

There are five others on the tour of the Homestead. The guide is a brisk handsome woman in her thirties, with short blond hair and lightly tanned skin. She introduces herself as Debbie.

'We're standing in what was the kitchen, in Emily's day.'

The room is now part ticket booth, part shop, the walls covered with shelves of books and greetings cards, decorated mugs, wall hangings, maps of old Amherst. Evidently there's a thriving Emily Dickinson industry.

From the outside the house looks like the photographs from Emily's day. The hemlock hedge has been replanted. The square yellow front with its green-shuttered windows and its welcoming porch hasn't changed. Emily's conservatory has gone, but the surrounding trees still stand. A path still runs through the trees to The Evergreens, no more than fifty paces away, where Austin lived.

But inside, the illusion fails. Emily's ghost is long gone, driven away by information displays, white walls, the intrusive flood of daylight.

'We are now entering what was the dining room,' says Debbie, leading the group into a space panelled with enlarged photographs. Here is Emily in the only known picture of her, at the age of sixteen: not at all what she looked like later, her sister Lavinia is said to have said. Too soulful, too pretty. The real Emily was not and never had been pretty, never expected to be admired, which is one reason why Alice loves her.

> *They might not need me – yet they might –*
> *I'll let my heart be just in sight –*
> *A smile so small as mine might be*
> *Precisely their necessity –*

Alice realises that this must be the room in which Austin and Mabel conducted their love affair. How? Or to be brutally practical, on what? The floor? The dining room table?

'Do we know how this room was furnished?' she asks.

'Not exactly,' says the guide. 'It was called the dining room, so we assume there were a table and chairs. But it was also used as a supplementary sitting room in the winter, when the parlours were closed off. There was a black horsehair sofa that stood here, we think.'

Alice makes a mental note. Sex on a sofa. But she doesn't raise the matter aloud.

The group passes down the passage, across a hall, into the two parlours. There's nothing in these bright well-kept rooms that evokes the half-lit Victorian world. There's a box piano that's similar to the one believed to have stood where it stands. Somewhere in this blank space Mabel Todd played and sang, while Emily listened from beyond the door: but the exercise of the imagination proves futile.

'Surely these rooms would have been darker?'

'Yes, certainly,' says Debbie. 'The wallpaper would have been darker. There would have been heavier drapes on the windows.

But there wouldn't have been much more furniture than we see here.'

On up the stairs to the landing, where in a glass case, on a headless tailor's dummy, there hangs a copy of one of Emily's famous white dresses. The group gathers round it. Alice hangs back. She can only think how frightened Emily would have been, to be trapped in a glass box.

Some say she took to wearing white to announce herself as a bride, though the bride of who or what remains obscure. But this is no wedding dress. It's a practical everyday garment. What else was she to wear? Black? Unthinkable.

Mine – by the right of the white election!

And through the next door is her bedroom, the room in which she sat at her little maplewood desk, mostly at night, and wrote her poems. The room with the bureau drawer where the poems were found after her death, almost two thousand of them, so many more than anyone had guessed.

No Emily here either; and yet she was here once. This is the view she looked at, through the front window. Except it isn't. In her day the land across Main Street was owned by the Dickinsons, it was called the Dickinson Meadow, and hay was harvested there. Emily would have been able to see almost all the way down the meadow to the plot given by Austin to the Todds, where Mabel and David built the house they called The Dell. From the side window of this room Emily would have looked out and seen her brother hastening down the path from The Evergreens to his liaisons with Mabel in the dining room below. What did Emily think of that?

Not seeing, still we know
Not knowing, guess —
Not guessing, smile and hide
And half caress —

And quake and turn away,
Seraphic fear —
Is Eden's innuendo
'If you dare'?

The poetry makes Alice shiver. Whatever else she might have been, Emily was on the side of passion.

The tour makes no mention of Mabel Todd. When it's over and they're back in the book-lined shop, Alice raises the matter of the notorious love affair. Debbie pulls a face.

'We don't talk about Mabel Todd very much,' she says. 'She was something of a troublemaker.'

'She came here, didn't she?' says Alice. 'For her meetings with Austin?'

The guide realises Alice is well-informed.

'So it seems,' she says, and raises her fine eyebrows.

'And Emily stood guard outside the door.'

'It's a disputed area,' says Debbie. 'Have you read Lyndall Gordon's book?'

'Yes,' says Alice. 'She suggests Emily was an epileptic. I can't see it myself.'

'I can tell you're not signed up to Team Sue.' Sue is Austin's wife, the woman wronged by Mabel.

'I'm not sure I'm Team Mabel either,' says Alice.

She tells Debbie about her planned screenplay. The others from the tour have trickled away.

'We have to be grateful to Mabel,' says Debbie. 'Without her, the poems would never have been published. But you can't help feeling sorry for Sue. You know what really made her mad? She couldn't stand the way Mabel demanded the love of two men. It just seemed to her to be unfair, and selfish, and greedy. But I guess that's not how you're going to show her in your movie.'

'I don't know yet,' says Alice. It's gratifying the way Debbie takes it for granted that her work, still little more than a few ideas for scenes, will turn into an actual film. 'I'm here to do the research.'

'Where are you staying?'

'At the Amherst Inn, over the road.'

Her phone pings. It's a text from Nick Crocker.

New idea. Why don't you stay in our guest suite?

Alice feels herself going pink.

'There's a coincidence,' she says. 'I've just had the offer of a guest room in someone's house.'

'Which house?' says Debbie. 'I know just about every house in town.'

Alice shows Debbie the napkin with the map.

'That's the Hills' house!' says Debbie. 'You know Peggy?'

'No. Nick Crocker.'

Debbie stares at her.

'You know Nick? From England?'

'I don't really know him at all. He's more of a friend of a friend.'

'And he's inviting you to stay at his house?'

'Yes.'

Debbie bursts into laughter. Alice smiles and feels awkward. Clearly there's something here she needs to know.

'Sorry,' says Debbie. 'I shouldn't.' She arranges her face into a more sober expression. 'It's just that Nick Crocker is a kind of legend here in Amherst. I know a lot of women who'd die to be offered a room in his house.'

'But I thought . . .' Suddenly Alice feels hopelessly naive. 'I thought he was married.'

'So?' Debbie's face breaks into a grin once more. 'Don't get me wrong. I'm a happily married woman myself. It's just that Nick Crocker's . . . well, like I said, he's a kind of a legend.' Then suddenly she looks concerned. 'I'm not offending you, am I? I just thought, seeing you're OK with Mabel and all, I thought . . .'

She trails away. Alice hastens to reassure her.

'No, I'm not offended at all. I'm curious. I had no idea. What sort of legend is he?'

'You've met him, right?'

'Yes.'

'So he's gorgeous, right?'

'OK.'

'The legend is—' She stops, blushing. 'This isn't according to me, OK? I've never taken a shot myself. But from what I hear, he's supposed to be – I don't know what word to use – irresistible?'

This is riveting stuff.

'Like Casanova, you mean? He's a great seducer?'

'I don't know that he has to bother with too much seducing.

Women just go for him. I've seen it myself. Smart mature beautiful women turn to jelly in front of him. Didn't you?'

'No,' says Alice, not entirely truthfully.

'Then you're made of stronger stuff than most. And he's asked you to live in his house! There's no justice in the world.'

A middle-aged couple come in, early for the next tour.

'Don't pay any attention to me,' says Debbie, touching Alice's arm. 'This is a small town, with too many people with time on their hands. You English girls have too much class to fall for that baloney.'

She turns to the newcomers.

'Welcome to the Emily Dickinson Homestead.'

Alice leaves. She crosses the road to her rental car, parked beside the Amherst Inn, and sits in it for a moment, needing time to think. When Luis Silva said to her, 'Don't fuck him,' it had seemed an absurdity. But the more she's told that other women desire him, the more desirable he becomes in her eyes. This is shaming. She has no intention of being added to the list of his conquests. He may be irresistible to others: she has some pride. And anyway, he showed no interest of that sort in her when they met for breakfast.

Why not?

If he seduces every woman he meets, why not her? It's not that she wants it. He's twice her age, he's married, it's out of the question. She recalls the girl in the café, a typical characterless blonde, the kind middle-aged men are supposed to chase after. How immature must he be, how insecure, to seek reassurance in the arms of girls half his age?

The more she thinks about it, the less she respects him. There's also some anger there. What about his wife?

She sits in the car with her phone in her hand looking at his text. He barely knows her. Is this invitation premature? Or is it simply an act of hospitality to a friend of a friend?

She looks again at the map. His house is so close she might as well take a drive past it, look at it from the outside.

She starts up the car and swings it round to exit onto Main Street. The very next intersection takes her onto Triangle Street, along one side of the Dickinson property. Ahead on the right, in the spot marked on the map, on a rising eminence of lawn stands a grand wedding cake of a house, with pillars and porticoes, great projecting eaves, ornate balconies, and a glazed cupola on its top. She pulls the car to a stop and sits gazing at it in awe. It's more than a house, it's a mansion. No shortage of rooms for guests there.

A screen door at the rear of the house opens, and Nick Crocker comes out. Before she can drive away she realises he's seen her, and is waving to her. He's beckoning her to drive in.

This is embarrassing.

She turns the rental car into the short drive, and pulls up in front of a large stable block. Nick comes over.

'I was only taking a look,' she says, not getting out of the car.

Nick doesn't seem to mind.

'I called Peggy to check,' he says. 'She's fine with it. She should be home tomorrow, she says.'

Somehow this changes the situation. The invitation comes from husband and wife. And Nick is, or was, a teacher of literature, who seems to know something about Emily Dickinson. And the truth is Alice would be glad to save on expenses.

'Are you really sure I won't get in your way?' she says.

'What way is that?' He's smiling at her. 'I'm not going anywhere.'

So she smiles back at him and tries not to think that her view of him has changed, and that all at once he's become, oh God, irresistible.

5

The camera is focused on a pair of clasped hands, the fingers working over each other. Move up from the hands, to look out of the bedroom window onto Main Street below. A cluster of people are spilling through the gate to The Evergreens next door, onto the high path: Sue and Austin Dickinson, Mabel and David Todd. The faint sounds of farewells. The Todds depart, walking up the path, away from the Homestead.

Quickly. Look after her as she goes. Perhaps she'll turn and look back.

I've become interested in Mabel. Is she beautiful? I need her to be beautiful.

She does turn. She does look back. Yes, she is charming. This is as it should be.

'She sings quite beautifully,' says Vinnie as she serves out dinner. 'Everyone says so.'

Now it's night, and the walls of the dining room are in deep shadow. An oil lamp stands on the table, illuminating Vinnie's pinched features. She looks like a bird, but all her love is for cats. I need my sister, and I pity her.

'And she paints charmingly, and I don't know what else she does, but all Amherst is in love with her, as far as I can tell.'

She takes her own food, murmurs a brief silent prayer, and begins to eat.

I say, 'She's certainly very pretty.'

'Young Ned is in raptures about her. I think her little husband had better watch out. And you should see Austin! He's turned into quite the gallant. Sue calls it a miracle to rival the raising of Lazarus.'

'Does she indeed?'

And what does Sue make of the new belle of Amherst? Does it suit her purposes to have her husband brought back to life? Does it suit mine?

In the parlour, later. My brother, the aforementioned Lazarus, sits at the piano, striking occasional keys. He's no pianist. When he turns to meet my watching gaze, he's more animated than I've seen him in a long time.

I say, 'I believe you're in love.'

'Who has told you such a thing?' he exclaims. But he blushes with pure pleasure. No one more vain than a man in love.

'I hope you know what you're doing.'

'How could I?' he says. 'Such a thing has never happened to me before.'

Did he not love Sue, then, in the beginning? He made a great cry about it at the time, but then his passion ran into the sand. Sue Gilbert's charm proved to be built on stony ground. And ever since he's carried his passion inside him, like a secret fire.

'Oh, Emily,' he cries. 'If only I could tell you.'

'You can tell me.'

'You ask me if I know what I'm doing. I have no idea what I'm doing. I open the shutters, I find the sun shining, I go outside to be warmed. What else should I do?'

I move nearer to him. I speak with soft deliberation.

'Go further. Go closer.'

'Do you think I don't want to? But I'm a respectable married man.'

I touch his arm. I do not allow such timidity.

'Do you want to die without having lived?'

He strikes a loud chord on the piano. The jangle of sound echoes in the room. I like that.

'God help me, I'm fifty-four years old! Why would she pay any attention to an old man like me?'

'Do you want her to?'

He gives no answer. He must be made to speak, and so to own his own desires.

'Do you want her to, very much?'

He stares back as if hypnotised. Of course he wants it. Just as I too want it.

'Go further, Austin. For me.'

6

Austin Dickinson's handsome phaeton, drawn by his horses Tom and Dick, was a common sight in the lanes round Amherst. His solitary drives took him along the banks of the Connecticut River, or up into the Pelham Hills. He was understood to be 'botanising'. Like his sister Emily, who tended a garden in the narrow conservatory her father had built for her along one wall of the Homestead dining room, Austin was knowledgeable about plants, and found consolation for his lonely life in the turning of the seasons. Every fall the great beech and maple woods turned red, then gold, then winter stripped them bare; but every spring life returned. There was comfort here, in the face of a disappointed life; and of course in the face of death. Austin thought often of death.

The town cemetery in the corner between Pleasant and Triangle Streets was already full. Austin was planning to purchase, on behalf of the town, a wooded hillside on the approach to the Belchertown railroad, to be dedicated as a new and very different kind of cemetery. The graves would lie among trees.

Here the turning seasons would remind mourners that their loved ones, though departed from view, would live again. As for heaven, Austin both believed and did not believe. He had never been drawn to the hysterical religious revivals that excited the women of the town every ten years or so; though to placate his wife he had scrambled together a conversion of sorts, and made his confession of faith to the congregation of First Church. That was twenty-five years ago now.

'It's so like you to want to build a graveyard,' his wife Sue said to him. 'Why are we to be always thinking about death?'

'I wasn't aware that you thought much at all on the subject,' Austin replied.

'You think me shallow.' Sue was irritated by his ponderous manner of speech as much as by his words. 'Why should a sad thought be any deeper than a happy one? Really, Austin, must you be so dull? You could at least try to be better company.'

Later, when Austin came down to join his family for dinner, as he paused at the closed dining room door he heard a peal of laughter from within. It was his daughter Mattie. Then came the answering laughter of his son Ned, and of Sue.

Is this happiness? he asked himself. Is it my fault that I don't share it?

He formed his face into a smile and entered the room, prepared to be light-hearted. At once the laughter died. All eyes were on him, apprehensive.

'Don't let me spoil the fun,' he said.

But the gay moment was past. Conversation through dinner was desultory. And when at last he left them he heard the bright chatter break out again in his wake.

Alone in his study, he put Sue's question to himself: must I be so dull? Is there no joy in me? But even as he framed the words, he knew the answer. There was joy in him, and laughter, and love, it cried out for release, but it was locked in his heart, and he did not have the power to set it free. He needed a word, a smile, a touch from another: from one who desired his love.

All at once Austin was overcome by a wave of desolation. It swept over him, shutting out all light and warmth. At such times he hated Sue. He hated her for being a wife who was not a wife. She filled the house with life and colour, but when she lay with him in his bed, it was a dead woman he held in his arms.

He threw the bitter reproof back at her. Must you be so dull?

If I am dull, it's as a volcano is dull while it remains dormant. When the eruption comes the land will be consumed with fire for miles around.

Strictly speaking it was not appropriate for Austin Dickinson to spend so much time with Mrs Todd. She was a little too charming, a little too beautiful. But where was the harm in it? He invited her for drives in his phaeton, and she accepted. They shared a love of nature. Like him, she had no fear of what others call bad weather.

'I love to see the great black clouds roll over the land,' she told him. 'I love to be in the woods when the clouds burst, and I press myself close to some great trunk, begging its shelter, as the rain draws its curtains all round me.'

Every word she spoke found an echo in his secret heart. He realised, almost for the first time, as he listened to her, that he loved nature because it was uncontrolled. Before knowing

Mabel he would have spoken of the rhythm of the seasons, and the consolation he found in the sense of a vast design. Now she showed him nature's other face: the wild, the explosive, the dangerous, the intensely felt. At once he knew that this was what he craved. This grave and orderly gentleman was hungry for storms.

They called each other Mr Dickinson and Mrs Todd. There was nothing indiscreet in their country rambles; they never spoke a word to each other that could not have been shared with their absent spouses. And yet over that summer and fall of 1882 a bond formed between them that astonished them both.

'I truly believe,' Mabel said to David, 'that Mr Dickinson is one of the most remarkable men I've ever met. He has such a sensitivity, such a delicacy – I don't know how to express it. I find I admire him more and more every day.'

'He's a fine fellow,' said David. 'A little on the gloomy side, perhaps.'

'You wouldn't say that if you knew him as I do,' cried Mabel. 'He's as gay as a child when the mood takes him.'

'Aha!' said David, drawing her onto his lap. 'I see you're falling in love with our venerable treasurer.'

'Would you mind terribly if I was?'

He kissed her, and eagerly she kissed him back.

'Not if it makes my puss happy,' he said.

She curled the ends of his moustaches in her fingers, and tickled his lips.

'Of course I'll always love my lover, my husband, my David.'

One September late afternoon Austin and Mabel drove into the Pelham Hills, and stopped at a turn in the road that opened out onto a wide view to the west. Nearby there stood a little timber-clad house painted a russet red. Mount Holyoke rose up to the south, the range of lower hills to the north; and before them, so framed, the wooded land fell away to Amherst and Plaineville and Hadley, and to the bright curling ribbon of the Connecticut River.

They left the carriage and stood side by side at an old two-bar fence, at the very moment that the descending sun dropped below the hood of cloud and flooded the valley with rosy light. They gazed at the scene in wonder, in reverence, as if this sudden glory had been arranged for their exclusive benefit. The sun dropped rapidly, changing the colours of the land minute by minute. There was no wind, and no sound in all the world but for the whiffling of the horses behind them. They neither spoke nor met each other's eyes. Mabel rested her hand on the bar of the fence, as if to steady herself against this assault from the sky. After a moment Austin's hand also gripped the fence. The sun deepened and darkened to a dull crimson, and touched the rim of the distant hills. They both became aware at the same time of the murmur of the crickets all round them, a sound that only served to intensify the perfect stillness of the evening.

The sun slipped behind the hills, and the sky burned, and the light among the trees where they stood by the red house faded almost to night. Austin's hand moved, and touched Mabel's. She stayed still, seeming not to have noticed the contact, but not withdrawing. Austin's heart beat fast, but his gaze remained fixed on the dying glow in the west. In that single touch lay all his hopes and dreams. Feeling the warmth of her hand against his, the long dormant yearnings of his body awoke, and he almost fainted with the ache of it. But still he didn't speak.

Then the twilight was deepening and they must be on their way, or they were in danger of finding themselves benighted.

'Thank you for showing me that,' said Mabel, as they set off back down the hillside road. 'It felt like it was our own private sunset.'

'So it was,' said Austin. 'I don't believe anyone else in Massachusetts saw it but us.'

'I don't believe anyone else saw it as we did,' said Mabel quietly.

Mabel found herself in some considerable state of turmoil. Every day that passed drew her closer to this remarkable man, this pillar of the community, this embodiment of all that was respected in the town; and yet to her, increasingly someone dear, someone precious, someone fragile. She felt his nearness like a flame, a flame that trembled in the wind and could so easily be extinguished. She knew beyond doubt that he loved her. Not as David loved her, not as a pet, not as an ally in a world of envy; Austin loved her fiercely, dangerously. She felt it in him, and it thrilled her beyond measure. He shook when he was near her. He went pale, and blushed. He sought her out at every opportunity. It was in her power to wake this sleeping man, to bring this dead man back to life. How could she refuse?

So do I love him? she asked herself. He was more than twice her age, but this seemed to have no relevance. His soul is no older than my soul, she told herself. Souls have no age, and do not die.

Is it permitted to love him? Is my love not promised to my husband, and to no other man?

She had no answer to this, except the knowledge that matters were otherwise. She found no difficulty in loving both Austin and David. She wondered if perhaps there was something wrong with her, some gap in her moral make-up. Of course she knew that in the eyes of the world she was not allowed to love two men. But the world was a sad fool, she had known that for a long time. The law of the world kept most men and women trapped in lives of loneliness and desolation. How could God have willed that?

The following Sunday Austin told her he had obtained an invitation for her to call at the Homestead.

'My sisters have heard that you're a famous singer. They would be honoured if you would sing for them.'

'A famous singer!' said Mabel, laughing. 'I think not. So am I to sing for both your sisters?'

'Vinnie will be your hostess,' said Austin. 'Emily will listen from beyond the door.'

Mabel was more excited than she liked to admit. Only a very privileged few crossed the threshold of the Homestead. Emily was a recluse, and Vinnie, though happy to go about the town, was the fierce guardian of her sister's privacy. In begging his sisters to receive Mabel, Austin must have given them to understand that she was a special person in his life.

Austin arrived promptly at the Amherst House to escort Mabel the short distance down Main Street to the Homestead. Miss Vinnie opened the door herself, a small fluttery woman with sharp noticing eyes.

'Oh, Mrs Todd, you're too good to us. We've heard so much about you. All the town seems to be in love with you at once.

Come in, come in. Though to be loved by the residents of Amherst is no great compliment, I'm afraid. Did you ever see so many sour faces in all your life?'

Mabel entered the dark hall, and followed Vinnie into the almost equally dark parlour, where there stood a low box piano. Austin followed.

'I don't know that our instrument will be up to your usual standard, Mrs Todd. I'm no musician myself. Our father bought it for us when we were girls, but I'm afraid we neglect it sadly. And Austin of course has not a single musical note in his body.'

'That's enough now, Vinnie,' said Austin. 'I'm sure you have a cup of tea and a slice of cake for Mrs Todd.'

Mabel set herself down at the piano and unfolded the music she had brought with her. Vinnie fussed about her, offering compliments and disparagement in equal measure, and throwing quick glances of fascination at Mabel's hair and dress and hands.

'You really are quite a wonder to us poor rustics, Mrs Todd,' she said. 'So much style almost dazzles us. Austin is half blinded. But then he never did see very well in the first place. As for Sue, all I ever hear is Mrs Todd this, Mrs Todd that. I fancy you are the perfect woman.'

'Oh, very perfect,' said Mabel. 'So please not to come too near me, or you'll discover I'm mortal.'

Mabel looked about her as she prepared her music, and found the home of the Myth just as it should be. The furniture old–fashioned, the lamplight feeble, the shadows deep. In such a lair, untouched by the busy world, a magician would be free to cast her spells. No husband to serve, no society to please, and a dragon at the gates to repel intruders.

But the castle gates had opened. She had entered. And when she sang, Emily would be listening at the door.

Tea was brought in by the servant.

'Thank you, Maggie,' said Vinnie. 'I'll pour.'

And so the time came for the performance.

'Your sister won't be joining us?' said Mabel, pretending not to know how matters stood.

'No,' said Vinnie, 'Emily doesn't go into company.'

But as she spoke she threw a meaningful glance at the closed door to the hall. Mabel felt a shiver of excitement. Was the Myth there now, hearing all they said?

'I understand she writes poems,' said Mabel. 'I'd love to read some of them.'

'One or two have appeared in the Springfield *Republican*,' said Vinnie. 'But other than that, Emily's poems are for herself alone.'

'I find that hard to believe,' said Mabel, hoping Emily was listening. 'Those who write do so to be read, and to be understood.'

Vinnie went a little pink at this, and glanced again towards the door.

'My sister's poems are unlike other poems,' said Austin. 'They're more in the nature of thoughts spoken aloud, thoughts without pattern or coherence, as thoughts can be.'

'Austin is a fool, as you can tell,' said Vinnie. 'He knows nothing at all about Emily's poems.'

'I grant you there are flashes of great beauty,' said Austin.

'Flashes of great beauty!' said Vinnie with scorn. 'What do you know about great beauty? Come, Mrs Todd, sing to us if you will. Austin, if you have nothing sensible to say, pray be silent.'

'I have no intention of speaking while Mrs Todd sings.'

Mabel opened the lid of the little keyboard and stretched out her elegant fingers. She arranged the sheet music on the stand before her, where it caught the light from the oil lamp. She looked round and saw Austin's eyes fixed upon her. She turned back to the piano, touched the keys, and sent her music out across the long room to the closed door.

She sang 'Drink to Me Only with Thine Eyes', and then 'The Last Rose of Summer'. As she came to the end of the last line she found Austin's gaze still on her. He seemed not to have moved a muscle.

She sang:

'Oh, who would inhabit this bleak world alone,
This bleak world alone?'

She played out the last few notes, and then closed the lid. Vinnie and Austin clapped softly. From beyond the door Mabel thought she caught the sound of scuffling feet.

Vinnie came to her with her hands reaching out, her face shining. Mabel offered her hands to be clasped.

'What an angel you are,' said Vinnie.

The servant entered, carrying a little silver tray.

'From Miss Emily,' she said, presenting the tray to Mabel.

On the tray was a glass of sherry and a small sheet of paper. Mabel took the paper and held it to the light. It was a poem.

'For me?' she said.

'You are honoured,' said Vinnie.

Mabel read the poem in silence.

Elysium is as far as to
The very nearest Room
If in that Room a Friend await
Felicity or Doom –
What fortitude the Soul contains,
That it can so endure
The accent of a coming Foot –
The opening of a Door –

'Do you think she wrote it just now?' said Mabel, convinced that it must be so.

'It's possible,' said Vinnie.

Austin took the paper and read for himself.

'The usual profligacy with capitals,' he said.

'Oh, Mr Dickinson,' said Mabel reproachfully.

'No, no,' he said, 'I think it has some fine lines – "*If in that room a friend await*" – that is very well done – but why will she never end a verse? See the way she leaves off in mid-effusion?'

'It's my poem,' said Mabel. 'I consider it perfect.'

Better than perfect: the poem had at once struck Mabel as true. She wasn't yet sure what this meant, she needed time to reflect, but here, she knew, was one who felt the vibrations of unspoken feelings between people even more acutely than she did herself.

'I would so like to read more of her poems,' she said.

'She keeps them tucked away,' said Vinnie.

'Please tell her I admire this beyond anything.'

As Austin escorted Mabel back across town, he complimented her on her singing, and she thanked him for his kind words, exactly as if they were in a public drawing room where everything they said was heard by others.

Then Austin said, 'That line in the song you sang, the last line. It haunts me. "*Oh, who would inhabit this bleak world alone?*"'

'And yet,' said Mabel, 'you remained unmoved by my poem.'

Already it was hers, written for her.

'I didn't say that. But there's something wilful in my sister's way of writing, as if she wants to obscure her meaning, which grates on me.'

'Why would she want to obscure her meaning?'

'To appear grander and deeper than she is.'

'Mr Dickinson!'

'I'm sorry if I shock you,' said Austin, 'but she is my sister, and I know her too well, perhaps. Emily has a tendency to pose.'

'I won't listen to you,' said Mabel. 'I'll have no more of your brute masculine intellect.'

They walked a few steps in silence. Then Austin sighed.

'Don't abandon me, Mrs Todd,' he said. 'My intellect is no friend to me. Truly I am one who inhabits this bleak world alone.'

'That is your choice, Mr Dickinson,' Mabel replied.

At the door of her boarding house, taking his leave, Austin reminded her that she was expected the following evening at his daughter Mattie's whist party.

'May I fetch you at seven o'clock?'

'You may.'

He watched until she was safely in the house, then turned to retrace his steps.

Mabel showed David her poem. David was very struck by it.

'It's certainly odd enough, but it's got something. I'm damned if I know what it is.'

'Truth,' said Mabel. 'We live our lives among lies, so the truth seems odd to us.'

'But you and I, puss. We don't lie to each other.'

'No, David. We don't.'

As they were preparing to go to bed, he saw that she was in an unusually thoughtful mood.

'So is my puss going to tell me what's on her mind?'

'Oh, so many things,' she said. 'I've been thinking about my father. He's such a wonderful man, David. I wish you knew him better. There was a time when he was a friend of Thoreau, and Emerson. He's a truly wise man. I wish he was here now.'

'What would you ask him, if he was?'

'I'd ask him to tell me about love. I remember him telling me once how God has created us with the power to love, and how it's the best of us, and we must never be ashamed of it.'

'A wise man indeed.'

'But our religion tells us we must only love one person.'

David said nothing. Mabel, half undressed, turned to look at him. He beckoned her to come to him.

'My darling puss,' he said. 'I've already made my confession to you. I know that I, as a man, am capable of loving more than one woman. Why should not you, as a woman, be capable of loving more than one man?'

She let him caress her, gazing into his eyes.

'Do you know what you're saying?' she whispered.

'I think so.'

She kissed him.

'You're a darling,' she said, 'and I adore you.'

The next day it rained without ceasing. Austin Dickinson presented himself at the door of the Amherst House armed with a large umbrella. Beneath its shelter, necessarily close, they walked down the street towards his house, The Evergreens.

'Our last evening,' he said.

Mabel and David were due to leave for Washington the next day.

'Must you go?'

'David says we must,' said Mabel. 'They are to decide who is to lead the expedition to photograph the transit of Venus. He says he must be there to have a chance. You know this is his big opportunity.'

'The transit of Venus, yes.'

'He hopes to be sent to the Lick Observatory in California.'

'Will you go to California with him?'

'That is not yet decided.'

They walked on through the rain.

'I will miss you,' said Austin. 'I'm not sure you appreciate quite how much. Your company has meant a great deal to me over these past few months.'

'And to me,' said Mabel.

'But you're young, and admired wherever you go. Your life lies fair before you. For me the prospect is very different.'

'And yet here we are,' said Mabel, 'on the same street, walking towards the same house, under the same umbrella.'

'What do you mean to say?' His voice shaking.

'We have the same prospect before us, if we so wish.'

They were on the high path now, with the picket fence and hickory hedge of the Dickinson properties on their left.

'Mrs Todd,' he said, speaking very low, 'I have never met anyone in all my life who I feel understands me as I believe you do. Perhaps I delude myself. I speak as I feel. You have become the one person in whose company I feel the possibility of happiness.'

They had now reached the gate into The Evergreens. At this point, where they should stop and turn into the path to the front door, Mabel did not stop. She continued walking, and Austin walked on by her side. In that moment, by that action, Mabel knew she had given him the answer he longed for, and had made her own irrevocable commitment.

'Tell me if I'm wrong to believe what I believe,' he said.

'You're not wrong.'

'You believe it too?'

'I do.'

'My dear Mrs Todd,' he said, 'you may not realise it, but I am a drowning man, and you have just saved my life.'

'I've done nothing,' she said. 'There's a power here that is stronger than both of us.'

'There is,' he assented fervently.

'I don't know what name to give it,' said Mabel. 'It may be God's will, it may be nature taking its course. All I know is we have been prepared for this moment, you and I, and this is what was meant to be.'

'Amen,' said Austin.

'But at the same time I'm frightened.'

'Of course. We've crossed the Rubicon. There's no turning back now.'

He sounded like a different man, younger, filled with a joyous energy. As he spoke the words 'there's no turning back', they both turned back, towards the gate. For a brief moment, beneath the umbrella, he took her hand, and their eyes met.

'Am I not too old?' he said.

She shook her head, struck by the blaze of his happiness.

'Let's be the same age,' she said. 'Both born today.'

7

The West Cemetery, where Emily Dickinson is buried, is up at the farther end of Triangle Street, beside Jones Realtor and facing Triangle Family Dental. Iron railings bound the grassy gravestone-studded hill. Emily lies within an inner iron-railed compound, one of a line of four family headstones, between her sister and her father. The other stones give the date of death beneath the one word DIED. Emily's date of death, May 15 1886, is headed CALLED BACK.

The day that Alice visits the grave is chilly, damp, grey. There's no one else in the little cemetery. She takes some photographs. Earlier pilgrims have tied a red ribbon to the railings by Emily's headstone, and on the stone itself have placed a half-burned candle and a small glass vase holding a white flower. The grass within the railings is weed-filled.

She tries to imagine the day of Emily's burial. Austin was there, of course, leading the mourners, with Vinnie. The accounts of the time make no mention of Sue. But Mabel was present, discreetly at the back.

Emily was familiar with graveyards. In their former house on Pleasant Street, before the family moved back to the Homestead, her bedroom had overlooked what was then the main entrance to this same cemetery. In so many of her poems she imagined her own burial.

> *Ample make this Bed –*
> *Make this Bed with Awe –*
> *In it wait till Judgment break*
> *Excellent and fair.*

> *Be its Mattress straight –*
> *Be its Pillow round –*
> *Let no Sunrise' yellow noise*
> *Interrupt this Ground –*

Alice feels half ashamed of how intensely she responds to Emily's death poems. She senses the longing for escape in them, escape from the unmeetable demands of life, that she be successful and beautiful and loved. In this surely Mabel stands as Emily's opposite. She was one who sought out the yellow noise, and, bathed in its flattering glow, demanded and received attention.

My story, Alice tells herself, is about Mabel, who chose life in all its mess and hurt, not Emily, who withdrew into the sepulchre of her own room. And yet in every picture she forms of Mabel, Emily is near, the listener behind the closed door. She's near even now. The words on her gravestone come from Emily herself, from almost the last letter she ever wrote: *Little Cousins. Called back. Emily.*

She leaves the cemetery by the old entrance, which comes out into a parking lot, and walks up the road beside the Mobil filling station onto Pleasant Street. She's beginning to get her bearings in the town. Left onto Main, past The Evergreens and the Homestead, the very walk taken so many times by Mabel and Austin, and so to the unlikely mansion where she now has her lodgings.

Her guest suite awes her. She has a bedroom with a wide bed, and a television, a bathroom where toiletries have been supplied as in a hotel, and a further room furnished with a writing desk, two armchairs, and a second television. She wants to tell someone about it, and realises that someone is Jack. After all, he's responsible, indirectly, for her presence in Nick Crocker's house. So she takes a photograph on her phone of the suite's sitting room, with a glimpse through the open door of the bedroom, and sends it to Jack with the message: *Not exactly roughing it. My guest suite chez Crocker, thanks to you.*

She wonders for a moment what he's doing. It'll be late evening in England. Is he sitting at a kitchen table marking essays, dreaming of pretty girls in headscarves?

She hears a car pull up outside and goes to her window, which overlooks the entrance drive. Nick's wife Peggy is due back from Boston any time. Alice is curious to meet her. But it's Nick himself, returning home in an old red truck. An odd vehicle for him to drive, as if he's pretending to be a builder. She watches him get out of the cab and cross to the back door of the house. Then he looks up and sees her, and she retreats from the window.

She sits down to work at last, at the writing desk, with her laptop before her and her books by her side: *Complete Poems of*

Emily Dickinson, and *Austin and Mabel, the Love Letters*. She opens up the document in which she has begun to write the first experimental draft of her screenplay, and reads through the notes she's made so far. But she finds it hard to concentrate. All she wants to do is go to sleep.

After half an hour or so she gives up and goes down to the kitchen to make herself coffee. Nick hears her and comes in, spectacles on his nose, book in his hand.

'I can't seem to keep awake,' she says.

'Why not have a swim?' he says. 'That's what I do to wake myself up in the mornings.'

'You have a pool?'

Alice has seen nothing as vulgar as a swimming pool in this part of historic Amherst.

'It's hidden away in the stable block. Come, I'll show you.'

She follows him across the backyard to the stable block. From the outside it's a handsome white-painted twin-gabled building, with two large doors painted russet brown. Inside, through a small lobby, an inner door opens onto a long shadowy space. A dark glistening pool fills almost the entire area. It's lined in black marble, and lit by shafts of daylight falling through glazed panels in the roof.

'Are you shocked?' says Nick.

'Why would I be shocked?'

'Well, conspicuous consumption and all that.'

'I think it's beautiful.'

'All yours, if you feel like it. Heated to eighty degrees.'

'I haven't brought any swimming things,' Alice says. 'I never thought I might be going for a swim.'

'So what? Swim naked. There's no one to see you.'

He waves towards a cubicle to one side.

'Plenty of towels in there.'

He leaves her alone in the great space. The heat from the water warms the air. She walks slowly down the side of the pool towards the changing cubicle. At first she has no intention of swimming. She kneels down and dips a finger in the water. It's pleasantly warm. As she stands up again she feels a little dizzy, no doubt the effect of jet lag. She looks round the long dark space and sees that she's all alone. Why not?

She strips in the cubicle. There's a tall mirror there in which she sees her naked body reflected. She feels a delicious surge of wildness possess her. She stands for a moment looking at herself in the flattering half-light. She may not be a beauty but she has a good body. She examines herself, twisting this way and that, trying to catch a reflection of her behind. Not a bad bum, all things considered.

She runs out of the cubicle and dives straight into the water, a clumsy dive that half winds her and makes a great splash. Then she drives down to the shallow end with a powerful crawl, and back again. She loves being naked in the water, she feels like a wild animal. Her sleepiness has vanished. She resolves to do fifty lengths. Somewhere after twenty she runs out of energy and turns onto her back to paddle lazily up and down. She closes her eyes and lets herself drift in and out of the shafts of light.

She becomes aware of a tapping sound. She curls her body round and opens her eyes. Nick has come back in and is standing at the far end.

'Sorry,' he says. 'I need to know if you're in for dinner.'

Slowly she lets her body sink below the surface of the water.

'Can I be?'

'Yes, of course. See you later.'

He goes. Slowly, like a sleepwalker, she emerges from the pool. She finds a towel and dries herself and dresses.

So he saw me naked. So what? He's seen naked women before. Did he enter silently, secretly, so he could see me? No, he announced his coming. He knocked on the door. Did I hear his knock? All she remembers is the sensation of floating on her back in water, the luxury of it, and the sweet relief of letting go.

And if he did see me, did he admire? Did he desire?

The dinner they share turns out to have been cooked by Nick himself. This takes Alice by surprise. Somehow she assumed there'd be a servant in this grand house. But no, they're alone.

He's made a stir-fry. Noodles, sugar-snap peas, finely cut strips of rare beef.

'You like wine?'

'Yes, I like wine.'

'This is a Syrah from the Walla Walla Valley, Washington state.'

The food and wine are both sublime. Alice feels intensely aware of taste and smell and touch. They eat in the kitchen, facing each other across the narrow Formica-covered breakfast bar. Nick's eyes remain on her with gratifying attention.

'So no Peggy?' she says.

'Maybe tomorrow. What are your plans for tomorrow?'

'Look around town. Get a feel for the geography. And I have to make contact with the library at Yale. I want to see some of the original letters and diaries.'

'I thought the archive was in Harvard.'

'That's Emily's poems. All Mabel's papers are at Yale.'

'You've done your homework.'

'A little. There's so much more to do.'

'Well, if you need any help, just ask.'

'Where I really need help,' says Alice, 'is in working out how to tell the story. I mean, the biographical facts are all there. We know pretty much who did what and when. What we don't know is why.'

'And that matters?'

'Totally. If Mabel was just a social climber, and all she wanted from Austin was status and attention, then why should we care about her?'

'Do you have to care about someone to write their story?'

Alice thinks about that.

'Yes, I think so. If I don't care about my heroine, why should anyone else?'

'She could be fascinatingly bad. Like Becky Sharp in *Vanity Fair*.'

'Yes . . .' Alice considers this too. 'But Becky Sharp always knew she was looking after herself. Mabel wasn't like that. She really did fall in love.'

'Whatever that means.'

'You don't believe people can fall in love?'

'Oh, you don't need my views on the subject,' says Nick with a laugh. 'But you, I take it, do believe in love?'

'Yes,' says Alice. 'Of course I believe in love. Not to believe in love is second-rate cynicism. It's just silly. Everyone experiences love. Even you.'

She stares at him fiercely, daring him not to agree.

'Then why not believe in Mabel's love?'

'I do, I do,' says Alice. 'And I don't, I don't. I don't know. I'm in a muddle. Can I read you some of the things she writes?'

'By all means.'

Alice runs up to her rooms to fetch the book of letters. Returning down the long stairs she feels a little giddy and realises she must have drunk more red wine than she thought.

Why did I go for Nick like that?

In the kitchen, she reads aloud to him.

'Oh! beloved! Are not our lives inextricably interwoven? And is it not bliss unutterable?'

'This is June 1885, Mabel to Austin.'

'Ah! dear, we did not know that it was God who led us by that gate, that rainy night! What else could make heaven to us but each other? Oh! darling. I am proud of our love – it is so great and strong and pure, so satisfying and so holy!'

'Strong stuff,' says Nick.

'They go on like that for pages, both of them.'

'What's this gate that God led them by?'

'The gate to Austin's house. They were going to a party there, but they walked on past. They called it "going by the gate". Austin wrote in his diary that night: *Rubicon*. Don't you love that? They realised their love was shared by that one simple action – not turning in at a gate.'

'Yes, that is good. I like that.'

She can feel his interest growing. In her story? In her?

'But what I can't work out,' she says, 'is why they felt so strongly about each other. I can see it from his point of view. She was young and pretty, and she knew all about sex. I expect he thought Christmas had come. But what was in it for her?'

'Now who's the cynic?'

'You think it's natural for a twenty-four-year-old to fall for a man in his fifties?'

'Very natural,' he says, keeping a straight face.

It's Alice who cracks.

'Sorry,' she says, laughing. 'I shouldn't get at you. You're being so kind to me.'

'Oh, I see. You're getting at me. I wonder why.' He pretends not to know, and then to remember. 'The girl in Rao's?'

'You do have something of a reputation.'

'Do I?'

His eyes are on her and she doesn't want to meet them but she does. She's filled with this absurd conviction that he knows exactly what she's thinking, and what she's going to say next, and none of it makes any difference, because the end is ordained. What end?

'You're supposed to be the Amherst Casanova.'

'Who told you that?'

'Isn't it true, then?'

'Does it matter?' He seems entirely unperturbed. 'No one's writing a screenplay about me.'

'No, it doesn't matter,' Alice says, 'and it's none of my business anyway. I'm a guest in your house. Sorry. Sorry.'

'That's a lot of sorry.'

'Well, I am sorry. You seem to me to be a nice man.'

'Oh, no, Alice.' He shakes his head, speaks gravely. 'Whatever else I am, I'm not a nice man.'

'OK.' She feels patronised. 'No need to be so proud of it.'

'I'm not proud.'

'Yes, you are. You think you're cool but really you're—' She puts one hand over her mouth, appalled at her bad manners, and shakes her head from side to side. 'Nothing. Nothing. It's the wine. It's the jet lag. Don't listen to me.'

'But really I'm what?'

'Nothing. Sorry.'

'A pathetic old lecher trying to reclaim his youth?'

'No, no.'

She groans and shakes her head. And the truth is, this is not how she sees him at all. So why is she going for him?

'Don't pay any attention to me. What do I know about anything?'

Then he does something that changes everything. Without preamble, and from memory, he recites an Emily Dickinson poem.

I shall know why — when time is over —
And I have ceased to wonder why —
Christ will explain each separate anguish
In the fair schoolroom of the sky —

He will tell me what Peter promised —
And I — for wonder at his woe —
I shall forget the drop of anguish
That scalds me now — that scalds me now!

A silence follows. He refills their wine glasses. Alice feels overwhelmed by a confusion of feelings.

'What was that for?'

'Do I have to tell you?'

'No.'

Emily Dickinson has said it, on his behalf. He's telling her that he too knows what it is to suffer pain, even if he doesn't understand the reason for the pain. And if he knows pain, he must know love. Or is that just sentimentality?

'We know so little of each other, don't we?' His brown eyes on her, smiling. 'Not just because we've only just met. It's the way we live our lives. We all live our lives in hiding.'

'Oh, Nick.'

'I'm sorry. I'm getting too serious, I know.'

She wants to say to him, Don't be too wise, don't be too understanding. Don't make me love you. It would be too ridiculous if that were to happen. It would be too commonplace.

She says, 'I think I should go to bed.'

'Off you go, then.'

'What about all this?'

She gestures round the cluttered kitchen table, the cluttered kitchen sink.

'The staff will see to it.'

She gets up, forces herself to act normally.

'You know what your screenplay is going to be about, don't you?' he says.

'What?'

'It's about two lonely people who start loving each other for the wrong reasons, the way we all do. But then a miracle happens. Their love turns into the real thing.'

'Is that what it's about?'

'It could be.'

'Is that what you think happened with Mabel and Austin?'

'It could happen in your film. You could write it that way.'

So that's Nick: he doesn't believe in love, but he wants to believe. He wants it to come true in a story.

'One of these days,' he says, 'I could take you to see their graves, if you like. They're not so easy to find, if you don't know where to look.'

'I'd like that,' she says.

She heads for the stairs.

'Are you as helpful as this to everyone?' she says, pausing, turning back.

What she wants to say is, Do you make every woman you meet feel you understand her? Is this why they fall for you?

'Everyone's different,' he says.

She goes on up to her room.

As she prepares for bed she hears him down in the kitchen, clattering about, doing the washing up.

The next morning he takes her to see the graves.

'Why do you drive a truck?' she says, climbing up beside him in the cab of the old Dodge Ram.

'It has its uses,' says Nick.

They head into town, and turn onto North Pleasant Street. It's still early, and the bars and restaurants on either side are quiet.

'You just know,' says Nick, 'when you go down a street called Pleasant Street, that something bad is going to happen. And sure enough, this is the way to the cemetery. You come down here on your last journey.'

He points out the Mobil filling station on their right.

'That's where the Dickinsons lived before they moved back to the Homestead.'

'You really are quite the tour guide,' says Alice.

'Down Pleasant Street to the grave,' says Nick. 'Only the best tours with me.'

A few blocks on and he turns onto Strong Street. They pass a collection of buildings that look like a light engineering factory but turn out to be an elementary school. The road winds on up the hill into the trees. A few hundred yards further and an opening in the trees to the left leads to a leaf-strewn track, marked by a modest sign: *Wildwood Cemetery*. Nick drives the truck down the unmade track, bumping between mature trees. The leaves clinging to the branches above are rust brown, the leaves on the ground yellow and copper. On either side of the track, widely spaced between the trees, stand headstones marking leaf-covered graves.

'This is Austin's cemetery,' says Nick. 'He picked out the site and got the town to purchase it.'

The cemetery goes on out of sight. Alice realises she could never have found the graves unguided.

'Lucky for me you're so well-informed,' she says.

'It used to feature in my course. I had a theory that Austin was working out an Arcadian myth with all his tree planting in Amherst.'

'And as well as that, you like Emily's poems.'

'Like isn't quite the word. But, yes.'

They're following the track round the hillside. He pulls up and cuts the engine.

'You see that boulder there? That's Austin's marker.'

They get out, crunch over the leaves to the boulder. One face has been cut flat, and onto it a metal plaque is screwed.

In memory of William Austin Dickinson,
April 1829–August 1895.

Self-forgetting in service for his town and college,
resolute in his convictions, at one with nature,
he believed in God and hoped for immortality.

'Not exactly a ringing tribute,' says Alice. 'You can tell they weren't sure he'd make it into heaven.'

'Actually the selectmen wrote it into the Town Meeting records.'

He moves across to some flat stones in the ground.

'This is where he's buried. And this is Sue beside him.'

'Where she can keep an eye on him.'

Nick walks on a little way up the track, beckoning Alice to follow.

'And here's Mabel and David.'

Two black slate headstones stand side by side, halfway down the tree-studded slope. The slate is as fresh and clean as the day it was cut.

In loving memory of Mabel Loomis Todd,
died 16th February 1932.

In loving memory of David Peck Todd,
died 1st June 1939.

On Mabel's headstone there's a verse by Emily Dickinson:

> *That such have died enable us*
> *The tranquiller to die —*
> *That such have lived, certificate*
> *For Immortality.*

Alice gazes on the graves, and at the hillside beyond. It's a beautiful cemetery. She moves a few steps back to take photographs of the tranquil setting.

'It almost makes me want to be dead too,' she says.

'That was the great temptation for the Victorians,' says Nick. 'The seduction of the last resting place. But I don't think Emily bought it for one moment.'

'No,' says Alice. 'Nor do I.'

Nick quotes some lines.

> *I don't like Paradise —*
> *Because it's Sunday — all the time.*

'You really do know the poems.'

'Only some of them. We pick out the ones that flatter our own preconceptions. It's what we do with all the great writers, isn't it? We each make an Emily in our own image.'

'What's your Emily like?'

'Lonely. Passionate. Without illusions.'

'So now I know the image you have of yourself.'

'How about you?'

'Oh, no. I'm not going to give myself away like that.'

'I haven't given myself away,' says Nick. 'It's only an image.

A pretty standard romantic image at that. Not very original, and certainly not true. But these pictures of ourselves that we conjure up, these idealised selves, they're powerful nonetheless. We act them out, we try to live up to them. Isn't that what Mabel was doing? She had a picture of herself as a certain kind of lover, and she did her best to make her life conform to the picture. Or am I being unfair to her?'

He turns to Alice with this last gentle qualifier, as if to acknowledge that she has more rights to Mabel than he has. They're walking back down the track to the car.

'She was certainly looking for a great love,' says Alice. 'Before she ever met Austin, I mean.'

'And after she had married David.'

'That's the puzzle. Did she love David? He doesn't seem to have been enough for her.'

'You think if she loved Austin, she couldn't have loved David.'

'No,' says Alice. 'I'm not sure what I think. I suppose that's what I'm trying to work out.'

Nick sweeps one arm round the cemetery.

'All these dead people,' he says. 'If they could speak, what would they say to us? They'd say, "Love all you can, love everyone you can, as much as you can, as often as you can. You're going to be old and alone soon enough. And you're going to be dead for ever."'

He opens the truck door for her to get in.

'Quite a speech,' says Alice. 'In praise of promiscuity.'

'Oh, please.'

He shuts the door, goes round to the driver's side.

'As far as I can tell from our brief acquaintance,' he says, 'you're not a fool.' He starts the engine, makes a three-point turn, backing among the graves. 'Spare me the herd-think.'

Alice goes red, mortified. They drive back in silence onto the metalled road. Alice thinks of Nick's wife, still not returned from Boston, and feels the stirrings of anger.

'It may be herd-think, but this free love of yours leaves a lot of hurt people in its wake.'

'Getting hurt comes with the package,' says Nick. 'You can have a life of hurt, or a life of hurt with some love along the way.'

'Getting hurt isn't the same as hurting. There's no need to go round deliberately adding to the hurt.'

'By loving?'

'By indiscriminate loving, yes.'

'Look,' he says, exasperated, 'I don't quite know why we're having this argument, but it seems to me to be perfectly simple. If I love my mother, must I love my father less? If I love one friend, must I love another friend less? Love isn't a limited resource. It's not a cake that's going to run out. It's the very opposite. The more you love, the more love there is.'

'Does your wife agree with you on this?'

'There!' He slams the steering wheel with both hands. 'Herd-think! Is that all you've got to offer?'

'I'm not offering anything.' Alice is rattled by the aggression in his voice. 'I'm just trying to work out what I think.'

'Why ask me about my wife? Because you've swallowed the whole consumerist agenda. Love as possession, love as owner-ship, love as property. You want status and security, fine. Sign your contracts. Enforce them. Just don't call it love.'

Alice can't think of a rejoinder to this. For a few minutes they drive in silence. Then she thinks of what to say.

'So how come you're lonely?'

He gives a snort of laughter.

'Is that supposed to prove me wrong? Loneliness, the ultimate failure?'

'Isn't it?'

'If you want it to be.'

They're back at the house. He gets out of the truck, avoiding her gaze.

'I'm not making it up,' she says. 'You said it yourself.'

'What did I say?'

'That you're lonely.'

'Yes, I did, didn't I? So I guess that means you can disregard everything I say.'

He strides into the house, letting the screen door bang after him. Alice follows, feeling bad.

She continues the argument in her head as she returns to her guest suite.

Free love! That old dinosaur! That fairy story from the high self-deluded days of the sixties! Ask my mum about free love. She'll tell you it's free enough, but the baby that follows costs you all you've got. Not that she ever grudged a penny. I should know, I am that baby, and I'll love my darling mum to the day I die. Who does Nick have to love him that much?

She wants to be told she's right and Nick's wrong but there's no one to ask. Then she remembers that Nick was once the boyfriend of Jack's mother. She sends Jack a text.

Amherst haunted by the ghost of Emily Dickinson. Nick Crocker full of old hippy nostrums. Is he real or fake? Do ask your mum about him. Still no clearer how to tell my story.

She half expects an immediate reply, but none comes. Perhaps he's in class, with his phone switched off. But then she works out the time difference and it's late in England. Most likely he's gone to bed.

Later it strikes her she's shown Nick a poor return for his hospitality, and she feels a wave of remorse.

Did I really mock him for being lonely?

She pulls out her edition of the poems and flips the pages. She finds some suitable lines and copies them onto a sheet of paper. Then she climbs the stairs all the way up to Nick's many-windowed study in the cupola above the roofs. He's at his desk, tapping at his keyboard.

'Peace offering,' she says.

He looks round, sees her standing apologetically halfway up the top flight of stairs, reaching out her sheet of paper over the handrail. He takes the paper, reads the lines.

> *The Soul selects her own society –*
> *Then – shuts the Door –*

'What's this? Permission to be alone?'

'From me and Emily both.'

'You remember the last lines?'

He pulls out his own copy from a shelf by his desk, and finds the poem with an ease that speaks of familiarity. He reads aloud.

I've known her from an ample nation
Choose one —
Then close the valves of her attention —
Like stone.

'Right,' says Alice.

'So I'm allowed to choose one,' he says.

He replaces the book on the shelf.

'I'm sorry if I made you cross,' she says. 'Would you like me to find a room somewhere else?'

'Why?' he says. 'We've only just started.'

8

In the depths of winter, Mabel Todd started work on a short story. David came up behind her as she was hard at work, and bent over to kiss her neck. At the same time he read part of the page on which she was writing.

'What's my puss so busily doing? Writing a story?'

'A love story,' she said.

'Of course it is,' said David. 'What else would she write but a love story?'

'I thought I might send it to the *Atlantic Monthly*.'

'So who's the hero? A handsome young fellow with a moustache and a wicked smile?'

'It's not about you, darling. I couldn't write a story about you. It wouldn't be fit to print.'

'But the heroine is you?'

'There may be some similarities.'

'So I'm to read about my puss making love to another man, am I?'

He kissed her cheek.

'You really are the most singular man in the world, David. Is there no jealousy in you at all?'

By way of an answer David read aloud a line from her handwritten page.

'He was past the first flush of his youth—'

'There, you see,' he said. 'My rival is an old man.'
He read on.

'—a youth which had brought him much pain, a good deal of endurance, many longings, which were principally unsatisfied—'

Mabel covered the page with her hands.
'Stop it!'
'An old man, and he's not happy. But my puss will make him happy.'
'Go away.'
David kissed her again and left her. Mabel returned to her love story.

She had given her hero the name of Henry Arnold, and made him an unmarried doctor with a great love for the sea. His only consolation in his sad life was the beauty of nature.

He had no definite grief – nothing upon which he could place his finger, saying: 'Here; were this removed, I could rise to joyousness!' But life seemed to hold so many possibilities – of which he could only dream. It might mean a garden of satisfying delights if he could but find the entrance.

As it was, he felt himself stumbling about vainly, outside of everything. He saw the high wall; he knew there must be a gate, and occasionally the scent of rarest blooms was wafted over to him. How he longed to enter! How he longed for even one person with whom to speak of the dainty fancies which throbbed through his heart and brain!

Occasionally a rebellious feeling appeared; and he wondered why Providence had been so cruel as to give him wants which were always unsatisfied; questions always unanswered. But in general he was content. Only his clear blue eyes were infinitely sad in their expression, if any had cared to notice – wherefore, he could scarcely have said himself. He thought he had found all that was for him to find, and yet sometimes a wild gleam of possible joy to come throbbed within him.

The story went on to tell how, while walking on a deserted beach, Henry Arnold found two sets of footprints in the sand, the tracks left by a man and a woman. This gave him a sudden vision of the possibilities of true companionship.

He walked onward through the glory of the sunset light, thinking great thoughts which completely overwhelmed him. He could hardly tell what had come upon him; he knew only that suddenly had been born a determination not to settle down into a placid self-content, satisfied with the husk, but missing the sweet kernel of life. He would have it all; and he would never give up the search, if he found it only upon his deathbed.

The search led to the young woman who had made one of the two sets of footprints. Mabel gave her the name of Mildred.

In the clear depths of this young girl's mind he saw an appreciative sympathy, an understanding of himself and his queer fancies which it had never occurred to him that anyone could have. The joy of being understood was something which had never before come to him. He saw as in a flash that the mysteries of life would be no longer cold and bleak if two could investigate them together. There would be mysteries always, of course; but it was only for one all alone to feel the dreariness of these riddles. This young girl, sitting so calmly beside him, with soft eyes gazing far out to sea, was the one person, the only person he knew, who had ever responded to his subtle thoughts, or to whom indeed it had ever seemed possible to express them. A wonderful joy and tenderness overflowed him; she belonged to him by divine right . . .

Mabel called her story 'Footprints'. She was still writing it when it was time for David to leave for the Lick Observatory in California, to photograph the transit of Venus.

'Tell me you'll miss me,' he said to her.

'Of course I'll miss you. But will you miss me? Do the astronomers in California have pretty daughters?'

'They won't be as pretty as you.'

'Maybe not, but they'll be nearer.'

He took both her hands in his and looked into her eyes.

'I've never lied to you, have I, puss? Don't ask me to start now.'

'I shall just have to find my own company without you.'

'So you shall. And when I'm home again, you can tell me all about it.'

Mabel's principal source of company in her husband's absence was Mrs Austin Dickinson and her ever-sociable home. Sue kept a bed made up for Mabel at The Evergreens, for those evenings when the partying went on into the late hours. Austin seemed more withdrawn than ever. At whist games and at musical soirées, it was young Ned Dickinson who was always by Mrs Todd's side, his eyes shining. When the first real snow came, and the sleigh was harnessed to faithful Tom and Dick, it was Ned who took the reins, and Mabel was always invited to join in the merry sleigh rides.

There were plans for putting on a play, though no one could agree which one it was to be. There were evenings of poetry readings, and more private evenings in which Sue read out to Mabel the few poems sent her by Emily.

'What do you make of that?' she said, offering Mabel a hand-written poem. 'Am I really so very mysterious?'

> But Susan is a stranger yet –
> The Ones who cite her most
> Have never scaled her Haunted House
> Nor compromised her Ghost –
>
> To pity those who know her not
> Is helped by the regret
> That those who know her know her less
> The nearer her they get –

Mabel felt a twinge of jealousy.

'I suppose we're all mysterious,' she said. 'I mean, none of us can ever be fully known, as we know ourselves.'

'How disappointing! I'd been congratulating myself on being uniquely unknowable.'

'You're so clever, Sue, I'm sure no one could ever get to the bottom of you.' Mabel hastened to soothe Sue's ruffled feathers. 'But even so, I'm sure you have a secret longing, as I know I do, for there to be someone, somewhere, who truly knows us.'

'Wanting is all very well. But what if there isn't?' She tucked the poem back into the envelope in which she kept it, folding the paper and inserting it with brisk, neat gestures. 'Emily does have a gift, I grant you. Her poems have a certain brilliance. But there's a lack of finesse. A little too much panting and gasping.'

'She wrote me a poem,' said Mabel. 'When I sang for her.'

'Did it make sense?'

'Oh, yes. It's wonderful. I want to do something for her in return. I thought I might paint her a picture.'

'Paint her a picture by all means. A picture of a ghost, being compromised.'

Mabel laughed a little guiltily. It felt wrong to mock the Myth.

'I'm better at flowers. I thought I could do Indian pipes.'

'You do know you'll never meet her?'

Mabel heard Sue's sharp words as a rebuke. She was not to expect any privileged treatment.

'Do you not think so?'

'Emily knows what she's doing. She has no husband, no children, no position. She's no beauty, and now she's middle-aged. A woman like that is commonly to be pitied by all the world, and Emily is proud. She understands very well that she does better to hide away and become a myth.'

'But she does see you?' said Mabel.

'I haven't set eyes on Emily in years. I don't go to the Homestead any more. I can't bear to listen to Vinnie's prattle. She doesn't have a kind word to say about anybody. She lives too much alone. I believe the only creatures she loves in the world are her sister and her cats.'

Austin now entered, followed by Ned. Austin stayed just long enough for politeness, and was gone again. Ned sat himself down by Mabel's side.

'How does your husband get along in California, Mrs Todd?'

'I can't really answer you, Ned. I ashamed to say he writes to me so rarely.'

'But I'm sure he thinks of you.'

'Are you? It may be so.'

'You aren't easy to forget, Mrs Todd.'

Ned spoke these gallant words in a mumble, looking at his boots and blushing. Sue saw this with some amusement.

'When does Mr Todd return?' she asked Mabel.

'Not for another two months at least.'

'Then we must make sure you don't have too lonely a time of it, mustn't we, Ned?'

When Mabel rose to leave Ned dared to shake her hand, and received in return one of Mabel's prettiest smiles. As she made her way down the path to the gate Austin came after her, to apologise for his earlier brusqueness.

'You must forgive me, Mrs Todd. Sue tells me I have never learned the social graces.'

As he spoke, he slipped a note into her hand, and returned to the house. On her return to her lodgings Mabel read the note, in which he spoke the words he dared not utter aloud.

I love you. I love you! Why should I! and why shouldn't I! Who made and who rules the human heart! Where is the wrong in preferring sunshine to shadow! Does not the unconscious plant lean toward light?

Mabel treasured these notes, which arrived daily. She and Austin were now living two parallel lives, one for the benefit of the world round them, in which Austin remained aloof and they barely spoke; and another secret life that found expression on paper.

Austin was in a state of ecstatic transformation. Mabel's love for him flooded him with wonder and gratitude. Time and again he told himself it couldn't be true. How was it possible that this beautiful young woman, who was admired and adored everywhere she went, could have chosen him in the autumn of his years?

When Mabel's story called 'Footprints' was completed, she gave it to him to read. He was astounded to learn how perfectly she understood his inmost heart.

'Every word is true,' he told her. 'I am Henry Arnold. I have despaired, just as he despairs. I have found happiness, just as he finds happiness.'

And if he was ever afraid and prone to doubt, there were Mabel's notes to him – not to some fictional character – but to his very living breathing self.

You too may be sure of me, of just what and how I am thinking of you and how infinitely I am trusting you. Through and
above every other feeling is this wonderful restfulness, expressed
by nothing so nearly as complete trust. And I love you – I
cannot say how much.

It was all still so new and so precious that he hardly dared
examine what was happening to him. All he knew was that
this late love, this coming into sunlight after the long years of
shadow, was a gift from God. Austin was not given to using
religious language, but now he thanked God every day. Mabel's
love had awoken in him a long-dormant self that he knew to
be his true being: he was born again, born in the spirit, through
the pure and powerful gift of love. This could only be God's
will for him. This was how he knew that it was right, it was
righteous, it was holy.

At the same time he understood very well that in loving Mabel
he was flying in the face of all that the world considered decent
behaviour. So much the worse for the world. He saw now with
new eyes the falsity, the hypocrisy, of the values of the world.
This propriety about which people cared so much, what was it
but vanity? His neighbours were so busy judging and despising
each other that they left no room for love. And in the end, what
else mattered? Austin was waking to the truth that he had been
made by God to love, and that in loving he was becoming his
truest highest self. Of course he loved Mabel as a man loves a
woman – he trembled at her very nearness – but this was only
one part of what was an act of spiritual surrender. Mabel touched
his soul. She understood him without words. The majesty of the
sky moved her as it moved him. She stood by his side and heard

the song of the crickets and told him they were saying, 'I want to live.' And in final proof of the seriousness of her nature, when every fresh-faced young man in town was aflutter about her, her choice had fallen on him. If all she wanted was a little flattery, a little distraction, she would not have turned to a man of his years. And turning to him, finding him waiting, their souls reached out to each other and knew each other, and would never now be alone again.

He wrote to her:

It nearly broke my heart to go through the day yesterday with only that passing sight of you.

She wrote to him:

I have been all alone since supper – but not in the least lonely. I thought it possible that you might look in for a moment – at least I knew you would if you could. But I am unaccountably tired. So I am going to sleep now, with the last word you said to me this morning in my heart. I love you more tonight than I have ever done before. It grows and grows into a wonderfully rare and beautiful something, every day richer and stronger and more all-pervading.

He to her:

I do believe you, my darling, and believe you love me as I love you. It was no fault of yours or mine that I could not take this in at first. My experience of life was too firm and encrusted to permit it. It contradicts everything, revolutionises everything, overturns everything with me — astonishes and overwhelms me as much as overjoys and intoxicates me. I love you, I admire you, I idolise you. I am exalted by your love for me. I am strong as not for a long time before — elastic, well. I walk the street airily and with high pride, for I am loved — loved as I love, loved where I love.

She to him:

It seems as if I cannot possibly bear it until you come. You have waked into an overbounding life things which will not let me rest away from you. It is wicked, as I said, said to you by word of mouth, how far away such bliss looks! To speak face to face with you at this moment. Heaven could hardly offer more.

And what of Sue?

Austin had no qualms on the matter. He had done his duty by his wife, given her a status she had never had before, and a home, and a family. He supported her in comfort. As the world went, he had fulfilled his side of the bargain. But Sue had never given him the deep love he craved. She had never awoken in him the power to love that now so electrified him. Therefore, he reasoned, his name and his worldly goods were owed to his wife; but his heart was his own, to give where it was wanted.

Mabel, however, did have qualms. She tackled Austin as he was escorting her back to Mrs Robison's boarding house on Pleasant Street.

'I love Sue so much,' she said. 'She's so lively and intelligent. She's the only fellow spirit I've met among all the ladies of

Amherst. And yet I see how she is with you. She seems not to mind if you come and go. Sometimes she almost laughs at you. It's very strange.'

'Strange, if you like,' said Austin. 'Common enough, I think. How many married folk live as strangers in the same house?'

'I mean strange that she should not love you. No, that's not kind. Who am I to say what goes on in her heart? It must be that she loves you.'

'Why must it be?'

'Because you're the most loveable of men!'

He took her hand briefly, and then let it go. It was dark, but who knew who might be passing, and might see? Their soft-spoken words, at least, were for themselves alone.

'My wife,' he said, 'does not care for me to touch her.'

'Not touch her!'

'All her life, I believe, she's had a great terror of childbirth. Certainly it took much persuading to venture down that path. When she was expecting Ned, she took certain measures – let's say, she wanted her condition to be over. She was not successful.'

'This is terrible,' murmured Mabel.

'It's many, many years since Sue and I have been man and wife in the fullest sense.'

Mabel was shocked.

'You poor, poor man. How have you borne it? I can't bear to think how you have struggled.'

Austin was moved by Mabel's sympathy.

'Do you truly understand? I thought this was something that women didn't feel as we men do.'

'Oh, yes! I understand. I feel for you. How else do we express love except through our physical senses? I see you, I hear you, I touch you. The more we love, the closer we come to each other, until one day there's no distance between us at all, and we're one.'

'Oh, my darling. My darling.'

And yet even now, standing on the snow-covered sidewalk on Pleasant Street, he was too shy to follow the promptings of his bursting heart, and take her in his arms. For all the effusions of their secret letters, they had not yet kissed.

'Be patient,' Mabel whispered. 'Our time will come.'

When Mabel visited the Homestead, carrying with her the painting of Indian pipes done for Emily, she talked with Vinnie about Sue.

'Why is it that Sue and Austin seem so distant from each other?' she asked.

'There's no mystery there,' said Vinnie. 'Sue's always had a sharp tongue. Would you want to be married to that old scratch?'

'But she's so lively! Her house is always so gay!'

'Gay, you call it? It's empty vessels make most noise. Poor Austin has to run away to us here. You should hear what Emily has to say about Sue! And they used to be the closest friends, back when she was Sue Gilbert.'

'What does Emily say?'

'She says Sue married an establishment. All she cared for was the house. Poor Austin! We've watched him shrink over the years, like a starving mouse.'

'How can anyone not love him?'

'You know that, my dear. I know it. Emily knows it. But

Sue has her carriage and her children and her parties, and need not trouble herself over Austin any more.'

'If that's really so,' said Mabel, keeping her eyes lowered, 'would you say he has the right to take love where he can find it?'

'I would say,' said Vinnie fiercely, 'that whenever any of us meet with love in this pitiful world, it is our right to enjoy it, and our duty to return it.'

'And does your sister think as you do?'

'Emily respects passion in all its forms.'

In response to Mabel's flower painting, Emily sent through a note for Mabel, containing a poem.

I cannot make an Indian Pipe but please accept a Humming Bird.

> *A Route of Evanescence*
> *With a revolving Wheel —*
> *A Resonance of Emerald —*
> *A Rush of Cochineal,*
> *And every Blossom on the Bush*
> *Adjusts its tumbled Head —*
> *The Mail from Tunis probably*
> *An easy Morning's Ride —*

That without suspecting it you should send me the preferred flower of life seems almost supernatural, and the sweet glee that I felt at meeting it I could confide to none — I still cherish the clutch with which I bore it from the ground when a wondering child, an

unearthly booty, and maturity only enhances mystery, never
decreases it –

Mabel didn't understand the poem, but she thrilled to the hint in the note that Emily felt her to be a kindred spirit. Now she could be sure that she had allies in the Homestead. At the same time, Sue continued to include her in all the gatherings she hosted at The Evergreens. At Sue's request, Mabel gave Mattie lessons on the piano. And unperceived by either of them, shy young Ned's admiration for Mrs Todd grew into a secret passion.

One crisp December day Mabel joined the family, which on this occasion comprised Sue, Ned and Mattie, on a sleigh ride. They bowled at a great pace down the Sunderland road and over the half-frozen Mill River, their breath smoky in the air, their cheeks pink. Mabel wore a fur-trimmed hood tight round her face, her eyes shining brightly with the excitement of the ride. Ned, who was driving, saw her delight and urged the horses on, until Sue had to call on him, laughing, to slow down.

'You'll have us all in the ditch, you foolish boy! What am I to say to Mr Todd when he returns, if he finds a wife broken in two?'

'What do I care for Mr Todd?' cried Ned. 'I don't care if he never returns!'

At the bridge they climbed down from the sleigh and threw snowballs over the ice, competing to see who could make their snowball slide the furthest. Ned discovered that the tighter the snow was packed, the further it slid over the ice. He made a snowball for Mabel, and she threw it, and by a lucky throw it outpaced all the others.

'But it was your snowball, Ned.'

'And your throw,' said Ned. 'We are joint victors.'

He took her gloved hand and looked, laughing, deep into her eyes.

'So you see, Mrs Todd,' he said, 'together we can overcome the world.'

Mabel enjoyed Ned's gallantries without taking them seriously. He was still a boy as far as she was concerned, though in plain figures he was only five years her junior.

On their return to The Evergreens, Ned said to Mabel, 'Now, in exchange for my driving I ask for some singing.'

But Austin was waiting. He expressed the intention of going out for a stroll, to see the winter sunset.

'We've just got back,' said Sue. 'Why would we want to go out again? Make up the fire. Mabel is going to sing for us.'

Mabel was standing by Austin's side. Austin turned to her.

'I know Mrs Todd shares my love for sunsets. I ask her as a kindness to keep me company, if only to the end of the street.'

Ned looked round to claim Mabel for the party in the house, and saw the way his father looked at her, and the way she looked back, and how they both quickly broke the look. There was nothing more to it, but in that moment, with the heightened sensibility of a lover, Ned understood that there was an intimacy between them.

'It's true that I do love the sunset,' said Mabel. 'I'm sure I shall sing all the more sweetly after I've watched the day end in all its glory.'

Ned looked on in silence. He saw Mrs Todd reach for her coat to go out again. He saw how his father helped her to put it on. He saw the door close behind them.

Mattie ran off to find her little brother Gib. Sue knelt on the rug before the fire to warm her hands. Ned crossed the room slowly, and stood in silence behind his mother.

'That was a fine brisk ride,' said Sue. 'But you must take care not to wear out the horses. You know how your father loves them.'

'Do I?' said Ned.

Sue looked round, surprised by his tone.

'What's the matter, Ned?'

'My father loves sunsets, too.'

'What of it? What's come over you?'

Ned knew he should say nothing, but he was unable to hold back the bitterness rising within him.

'My father is very attentive to Mrs Todd,' he said.

'Why should he not be? She's a charming friend to us. To you most of all, I should say.'

'No, Mother. Not to me most of all.'

'To who, then?'

'You may choose to be blind if you wish,' exclaimed Ned. 'I wish I could be blind.'

With that he left the room.

Sue was not altogether blind. Prompted by Ned's outburst, she set to reviewing recent events in a fresh light.

By the time Austin and Mabel returned, it was fully dark outside.

'It must have been a fine sunset,' said Sue. 'I began to think you were waiting for the dawn as well.'

'We stayed to see the last light fade in the sky,' said Mabel. 'And now I'm back, and ready to take my place at the piano.'

'I think perhaps we've had enough excitements for the day,'

said Sue. 'We take up far too much of your time as it is, Mrs Todd.'

Mabel looked at Sue in some surprise.

'You know you have only to ask,' she said.

'What's the matter, Sue?' said Austin sharply. 'Are you sending Mrs Todd away?'

'Ned has a headache,' said Sue. 'I think it would be better if we were quiet this evening.'

'It would be better if we were quiet every evening,' said Austin angrily.

'Please, Mr Dickinson,' said Mabel. 'Don't concern yourself over me. I have so many letters to write. I'll take myself off, and sing another day.' To Sue, 'My sympathies to Ned.'

'Then I'll see you home,' said Austin.

'Perhaps you can watch the moon rise,' said Sue.

To this Austin gave no answer.

For a while they walked in silence up the street. Then Austin said to Mabel, 'I'm not surprised. I had expected something of this sort sooner.'

Mabel, distressed, said very low, 'What are we to do?'

'Nothing.'

'I don't want Sue to hate me.'

'If she believes I love you, then she will hate you. There's nothing to be done about that.'

'Why must your love for me make you love her any the less?'

'It doesn't. If anything, loving you makes me feel more kindly towards my wife. But that's not how Sue works. She'll assume that any love I give to you is taken from her. Dear God! If only she knew! I have no love for her to take. There has been no love in my life, until you.'

A whisper: 'My darling.'

'If Sue starts to hate you, will you stop loving me?'

'Never, ever. But must she hate me? How will that make her happy? I wish we could all love each other. Why can't she be like David? He understands.'

'How much have you told him?'

'Nothing, and everything. We haven't spoken of it openly. But we will.'

'I envy you that.'

'Can't you speak to Sue? Can't you make her not be afraid?'

'My sweet darling,' he said with a sigh. 'Not everyone has your open loving nature. Sue will see as the world sees. I'm afraid this means we must be even more careful. We must never be seen alone together.'

'Never alone!'

'Not where we can be seen.'

'Where, then?'

'There is one place where we can meet,' said Austin, 'where our secret will be kept. We can meet in my sisters' house.'

'Will Vinnie not think it improper?'

'Vinnie? She's not a booby like the rest of them.'

'And Emily?'

'Emily is our friend.'

This sent a thrill through Mabel.

'You've told her?'

'I've told her of my unhappiness. And I've told her of my happiness. Emily no longer lives in Sue's world.'

'I know it,' said Mabel. 'When I'm sitting with Vinnie, I can always feel her there. I expect it's foolish of me, but I do feel as if she's my friend.'

'Emily knows you've given me back life itself. She loves you for that.'

This was what Mabel had longed to hear. Emily had come to represent to her the higher truth that stood in judgement over her actions. Once she had found this in her father. A part of it now resided in Austin. But both her father and Austin, being men, were subject to female charm, and so their approval was not to be taken as without bias. Emily was beyond fear or favour. She had never set eyes on Mabel. She was the Myth. She lived apart, accepting the pain and the freedom of loneliness. For all these reasons, Mabel bowed her head before her, almost in worship. And now, she learned, her deity graciously received her prayers, and smiled upon her.

'I wish so much that I could meet her one day,' she said.

From now on, Mabel was an infrequent visitor at The Evergreens. Mattie ceased coming to her for piano lessons. Ned avoided her. Instead, Mabel took to calling more often on the sisters in the Homestead. And Austin trod the path between the trees, from the side door of The Evergreens to the kitchen door of the Homestead. Now that winter had come half the house had been shut down, and only the rooms close to the warmth of the kitchen were in use. The parlour couch had been moved into the dining room, and here the lovers were able to be alone together. With the shutters closed and the new iron stove warming the winter air, they could sit and talk to their hearts' content.

For all the passion of their words, spoken and written, they maintained a curious formality when in each other's presence. They called each other Mrs Todd and Mr Dickinson. They observed all the customary politenesses. For both of them this was a matter of pride. They wished it to be understood that while their love was illicit, they remained respectable people. It was their pride to claim their love as something finer than the commonplace proprieties of others. Theirs was not some mere abandoned debauch, driven by the base appetites.

This was all well and good, but it made it hard to move on to the next phase. The shift into physical intimacy had, of course, to be initiated by the man. Austin was shy. He had no practice in the business, and was afraid he would be clumsy. He was afraid he might appear ridiculous. And secretly he was not sure Mabel would welcome such a development. Austin had his share of vanity about his personal appearance; in his youth he had been considered a handsome man. But the long loneliness of his marriage had worn away his confidence, and he no longer believed he possessed physical charm. Even now, in this astonishing flood of answering love, it was all rapture of the spirit, with no mention of the body.

Austin was now fifty-five years old. His face was pouchy and lined, his body had lost the firmness of youth. Mabel Todd, so vital, so young, could love him for his mind. But if he were to invite her to touch his body, might she not recoil?

Fortunately Mabel understood this. She too was proud and protective of the nobility of their love. But David had taught her a great deal about the nature of men, and she had no intention of allowing her intimacy with Austin to fall short of the fullest physical expression. She knew how the bond of sexual love held David tight to her, and she wanted the same with Austin. She wanted to please him as no woman had ever pleased him before, knowing that if she succeeded in this he would love her for ever.

She was happy to let matters proceed slowly, because she was aware of all the obstacles Austin had to overcome in his own mind. Also there was a piquancy to this *time before* which she sensed gave their love its particular intensity, its pure gemlike flame. But one can't be sighing and longing and holding back for ever.

One evening in February, in the dining room of the Homestead, she said to him, 'I dreamed last night that you kissed me. Do you know, you have never kissed me?'

'And how was it, in your dream?'

'It was just like yourself. Tender and true.'

'I must ask my dream self how he goes about such a thing. It's been so long since I attempted it, I would hardly know what to do.'

'There's no secret to it,' said Mabel.

She took his hands in hers and stood up, drawing him to follow her. Then she turned her face up to his. She was smaller than him, and he had to bend to reach her. His side whiskers tickled her cheek. Then his lips brushed hers.

Ashamed of his awkwardness, he moved away again.

'I'm no better than a boy of sixteen.'

'Come,' said Mabel. 'Come back to me. Tell me you love me. Just not with words.'

She drew his face to hers once more, and let her lips gently nuzzle his, making the smallest of movements. Little by little he relaxed, and his lips moved in response. In this way, wordlessly, they whispered their love to each other.

Then he kissed her cheeks, and her brow, and her closed eyes.

'I adore you,' he murmured. 'I worship you.'

He was frightened by the intensity of his feelings. They swept through every part of him, taking possession of him. He was filled with wonder and gratitude.

'I give all I have and all I will ever have just for this moment.'

Mabel accepted his love joyously. Here was a passion that transcended all other attachments. She rejoiced to know that she had awoken in this good and noble man a power of loving that made his life complete. And through him, through his love for her, her own life now had meaning.

While they kissed in the dining room, was Emily in the passage outside? Was she on the stairs? There were moments when Mabel thought she heard the rustle of a skirt on the far side of the door.

9

The dark of the passage, moving towards the closed dining room door. Nearer now, faint sounds become audible from within: the hiss of clothing, the hiss of breath.

Hands reach up to touch the panels of the door.

I listen. I hear. I feel.

Does he touch her? Does he feel her?

Later, in the bedroom. The only light in the room is faint moonshine through the windows. The silver glow reflects in a dressing table mirror. Indistinct in the frame there stands a shadowy form, hand touching cheek.

My cheek is warm.

The pen writes by the light of an oil lamp. Follow the writing, letter by letter:

Seraphic fear

Each night I die, each morning I am born again.

Bright light falls on green plants. A spray of glittering water bursts from the rose of a watering can, throwing a sudden rainbow in the little conservatory. I call this my Garden of Eden. Vinnie approaches, bird-like, ever-present.

'Do you believe in the Fall, Vin?'

She shakes her head, says, 'I'm not clever enough for that.'

'I don't believe in the Fall. I find no snake in the grass.'

'Sue will have nothing more to do with Mrs Todd.'

That makes me smile. I speak of original sin, the great lie invented by priests, and Vinnie speaks of Mrs Todd. *And priests in black gowns are walking their rounds, and binding with briars my joys and desires.* Blake's garden of love is filled with graves.

'Austin will not be bound,' I say.

Vinnie thinks I speak of Sue and the wagging tongues of the village, but I speak of briars, with their lacerating thorns. The crown forced onto the bleeding head of a saviour long ago. Only he failed to save me, so I mean to do the job myself.

'Austin,' says Vinnie, awed, 'is in love.'

'And Mrs Todd too? Is she in love with Austin?'

Vinnie looks perplexed. The question has not occurred to her. If a man deigns to offer a woman his love, the woman is honoured and grateful, and gives her love in return.

'She could never allow his attentions if she were not.'

'Perhaps,' I say, 'she's an adventuress.'

'An adventuress!' Vinnie is shocked. 'I hope not! Poor Austin!'

'Happy Austin!'

I believe Mrs Todd to be an adventuress. I have an adventure for her.

10

Alice sets out for Yale early in the morning, to be at the Sterling Memorial Library as it opens at 8.30 a.m. It's still dark, and a deep mist hangs over the roads. She drives slowly. By the time she reaches the interstate at Northampton the sun is rising, and the mist lifting, but the traffic is building up with the morning rush. All through Hartford her progress slows to a crawl. Such immense roads, and so little movement.

Her mind is full of Mabel and Austin, and the puzzle of how to tell her story. It seemed so simple when she pitched the outline to her stepfather and his producer, back home in the summer. But it's turning out to be more complicated than she bargained for.

'It's the ending that defines the story.' All very well for Jack to pronounce in his teacherish way, but real life doesn't go in much for endings, other than death. And even death can leave you up in the air. Contemplating the way Mabel's great love affair unfolded, Alice finds herself helpless in the face of brute dates. Austin died in 1895. Mabel lived on for almost forty more years, half a lifetime without her great love. What sense does that make of a life?

One answer is that life makes no sense. Things just happen. This is Nick's view of the world. You do what you want, insofar as you're able, and then you die.

Every instinct in Alice rebels against this conclusion. Somehow, somewhere, there's a way to tell Mabel's story that grants dignity to her passion. In the Sterling Memorial Library Mabel's letters and diaries are stored. There are far too many documents to read all she wrote, but in the course of this coming day Alice hopes to find a key that will open a door; or perhaps a key that will close a door, and so permit the final credits to roll.

The interstate delivers her with a disconcerting suddenness into the heart of patrician Yale. She finds herself cruising past immense nineteenth-century buildings separated by wide green lawns. She leaves her car in a parking lot on College and Crown. It's coming up to nine in the morning as she walks back up New Haven Green with its two island churches, past Bingham and Welch, grand complacent halls built in an age when privilege was a virtue. Little Amherst College, founded by Emily's grandfather, is humbled by the comparison. Here in Yale is the full pomp of learning.

A sharp cool sun shines on the campus, lightening its sombre air. She passes through the Phelps Hall arch and crosses the lawn within, following the map she has printed from Google. So out onto High Street, across Elm Street, to her destination.

The Sterling Memorial Library towers above her, its two great arched doorways, topped by even taller stained-glass windows, rising up to a pinnacled façade: a veritable cathedral of knowledge. How the founders must have believed in the power and glory of the written word! It seems almost quaint now, an act of touching folly, like the building of the pyramids.

Inside the library, Alice is directed to the far end of the shadowy nave. There a narrower hallway runs off to the right, past the Music Library, to the Manuscripts and Archives Department. She presents her identification, deposits her bag in a locker, and passes through to the inner room where her requested documents await her. They stand numbered on a trolley: nine boxes from the Todd–Bingham bequest. Here are Mabel Todd's letters and diaries, and Austin Dickinson's letters to Mabel. The very notes they sent each other with such secrecy now made available to a stranger from across an ocean, who is hoping to understand a little of the love that burned so brightly, a hundred and thirty years ago.

She opens Box 94, which contains letters from Austin: each letter folded in a protective outer sheet of paper. The pen strokes are faded now, the nib lines narrow in the vertical, broad in the horizontal, the bars of the Ts hurrying over the other letters to reach the next word. She can read My dear Mrs Todd – but his hasty handwriting is hard to make out.

She opens a box of Mabel's letters. Mabel writes in a big looping script which is far easier to follow. Her letters too begin in the same oddly formal way: My dear Mr Dickinson. But there among them, as if to give the lie to such respectability, she finds a scribbled note from Austin:

Vin – If anything happens to me burn this package at once without opening. Do this as you love me.

Most of the letters have no salutation and no signature, though often there's a date and a time.

From August 1884:

Now I am going to sleep with the crickets' mysterious song for my lullaby, and your divine love for my canopy and safeguard. Oh! I love you, and I love you, and my soul is in your tender keeping. Tuesday 10:45pm.

Alongside one letter lies a slip of paper on which is written: *A M U A S B T E I L N*. Alice knows from her reading that this was the way they merged their names, one letter at a time, to make visible their union. And here it is, the paper on which Mabel nested the curling letters, with the date, December 9 1888. It's stored with a sheet on which is written out a love poem of her own devising, that she called 'P. S. First':

> *You are all that I want to live for,*
> *All that I have to love,*
> *All that the whole world holds for me*
> *Of faith in a world above . . .*

Not quite Emily Dickinson, but Alice is moved by it even so. This was the paper Mabel held steady with one hand. These curls of ink were laid down by her pen, to express the overflow of her heart. There is an innocence about it that defies cynicism.

She opens Box 46, which contains Mabel's diaries. She takes out a stiff-boarded marbled notebook, and reads from 1881:

What is there in me which so attracts men to me, young and
old?

And later, from November 11 1883, her birthday:

Twenty-seven! I! It seems impossible – in most things I feel
like a child – in fact it always seems to me that I'm eighteen, and I suppose I act so.

It becomes clear that she used her diary to send messages to
Austin.

Monday 25 May 1885. I am going away, and here is this
book for you to read – full of everything under the sun
– but reaching at last the real peace and joy and unutterable happiness in my life – in you, Austin, whom I love so
that I am lifted solemnly to God by it – so that, as you
said yesterday, neither of us can ever be lonesome again.
Oh darling, darling!

She must have handed it to him to keep while she was away,
on one of her periodic visits to her parents and daughter in
Washington. If so, he would have taken care to hide it where
Sue could not find it; most likely in his law offices in town.
Alice reads on, not attempting to follow every page, taking
out volume after volume, immersing herself in the living
moments in which Mabel poured out her love. She stays at the
library table among the boxes all through the middle of the day,
not breaking for lunch. Sometime in the early afternoon she
comes upon a small copper-coloured booklet, on the cover of

which is printed a title, 'Footprints', over the author's name, Mabel Loomis Todd. Inside she reads that it's a reprint from the *Independent*, 27 September 1883. The print is laid out one narrow column per page, for forty-four pages. She reads the story from beginning to end.

It is of course Mabel's own love story. She has chosen to tell it from the point of view of the man. The heroine charms him 'by her beautiful combination of light-hearted girlishness and deep womanly feeling.' There's no suggestion of physical attraction: this is the story of soul meeting soul.

It's absurd in its plotting, with its brief shadow on their love, and its brisk and convenient removal. It's sentimental, and heavily reliant on the pathetic fallacy: 'The heavens, which had been as brass, became a tender blue . . . The sea had fulfilled the promises he used to hear in its most hopeful songs, and had brought him this magnificent happiness.' But take it as a love letter, and Alice finds it touching. How Austin must have treasured it!

Strange to think it was published in a New York newspaper for everyone to read. Did Sue read it?

She returns the booklet carefully to its box and continues with her explorations, making pencil notes as she goes. Just as she begins to think of packing the archives away, so that she can drive back in daylight, she comes upon a passage in one of Mabel's diaries that makes an impression on her. She copies it out in its entirety.

6 February 1890: I had a passionate longing to be loved for my own individual aroma, not because I was a bright and pretty woman, of whom there are many similar, equally

attractive. If I should die David would soon marry again. But I am the one woman for all time to Austin, I, just myself, and because it is I.

This is the passage that is on Alice's mind as she heads back up the interstate to Amherst. It's no answer to her puzzle over how to end her story, but it is something important nevertheless. It's the beginning of a whole new line of thought about the nature of Mabel's love affair; and more than that, about the nature of romantic love itself.

What if we seek love not because we long to be discovered by another, but because we need to affirm ourselves? This makes it a very different enterprise, and one that is not negated by the death of the lover.

Alice is excited. New ideas swarm in her brain.

I, just myself, and because it is I.

Mabel was seeking to know herself and believe herself to be uniquely valuable. She was driven to assert her own worth against the greater meaninglessness of life. Did she delude herself? In her extreme need, did she fabricate a noble passion, and then call upon it to give her life a glory it otherwise lacked?

There's something else here, something more. Alice knows it, but her mind can't quite grasp it. To say that romantic love is a form of egotism is merely banal. She has held in her hands all day the relics of a passion which transformed several lives. It's not good enough to mock the claims of the lovers, to know better than they knew themselves what they were feeling. They used the words of their day to give voice to their emotions. 'I am to him the holy of holies,' wrote Mabel in her diary. 'The inner sacred temple.' No use snickering over the unconscious sexual imagery. Something true and powerful is at work here. What if it's something bigger than love? What is there that's bigger than love?

She reaches Amherst with enough light left in the sky to enable her to find her way home through the still unfamiliar town. This time she succeeds in making the turn off Route 9 onto Pleasant Street, and so down Main, past The Evergreens and the Homestead.

The house on Triangle Street appears to be silent and empty. Thirsty, she explores the fridge for something to drink. She finds a carton of apple juice. She's sitting at the kitchen table writing up her notes when a young woman appears, her cheeks flushed, her long blond hair dishevelled.

'Oh hi,' she says. 'Great. Apple juice. Just what I need.'

'I didn't know Nick was home,' says Alice.

'Yeah, he's home.'

The young woman gulps her juice and stares at Alice.

'Oh, right. You're the English girl.'

'Yes,' says Alice.

'Well, I gotta run. Nice to meet you.'

And she's gone. Alice hears her bare feet pattering up the stairs.

She tries to return to her notes, but she's distracted. The nameless young woman is about her own age, maybe younger. Attractive in a simple enough way. If she wants to spend the late afternoon with Nick, and he with her, that's their business.

So why does it piss me off?

She's embarrassed by her own reaction. It makes her seem prudish; or jealous, which is worse. She doesn't like finding she thinks the worse of Nick for his casual approach to sex. It's not as if he's pretended to be any other than he is.

The fact is she can't make Nick out. He doesn't add up. One minute he comes across as sensitive, even wise; the next minute he's acting like a jerk. Surely there's a disconnect between reading Emily Dickinson and having sex with students?

Noises from the hallway. Voices on the stairs, a door opening and closing.

Then Nick comes into the kitchen.

'I didn't expect you back till later,' he says.

'I don't like driving in the dark,' says Alice.

'So how was it?'

'It was good.'

He gets himself a beer from the fridge. Drinks from the bottle.

'You met Marcia.'

'Apparently. She didn't introduce herself.'

'She said.'

'She said she didn't introduce herself?'

'No. She said she met you.'

'I'm sorry if I was in the way,' says Alice.

'Not at all. She wanted to know about you.'

'What about me?'

'What you're doing here. All the way from England. How I know you.'

'How well I know you.'

'That too.'

'I hope you were able to reassure her,' says Alice.

'Up to a point,' says Nick. 'Marcia takes a fairly simplistic view of these things.'

'That no girl can resist you?'

'That what can happen usually does happen.'

'And I'm sure with Marcia it does.'

As soon as she says it she regrets it.

Nick finishes his beer in silence.

'Sorry,' says Alice. 'None of my business.'

'So tell me about Yale. Did you get what you wanted?'

They start to talk about Mabel and Austin, and pretend the crackly little exchange didn't happen. He's interested in all she has to say. Telling him makes it take on a shape in her mind.

'The more I read Mabel's diaries,' she says, 'the more I get the feeling of what it was she was really looking for. The strange thing is, I'm not sure it was love at all.'

She reads him the passage she's copied out: '"I had a passionate longing to be loved for my own individual aroma . . ." It's more than wanting to be loved. It's as if she wants to know she exists.'

'Is that something bigger,' says Nick, 'or something smaller?'

'It's bigger. It has to be bigger.'

She can see him thinking about that.

'You think it's smaller?'

'No,' says Nick. 'I'm wondering about something else. You know how we're always looking for hidden motives, and deeper drives? We've been taught to take it for granted that what people say they want is just a cover for something else, for some more potent unadmitted need, like sex or status or identity. I'm thinking now how that carries an assumption with it, a sort of hierarchy. At one end are all the little desires, and at the other end is the big engine that drives the train. Sorry, my metaphor's collapsing. A train isn't a hierarchy, is it?'

But Alice is interested.

'Do you mean the little desires might be as significant as the big ones?'

'I don't know,' says Nick. 'I'm just not as respectful of Big Theory as I once was. It doesn't seem to be the way I lead my life.'

'How do you lead your life?'

'I think I lead it moment by moment. A chain of tiny impulses, and decisions. I'm not sure they add up to anything greater than themselves. Or rather, if you add them all up you don't get one single big thing, you just get a bag full of lots of little things.'

Alice is disappointed. He reads the look on her face.

'Look, it doesn't matter. Let's get back to Mabel and Austin.'

'No, I want to get it,' says Alice. 'It sounds like you're saying we shouldn't bother to try to make sense of our lives.'

'Like, make a screenplay of our lives.'

'No, that's something else.'

But suddenly it seems to her it isn't something else at all. Why should her attempt to make sense of her own life be any different from turning Mabel's life into a story?

'So you don't think your life makes any sense?' she says.

'I don't even know what that means,' he says. 'I'm not disagreeing with you. I just can't make that sum add up any more. My life is in too many pieces.'

'OK.' She thinks about that. 'So it's all random. Doesn't that do your head in?'

'Not any more,' he says.

'Everything is just for nothing?'

'Or for itself.'

'Oh, OK, I get it. You live from moment to moment,

meaning you just do whatever you feel like. Live a life of passing pleasures.'

Like sex with Marcia.

'Does that seem so worthless to you?'

'I don't know. I don't know.'

And she doesn't. She wants there to be a journey and a destination, but maybe that's just childish. Like wanting there to be a father God and a life after death where all the sacrifice finds its reward.

So what about love? Is that just one of the little pleasures that fills our dwindling store of days? She wants to ask Nick what love means to him, but somehow it feels too personal. To him or to her? So she asks him about Mabel.

'Do you think Mabel was fooling herself?'

'No more than any of us,' says Nick. 'I like the idea of being loved for . . . what was it? Her individual aroma.'

'I'm beginning to think she was just seriously insecure. She's forever writing about how attractive she is, and how men can't keep off her.'

'What was her relationship like with her father?'

'Oh, her father loved her, if that's what you mean. He adored her. But he was a disappointed man. One of those self-made intellectuals stuck in a job inferior to his talents. He was a clerk in some office attached to the Naval Observatory. Mabel always called him Professor. I think he may even have given himself the title, but he wasn't a professor. Do you think that might have affected her?'

'Fathers matter to daughters,' says Nick. 'Doesn't your father matter to you?'

'My father's a selfish womaniser who never wanted me in the first place,' says Alice.

'Oh, boy,' says Nick.

'So what? My mother loved me. I have a fantastic stepfather. I'm fine.'

'I believe you.'

'I suppose you think Mabel had a father-thing for Austin?'

'Don't you?'

'Yes,' says Alice, 'but I hate the way Freud's made us all reduce relationships to these corny stereotypes. You're the one who wants to junk Big Theory. Couldn't she have fallen in love with him because he was a fellow spirit?'

'So you still want to believe in love. For a while back there I thought you were moving on.'

'Moving on where? To some sad little conclusion that love is just a bundle of neurotic itches that we want to scratch? I don't like that. Do you like that?'

'No,' says Nick. 'I don't like it. Just like I don't like Santa Claus being my dad in a false beard.'

Suddenly a real personal detail. Alice is disarmed.

'Did he really do that? Your dad?'

'Yes, he did. He kept the beard in a bottom drawer in a chest in the passage where we hung our coats and lined up our wellington boots.'

'And you found it.'

'There you go. End of innocence.'

He's grinning as he says it.

'I don't believe that,' she says. 'I bet you knew already.'

'Yes, I knew. I recognised his special dad smell. Cigarettes, coffee. His individual aroma. No false beard could hide that.'

Alice thinks how she never knew a special dad smell. It was always her mother who snuck her stocking onto her bed the night before Christmas. She thinks how much she loves her mother, and suddenly she misses her with a terrible ache.

'I do want to believe in love,' she says. 'Don't take it away from me.'

'I could never do that, Alice.'

He hardly ever calls her by her name. There's no need when there's only the two of you in the room. The effect is unexpected, as if he's touched her.

'I don't want to think love's just egotism,' she says.

'It would make a rotten screenplay.'

'And a sad life.'

'That happens whether you like it or not,' he says.

'To you, maybe. Not to me.'

'Good for you. Rage against the dying of the light.'

'That's Dylan Thomas,' she says. 'Haven't you got an Emily Dickinson line?'

Straight off he gives her a verse.

> *Behold this little bane*
> *The boon of all alive*
> *As common as it is unknown*
> *The name of it is Love.*

Alice gives a shrug, and pulls a face for him. What can you say?

'Don't you just love her half-rhymes?' he says.

'I love everything about her,' she says. 'Emily believes in love.'

'But she calls it "this little bane",' he says. 'And "the little toil of love".'

'I don't care. I say she wanted to love. I say she did love.'

Alice's defiance, based on nothing. Nick's response takes her aback.

'I wanted to love. I did love.'

What can you say to that?

'I just didn't know it at the time. Then the time came when I did know it. But it was too late.'

'This was Jack's mother?'

'Yes. Laura.'

'There must have been others.'

'There've been others, yes. But not like that.'

'It's not as if you haven't had your chances. And by the way, you are married.'

'So you're still angry with me.'

'Why should I be angry with you?'

'Because of Marcia. Because of your dad.'

'Oh, for God's sake!' She jumps up, gathers her papers together. 'Your sex life is your problem. My father's my problem. I don't need this.'

Ridiculously, she finds herself in the grip of a tantrum, like a two-year-old child. She knows it's entirely unnecessary but she can't control it. Sensing she's about to burst into tears, she runs out of the kitchen and up the stairs.

In the safety of her room she does cry, a little, but it's mostly out of frustration with herself. What was that all about?

About Marcia. About my dad.

She hates Nick knowing she resents his afternoon with Marcia. She hates him knowing she has a father who didn't love her, which makes her into someone looking for love from an older man. She hates being understood more than she understands herself. She hates the feeling that he's in control and she isn't.

That's a lot of hating. Who knew I was so wound up?

She decides to get out of the house. She needs some kind of supper anyway. She pulls on a coat against the night chill and goes out, not looking to see if Nick's still in the kitchen, not announcing her departure.

She walks up Main Street and goes into a pasta restaurant near the centre of town. It's a plainly furnished place, priced for a student clientele, and only about a quarter full. She sits at a table by the window and orders herself a large glass of Pinot Grigio and a bowl of carbonara. Her wine comes and she drinks it fast, staring at the street outside, seeing nothing.

This wasn't meant to turn into my story.

She's angry at herself for being angry with Nick. She replays their conversation in her mind, seeing as she does so his quiz-zical face gazing so steadily at her, silently interrogating her, finding answers she does not mean to give.

Not many people passing on the sidewalk. But there's one who has come to a stop and is looking back at her through the glass. Then the ghostly onlooker gives a little wave. Alice stares.

It's Marcia.

Now she's coming into the restaurant. To her table. Why?

'Hi,' she says. 'I thought it was you.'

'Hi,' says Alice.

'Mind if I stop for a few minutes?'

'No, sure,' says Alice.

Marcia sits down at the table facing Alice, puts her elbows on the table top and her face in her hands, and starts to weep. She cries noiselessly, helplessly, her tears running down between her fingers.

'Sorry. I'll be OK in a minute.'

Alice drinks her wine and waits. Marcia snuffles, and dabs at her eyes with a tissue, and gives Alice an apologetic grin.

'That wasn't the plan,' she says.

'Is this Nick?'

'No. Well, yes, I came in because of Nick. But I'm not crying over Nick. What's that you're drinking?'

'Pinot Grigio.'

'I need some of that.' She waves at the waitress.

'I'll have another one,' says Alice. 'You want something to eat?'

'I'm never going to eat again. I am so fucked up you wouldn't believe. You know about body dysmorphia?'

'Yes,' says Alice.

'I've got body dysmorphia and mind dysmorphia and spirit dysmorphia and anything else you want to name. I have scaled heights of self-hatred that aren't even on the map.'

She sees Alice's bewildered look.

'Too much information, right? Listen, all I wanted to do was tell you about Nick. I owe him my life. He has saved my life. Quite literally.'

'How did he do that?'

'I've been planning to kill myself for months. I've got the pills. I've written the letters. Farewell cruel world and all that crap.'

She's laughing as she speaks and running her hands through

her blond hair and looking so pretty and full of life. Nothing makes any sense.

'But I'd made Nick this promise that I'd say goodbye in person, right? So I go to say goodbye. And he talks me out of it.'

'How did he do that?'

'Hey, guess what? He talked me into it!' She shakes her head and bites her lower lip and starts crying again. 'He sat me down and he held my hands and he said to me, OK, let's do it. He made me act it all out in front of him. I acted out drinking down the pills, and getting sleepy. Now you're falling asleep, he says. Now you're asleep. Now your heart's stopping. Now you're dead.'

Alice listens, awed. Her pasta comes. She doesn't eat.

'Now you've died, Nick says. All that stuff that bothered you doesn't matter any more. It's gone. It's over. Do you see that? And the crazy thing is, I see it! I'm like, what the fuck! I'm dead! I don't need to give a shit any more! And ever since I've been walking round town like I'm in a dream, and I don't know how to tell anyone that this miracle has happened, but I want to talk about it. And then I saw you, and you're Nick's friend, and I just had to . . . I'm sorry, I know this must all seem pretty wild to you – but I had to tell someone. I needed, like, a witness, before it all goes away.'

She starts crying all over again.

'That's OK,' says Alice, not knowing what to say. Marcia's mood has infected her, and she wants to cry too.

'Isn't it something else?' Marcia says. 'How did he know to do that? You know what he said when I left? He said, "You'll feel bad again in a while. This isn't going to last. So when it

138

comes again, do what we've done again. Die again. Then you'll be free.'"

'Wow!'

'I think he's an old soul.'

She reaches across the table and Alice gives her her hands to hold.

'I'm dead' she says. 'I'm free.'

Alice smiles. It's all insane but she can't help being moved.

'I thought you were up there having sex,' she says. 'And all the time he was saving your life.'

'Oh, we've done that,' says Marcia. 'Way back. Not for a long time now. He's too smart. He knows I'm crazy.'

'What went wrong, Marcia? How did it get so bad for you?'

'Give my mom a call. She'll tell you. Hey, you know what?' Now she's laughing again. 'I should kill my mom. Not for real, but the Nick Crocker way. Get a gun. Bang! You're dead now, Mom! Get off my back!'

She lets go of Alice's hands and stands up.

'You eat. I'm going. Thanks for being my witness.'

Walking back to the house, Alice thinks she'll make Nick some kind of apology. But what can she say? There's no form of words that doesn't get into assumptions she had no right to make. It's hard enough dealing with her own confused responses to Nick, without inviting him to join the party.

He's in the big room downstairs, stretched out on a couch in a pool of lamp light, reading *Don Quixote*.

'Sorry I went off like that,' she says. 'I think it must have been a blood sugar low.'

'You got something to eat?'

'Yes. I've had a bowl of pasta and a glass of wine.'

He smiles up at her, his reading glasses pushed high on his brow.

'It's my opinion,' he says, 'that there are no griefs that can't be assuaged by a bowl of pasta and a glass of wine.'

'Marcia joined me for a while.'

'Marcia!'

'She saw me through the window. She told me what you'd done for her.'

'That poor kid is in big trouble. She needs more help than I can give her.'

'You were good, Nick. You did a good job there.'

He gazes at her and she sees that he understands. This is her apology. Her peace offering.

'How was the pasta?'

'Not great.'

'Amherst can do better. Let me take you out to dinner one of these nights. We can go on with our conversation.'

'Sure. I'd like that.'

'I've none to tell me to but thee,' he says.

More Emily Dickinson.

'I don't think I get you, Nick.'

What she means but can't say is, I don't get how I feel about you.

'Don't worry about it,' he says. 'People are ungettable. That's just how it is.'

Up in her room she goes through the *Collected Poems* until she finds it.

I've none to tell me to but thee
So when Thou failest, nobody.
It was a little tie —
It held just Two, nor those it held
Since somewhere thy sweet Face has spilled
Beyond my Boundary —

11

Sue Dickinson maintained her pose of not being aware of the rumours. Mrs John Jameson, a near neighbour, asked after Austin when she met Sue on the high pavement, adding as an apparently casual afterthought, 'I passed him the other day out driving, and with charming company.'

'You mean Mrs Todd, I suppose,' said Sue.

'I'm sure they had a delightful outing. We all so admire Mrs Todd. I always say she brings a touch of Paris to our little village.'

'I wouldn't know,' said Sue. 'I've never been to Paris. Nor, I believe, has Mrs Todd.'

Sue was busying herself at this time with the redecoration of The Evergreens. She had decided that the great central hall-way, which rose up through two storeys, must have new wallpaper. Austin came home from his college office to find her taking measurements, with the help of Ned.

'I can't bear this old paper any more,' she told him. 'It must all come down.'

'Come down!' exclaimed Austin. 'Have you any idea of the cost? I forbid you to do any such thing.'

'You forbid me?'

Sue trembled as she spoke.

'It's an unnecessary extravagance,' said Austin.

'You dare to talk to me about what's necessary?'

'There will be no new wallpaper. I have nothing more to say.'

Austin retreated to his study. Sue remained standing where he had left her. Ned looked on in trepidation. Then Sue went to the nearest wall, the wall that framed the door to the parlour, and prised up a section of the wallpaper with her fingernails. When she had enough to grip, she tore it from the wall in a long strip.

Ned cried out in alarm.

'Don't!'

She tore off a second strip. Then climbing the stairs, she began to rip at the paper wherever she could, tearing out patches all the way up.

'He forbids me!' she cried as she tore. 'He forbids me!'

When she reached the landing she sat herself down on the top step of the stairs, breathing rapidly. Ned came to her, dismayed.

'You mustn't mind so,' he said. 'You mustn't.'

'He was never like this before,' Sue said, speaking in a low hurried voice, as if to herself. 'She has done this to him. She has poisoned him. He's too unworldly. He's a good man, but he's weak. She has taken advantage of that. There is such a thing as evil in the world. We must fight against it. We must not let it win.'

★

From this day on, Sue chose to act as if Mabel did not exist. Her name was never mentioned. When encountered on the street, she was cut. Mattie and Gib, the younger children, without ever being told the reason, understood that Mrs Todd had become someone to fear and shun. Ned, deeply conflicted, withdrew into silence.

At the other house, the Homestead, Sue's declaration of war on Mabel had the effect of confirming the Dickinson sisters in Mabel's support.

'Any friend of our brother is a friend to this house,' said Vinnie.

Mabel clasped Vinnie's hands in hers and allowed a shine of incipient tears to brighten her eyes.

'I don't know what I'd do without you,' she said. 'I thought Sue was my best friend in Amherst, and now I've lost her.'

'Sue is nobody's friend for long,' said Vinnie. 'She contrives to quarrel with everyone in the end.'

'So I can go on calling on you?'

'You must call, and Austin must call, and Emily and I open our arms to you both. Our house, as Emily says, is a house of love.'

The fact was that Mabel, accustomed to being loved by all, was bewildered by Sue's hatred. Somehow without ever addressing the matter clearly, she had persuaded herself that Sue would come to understand and allow her love for Austin.

'If she truly loved you,' she said to Austin, 'she'd be proud that others love you too.'

'That's not Sue's way,' said Austin.

'Can't you talk to her? Make her understand that our love takes nothing away from her?'

'I wish that were so,' said Austin.

'What is it she wants? You're still her husband. You still go home to her every night. If anyone has a right to feel unhappy in these circumstances, surely it's me. I'm the one who can never be alone with you. I'm the one who must hide your letters, and send you mine in secret, unsigned. She has the most of you. In public she has all of you. Why can't she be content with that?'

'She wants my love,' said Austin, 'and she knows it's you who has that.'

'Did she have it before? Did I take it from her?'

'There was no love in me before. I've learned to love because of you.'

Austin's understanding of his wife's mind was no more than guesswork. Sue never cross-questioned him, or spoke about Mabel in any way. She had decided to act with Austin as if there were no shadow over their marriage and nothing had changed.

'Ned and I have a mind to take out the sleigh,' she said one Saturday. 'It's a fine afternoon, it's a crime to moulder indoors. Ned fancies a run to Hadley and back before we lose the light. Will you join us?'

'I have papers to read,' Austin replied.

As soon as Sue and Ned had set off, Austin was on his way to Pleasant Street to suggest to Mabel that they take advantage of the fine afternoon. He proposed that they walk up the Leverett road. Mabel understood that Sue was otherwise engaged, and at once put on her outdoor boots and fur-trimmed coat.

As they walked through the town, keeping a little apart,

conversing politely, there was nothing in their manner to give rise to any suspicion. If gossip had already begun to remark on Mr Dickinson's preference for Mrs Todd, gossip had no actual indiscretion on which to feed. Austin himself had a clear conscience. He had done nothing against the laws either of God or man. His love for Mabel contravened no statute. If Sue chose to make herself miserable over it, that was her affair.

'Even so,' said Mabel, who couldn't be as easy as he could, 'how long are we to go on like this? You don't feel it, perhaps, but I can assure you that I do. Am I to be treated like a pariah for as long as I live in this town?'

'I do feel it,' said Austin, 'but what are we to do? Sue supposes that she can make me give you up. I will never give you up.'

They had left the town now and were walking between snow-covered fields. There was no one to overlook or to overhear.

'Have you told her so?' said Mabel.

'We never discuss the matter,' said Austin. 'What purpose would be served? My mind is made up.'

'If she knew that, perhaps she would learn to accept matters,' said Mabel. 'David and I talk about everything. He doesn't go about looking black as thunder just because I choose to love you.'

'David is a wise man. Sue is not wise.'

'Even so, Austin. I think you might talk to her.'

'What am I to say?'

'Ask her to be civil. Tell her she gains nothing by this petulance. Order her to be civil. You are her husband.'

'She won't take orders from me.'

'So am I to be snubbed and cut and humiliated for ever more?'

At this moment they heard the sound of horses' hooves, and the Dickinson sleigh came up behind them. Ned was driving, with Sue by his side. It was clear from the shock on their rigidly averted faces that they had not expected to encounter the walkers.

Austin raised his hat. Mabel gave a bow. Neither Sue nor Ned made any acknowledgement in return. The sleigh swept on towards Leverett.

Once it was passed Mabel exclaimed, 'It's unbearable!'

They stopped, and turned, and retraced their steps.

'She told me they were to take the Hadley road,' said Austin. 'You must see it!'

'Yes, I see it. Of course I see it.'

'You must say something to her!'

Austin was silent for a long moment.

'I will do what I can,' he said. 'I think she must speak to me now.'

Austin was waiting in the parlour of The Evergreens when Sue and Ned returned. He stood grave and ominous before the fire, saying nothing at all, waiting for the accusation. Ned removed himself, glancing unhappily at his father as he went. Sue called for a pot of tea, and settled herself down with some embroidery. For a while neither spoke. Then Sue broke the silence.

'Are you not going to ask me how I enjoyed our sleigh ride?'

Austin said nothing.

'I take it you found a way to pass the time.'

Still he said nothing.

'Why won't you talk to me, Austin? Have I done anything to displease you? If so, please tell me.'

Still Austin said nothing. So Sue took a step nearer the abyss.

'Have you seen Mrs Todd recently?'

'You know I have,' said Austin.

'Will you be seeing her again?'

'Of course. Why should I not?'

'I never said you should not.'

A silence. Austin had expected an accusation, and in its absence he was unsure how to proceed. He had his defensive indignation ready, like a pile of dried tinder, but it needed a match.

'You are free to walk with your friends whenever you choose,' said Sue.

'I should hope so.'

'Of course, if you show too marked a preference, you must expect to give rise to rumours.'

'I can't be responsible for the fancies of idle minds.'

'But you would not wish me to be insulted.'

'How have you been insulted by any word or action of mine?'

His cold gravity was designed to force his wife into either acquiescence or an open breach. But Sue knew that in one respect at least her position was unassailable.

'You've never meant to insult me, Austin,' she said, 'and I know you never will, because I am your wife. An insult to me is an insult to you.'

'Just so,' said Austin.

'I know you value your position in society. I know you're a man of principle, and a man of faith. I know that you never would or could betray your marriage vows. That must be my consolation. You are my husband, till death do us part.'

To this Austin gave no answer at all.

That September Mabel Todd's story, 'Footprints', was published in the New York *Independent*, to general acclaim. The Amherst *Record* reprinted it. David Todd ordered a private printing, and gave out copies as gifts to friends and colleagues.

'I don't expect you to have read it, my dear,' said Mrs Jameson to Sue Dickinson. 'It's not your kind of thing at all. The writing is surprisingly sentimental for one who sets up to be sophisticated. But the great wonder is how the husband can bear to have it read by all the world!'

'Only a little wonder, I think,' said Sue drily. 'And not quite all the world, surely? They say the *Atlantic Monthly* turned it down.'

Alone with Austin, she broke her vow of silence on the subject of Mrs Todd enough to say, 'I hear you've become the hero of a work of romantic fiction.'

'Mrs Todd has published a beautiful story,' said Austin. 'Have you read it?'

'Do you advise me to?'

'My advice has very little success with you.'

'You are my husband. I respect your opinions.'

'Except in the matter of wallpaper.'

'I may go my own way when it comes to the decoration of the home in which I live and over which I preside,' said Sue angrily. 'But I hope I know how to behave when it comes to matters of law and decency.'

'I know of no law against the writing of stories. Yes, I advise you to read it. Her hero is a man who has lived too long with loneliness. Mrs Todd imagines his feelings with great delicacy.'

'Does this lonely hero have a wife?'

'He is unmarried.'

'Then Mrs Todd can get him married, and he'll not be lonely any more. Does she marry him off by the end of the story?'

'A marriage is in prospect.'

'A happy ending! Marriage is always the happy ending, isn't it? How could it be otherwise?'

Her voice trembled a little as she spoke. Austin caught a sudden glimpse, through the cracks in the armour of her bitterness, of the wounded creature within. But he had gone too far, and the gulf between them was too great. He gave no answer.

'I have work to do.'

He retreated to his study.

He had gone too far, and yet not far enough. He found himself locked in daily struggle with a terrible temptation. His love for Mabel was a love of the spirit; it was the joyous discovery of a sympathetic companion on life's bitter journey. The ecstatic release he felt in her company was pure, and holy, and surely a gift from God. His marriage was not negated, it was complemented. However, when he took Mabel in his arms and kissed her, when he felt the soft yielding pressure of her body against his, he knew that there lay waiting a deeper love, and one that he craved more with every day that passed.

He had never spoken aloud of such hopes to Mabel, but his instincts told him he was not wrong to hope. He sensed in her every touch the invitation to further touch. Still he hesitated. If he were to ask, and she were to grant, what then? He felt himself to be standing on the edge of a cliff. So small a step, so great a fall.

It was impossible. It would be a crime, and it would be a sin. It would shatter the whole edifice on which he had constructed his life. His love for Mabel must remain for ever unconsummated.

'I believe our love comes from God,' Mabel said to him, understanding every turn of his thoughts. 'If God has brought us together, God will find a way to join us in sacred union.'

They both found it comforting and exciting to co-opt religious terms in this way. Mabel wrote to Austin:

> I trust you as I trust God. The way in which you love me is a consecration – it is the holy of holies, and a thought, even commonplace, would desecrate it. I approach it even in my mind as a shrine, where the purest and noblest there is in me worships.

Secretly – this she dared not say openly even to Austin – Mabel hoped that Sue would die. Austin, released from his marriage vows by death, would then be free to marry her. Quite what would happen to David she did not consider.

In the end it was a death that brought about the sacred union, but not Sue's death. Little eight-year-old Gilbert, known as Gib, the sweet-tempered joy of his father's heart, contracted typhoid fever. Austin abandoned all his legal and college affairs to sit by the boy's bedside. He hardly saw Mabel at all. Sue, in terror for her youngest child, nevertheless felt that the illness had restored her husband to sanity. Wracked with suffering for his boy, he had become the father of the family again.

Doctors were sent for, and all was done for the child that could be done. Day followed day, and the fever did not abate. The doctors looked ever more solemn. Sue prayed by the bed-side, and Austin prayed with her, his doubts overwhelmed by his need.

'Let him live, Lord,' he prayed. 'He's without sin. Let others pay for their transgressions. Let my little one live.'

Gib himself bore his illness with such exemplary sweetness that his father was harrowed.

'He never complains,' he said to Sue.

'Why should he complain?' said Sue. 'If he leaves us, it'll be to run straight into the arms of God.'

Sue was magnificent: the strong centre of the household as they waited night after night for the denouement. She managed Gib's medicines, fed him such food as he could eat, washed him. She never seemed to need sleep herself, and she never seemed downcast. She went about her duties with a shining face, her head held high.

She only spoke of Mabel once, and indirectly.

'I hear the theatricals are going ahead,' she said to Austin.

The village was to have an amateur production of Mrs Bur-nett's *A Fair Barbarian*. Mabel Todd had agreed to play the leading part.

'I care nothing for that,' said Austin.

This was sweet for Sue to hear. While she nursed their sick child, Mabel was making a spectacle of herself on a public stage. This would not be lost on Austin.

Then after six weeks, uncomplaining to the end, little Gib died.

Austin was devastated. His grief was compounded by guilt. Was this God's punishment for his illicit love? He withdrew from all society, including Mabel's, and for a while lost himself in solitude and silence.

The Evergreens entered deep mourning. Sue dressed in black like a widow, and seemed to age beyond her years. Death possessed the house and the family, and it seemed as if they welcomed it.

Emily sent a letter of condolence, one of her strange unfinished notes:

His life was full of Boon, I see him in the Star, and meet his sweet velocity in everything that flies – His life was like the Bugle, which winds itself away, his Elegy an Echo – his Requiem ecstasy –

When Austin emerged at last from the paralysis of grief, Sue was waiting. She expected her husband to be a chastened man, ready to join her in the shared solemnity of mourning.

'Dear Austin,' she said to him, 'our boy is gone for ever. But he has left us the great gift of his sweet love. We have Ned, we have Mattie. We have each other.'

Austin stared at her uncomprehendingly.

'Austin?'

She took a step towards him, reaching out her hands. To her horror he let out a cry and drew back.

'What is it, Austin? I'm your wife.'

'Leave me alone!'

'Husband! We must stand by each other!'

'He's dead,' said Austin. 'Let the dead bury their dead. I want to live!'

With these terrible words, he left the house that had now become for him a tomb, and ran through the trees to the Homestead. There he begged Vinnie to send for Mabel. Mabel came, and took him in her arms, and there he found the life he craved.

'I live for you now,' he told her again and again. 'Only you. I have only you. You are life to me, my darling. Only our love is real now.'

It was as if he had abandoned all his former constraints, and was born again. He no longer cared for his reputation, or for his wife's feelings. He was possessed by a single overwhelming conviction: death is near, now is the time to love.

'I have no more doubts,' he told Mabel. 'Why should there be any barriers between us? Why should we not come as close to each other in body as we are in soul? Is this not what we were made for?'

His love for Mabel was more intense than it had ever been. He had overcome his scruples. He stood within reach of the joy he had been denied for so long. He trembled with longing, and found in his own ecstatic surrender the sure evidence that this was the true path, that this was life, and everywhere else there was death.

Mabel understood and rejoiced. She wanted to bind Austin to her for all time, and she knew that the closest bond was not a wedding ring. She had it in her power to make him the gift of her body. Once given, there was no way back. They would be lovers. They would be one.

But first, following the dictates of her own private morality, she sought David's permission.

'My dearest,' she said to him, 'you know how Mr Dickinson has been broken by his boy's death. The dear man nearly died himself. But now he wants to live. He wants to find comfort in the world. I know I can give him that comfort.'

'Of course you can,' said David. 'Who would not be comforted by my sweet darling?'

'You're my own husband, and you know I love you, and I always will. But you know how close I've grown to Mr Dickinson. You know there's so much love in me that I can love him too.'

'I'm proud to call Mr Dickinson a friend. Your love for him does you honour. He's a remarkable man.'

'My best husband in the world! How many husbands would understand as you do?'

'My sweet,' he said, 'you and I have always been open with each other. Before we were married I made you a confession. A lesser woman might have broken the engagement for that alone. But you chose to understand my nature, and to love me as I am. I have loved others. I have never denied it. Why should you not do the same?'

Mabel kissed him and was almost reassured. But she wanted to be quite clear that he understood and approved her intentions.

'Before this latest blow,' she said, 'Mr Dickinson held back from the final proof of his love for me. His noble nature caused him to feel that the obligations he had undertaken forbade taking that step. Now, his spirit half crushed by grief, he turns from death to life, and finds it in me. In my arms. In my love.

In my fullest love. In all that lies in my power to give. How can I deny him what he asks?'

'You cannot, and you should not,' said David. 'Love him as you love me.'

'Darling! Darling!' She covered him with kisses. 'What have I done to deserve so perfect a husband? How can I repay you?'

'Keep no secrets from me, my sweet. There need be no false shame between us. Let's all three give love and receive love, as nature has made us, openly and joyfully. Love him for me too.'

Secure in David's approval, Mabel and Austin prepared themselves for the final consummation of their love. Three days after the conversation with David, on the evening of December 13 1883, the lovers met in the dining room at the Homestead. Vinnie and Emily were accustomed by now to their trysts, and made sure to allow them the privacy they needed. The spinster sisters had no way of knowing, now or later, exactly what transpired behind that closed door.

The iron stove burned bravely, warming the dining room. An oil lamp on the table sent out its soft, flattering glow. They drew the sofa close to the heat, and sat there, side by side. Slowly, with trembling fingers, Austin unbuttoned Mabel's dress, and unlaced her undergarments. When she was partially unclothed he came to a stop, overwhelmed by wonder. He gazed at her body in the lamplight, unable to believe that such joy was permitted him. Gently she took his hands and pressed them to her breasts, saying without words, See, my body is yours. I give it to you.

He slipped down onto his knees before her. For both of them it was an act of worship.

It had been a long slow courtship. From the evening of 'going by the gate' to the night of the consummation of their love fourteen months had passed; four hundred and twenty-eight days of ever-intensifying passion. From now on, Mabel regarded her relationship with Austin as a second marriage.

On December 20 the Todds left Amherst for a long stay in Washington. From her parents' house, Mabel wrote Austin a poem of her own devising. She added it to the end of a letter, and she called it 'P. S. First':

> You are all that I have to live for –
> All that I want to love,
> All that the world holds for me
> Of faith in a world above.
>
> You came – and it seemed too mighty
> For my human heart to hold;
> It seemed, in its sacred glory,
> Like a glimpse through the gates of gold.
>
> Like life in the perennial Eden,
> Created, formed anew,
> This dream of a perfect manhood
> That I realise in you.

12

Stand at the top of the stairs. Look down into the dark hallway below. She's there with him, the one he loves, the one I need. A door opens. The rustle of a dress as a half-glimpsed woman passes quickly down the passage, and out of the back door. Don't move yet. Wait.

He comes out more slowly, as if deep in thought. Halfway across the hallway he stops. He knows he's watched. He looks up, and there's wonder on his face.

Come down the stairs now, holding tight to the banister, taking each step carefully.

'Why, Em, you're not well!'

This is true, but it's of no account. Reach out to him, press one hand to his arm.

'Are you happy, brother?'

He says, 'I have no words.'

'But you're happy?'

'I never knew such happiness was possible.'

This is good. This is as it should be.

I say, 'Make me feel it.'

'What can I say?' But the glow of his face speaks for him. 'An explosion – of joy . . .'

An explosion. Like the firing of guns. His arm trembles beneath my hand.

'She loves you too, Em. She feels so close to you.'

I say, 'She must come closer.'

He thinks I mean something else.

'Will you see her? She wants so much to meet you.'

'There will come a time,' I say.

He goes on his way, to make his shout in the noisy world. I climb back up my mountain to my lookout. Every day the path a little steeper, until the day I take wing and fly.

Just my little toot of vainglory. There'll be no playground in the sky when the time comes. Down I shall sink, and the darkness will close over me.

But I do not mean to be silent.

13

Chez Albert on North Pleasant Street is a small homely restaurant that makes an attempt to recreate the atmosphere of a Parisian bistro. Amber wood floors, candles glowing on copper-topped tables. The front-of-house manager greets Nick as an old friend.

'How is it, Nick? Good to see you again. I heard you were leaving us.'

'You'll have to put up with me a little longer, Emmanuel. Seat us somewhere where we can hear ourselves talk.'

Emmanuel leads them to a booth at the back. Alice, following, wonders how many young women have come this way in the past. She registers Emmanuel's brief appraising glance, and feels herself bristling at being presumed to be the next in a long line of dates. For a moment she regrets agreeing to come. Then she looks at the menu and changes her mind. At least she'll eat a good dinner.

'Paul got anything special on today?' Nick asks.

'The oysters are fresh in. And we have veal sweetbreads with plum marmalade.'

He leaves them to make their choices.

'Emmanuel comes from the Loire valley,' says Nick. 'His second name is Proust. How can you not like a restaurant run by a man called Proust?'

'You come here a lot?'

She's looking at the menu. The dishes are pricey for Amherst, beyond the reach of students.

'Enough,' says Nick. 'Thanks to Peggy, I'm one of the idle rich. For now at least.'

Alice frowns, more in confusion than disapproval. The invisible wife has still not returned. Would she approve of this evening out, which looks so much like a date?

Emmanuel brings a basket of warm bread and a dish of olive oil. Nick orders wine. They make their menu choices. Alice chooses the butternut squash soup and pork confit. Nick chooses the veal sweetbreads and scallops. They talk about Mabel and Austin.

'Now here's a leading question,' Nick says. 'Do you actually like Mabel?'

Alice tries to answer truthfully.

'I want to like her. I want to believe in her great love. But it's not easy. She's so self-centred, I suppose. But then, why shouldn't she be? I mean, aren't we all?'

'I think we are,' says Nick, smiling.

'Why is that funny?'

'I'm sorry. I don't mean to tease you. It's just the sight of you struggling with the shapelessness of life.'

'The shapelessness of life? I don't even know what that means.'

'It means that we want things to fit the clothes we dress them in, but they don't.'

'Oh, right. Like, life is complicated.'

'Well, isn't it?'

'For a moment there I thought you were saying something original.'

He gazes at her across the candlelit table, the smile lingering.

'You're very beautiful.'

She flushes.

'Why say that?'

'I was hoping to surprise you.'

'Say that to your girlfriends. Say it to your wife.'

He just goes on staring at her, apparently not offended by her sharp response. It feels as if he's studying her.

'You're beautiful in the way the young Virginia Woolf was beautiful.'

'Why are you doing this, Nick?' She has to stop him. 'Is this your famous technique in action? Don't try it on me, it won't work.'

Don't try it on me, it might work. What fools we are. A little flattery, and resistance crumbles.

'My famous technique? No. I have no technique.'

'They just throw themselves at you, I suppose.'

'That does happen,' he says. 'Doing nothing to attract people is an attraction all by itself. For a certain type.'

'I'm fascinated.'

She means to be sarcastic and he understands her, but he doesn't seem to mind. How can he be so relaxed?

'Would it help if I told you my love life has been one long catalogue of failure?'

'Would it help what?'

'Would it stop you wanting to punish me?'

Their first course arrives. Under cover of the clatter of dishes Alice reflects that Nick is right, and she does want to punish him. This is embarrassing. However he chooses to conduct his love life, it's not her job to judge him.

She starts on her soup.

'All right. Tell me about the catalogue of failure.'

'I'm not asking for pity. Just shifting your perception a little.'

'I don't pity you, Nick,' she says.

'I expect you can guess. I make no claims to originality. The truth is that from a very young age, I've felt I'm alone. I've not wanted to be, I've tried not to be, but that's how it's gone on. For a short time, with Laura Kinross, it didn't feel that way. But that was long ago, and I was young, and I didn't know how rare it was to love like that. So I blew it, the way you do. Since then there've been others. There've been good times. But I've always been alone.'

'What about your wife?'

'My wife,' says Nick, 'finances cancer research, and a scheme to promote literacy. She's on the board of trustees of Amnesty International, and the Register of Historic Houses, and the Emily Dickinson Museum. I'm the least of her charities.'

'Oh, please.'

'Actually, she describes me as her leisure activity. In jest, of course.'

'You chose to marry her.'

'So I did.'

He stares back at her, entirely unashamed.

'I still don't understand,' says Alice.

'Think of it as a genetic defect,' he says. 'Some people are born colour blind. Maybe I was born missing some essential ingredient.'

'Except you did love Laura.'

'Yes, I did. I tell myself that. I hold on to that.'

So he's telling her he can't love but he wants to love.

'That line from Emily Dickinson,' she says, '"I've none to tell me to but thee." Where did that come from?'

She's not asking about the poem. She's asking why he said it to her. He understands.

'A sense of fellow feeling, I suppose.'

'But you didn't mean I was the one you could tell yourself to.'

'Didn't I?'

'You don't know me.'

'That's true. I don't know you at all. But I know what interests you, because you've told me. Do you think I talk like this with all my so-called girlfriends?'

'You might.'

'Take it from me, those conversations do not last long.'

'But then I guess you don't want them for the chat.'

'So I talk to you.'

Great. They get the sex, I get the confession. Who's more used here? It's a close-run thing.

'Some people manage to combine the two.'

'Like Mabel and Austin,' he says. 'Which is what makes them so interesting. We want to know how they did it. That's why I'll go to see your movie when it comes out.'

'If it comes out.'

'Come on. Have faith.'

He's navigated them back onto safe ground. After a danger-ous lurch into real emotions, the non-date can resume.

He's tucking into his sweetbreads.

'I'm not sure I'll ever find out how they did it,' Alice says. 'Here's one of the twists in the story. I don't think they would ever have become lovers if Austin's little boy hadn't died.'

'You think they would have gone on talking love but never doing it?'

'The shackles were on him, weren't they? Adultery was beyond the reach of his imagination. And then Gib died, and it's as if he just rose up, like a mythical hero chained to a rock, and ripped himself free.'

'The opposite of death is desire.'

'Is that a quotation?'

'Blanche, in *A Streetcar Named Desire*.'

'Well, it's true.'

'You mean even if written by a metaphor-drunk pansy like Tennessee Williams, it's still true?'

'Oh, God. Is that how I sound?'

'He was a metaphor-drunk pansy. But it's still a fine play. And desire is the opposite of death. That's a big, big truth.'

'And a big, big get-out.'

Emmanuel comes to their booth to ask if the starters are good. Nick raises one hand, puts thumb and forefinger together. Emmanuel leans a little closer and speaks in a sympathetically low voice.

'I heard about you and Peggy. I'm sorry about that.'

'So it goes,' says Nick.

'She's a great lady.'

'And always will be.'

Emmanuel departs. Alice stares at Nick.

'What was that about?'

'Oh, me and Peggy have been in here together a few times. Peggy's a generous tipper.'

'Nick, are you and Peggy going through a bad time?'

Now, for the first time, he's not looking at her. His eyes on the copper glow of the table between them.

'Not any more,' he says.

'She's supposed to be coming home, but she never comes. I mean, I know it's none of my business, but what's going on? I am staying in her house. I feel really confused.'

He's nodding, accepting the justice of her complaint.

'I know,' he says, 'I know.'

'So what am I supposed to think?'

'Does it matter what the situation is between Peggy and me?'

'No. Not to me. Except that you're the one who gave me that Emily line. You're the one who's saying we've got this fellow feeling, and telling me all your life you've been alone. You're the one who talks about big truth. And behind it all I hear is silence.'

Silence.

'You're right,' he says at last. He looks up. He's so handsome in the candlelight, his face so frank, his gaze so gentle. 'It's no secret. Peggy and I are getting divorced.'

'Divorced!'

'All very amicable. I think it's come as a relief to both of us. We're really very good friends now.'

'Divorced! Why didn't you tell me?'

'Should I have told you?'

'Well, I would have thought . . . I mean, you offered me a

room in your house – naturally because I knew you were married . . . I mean . . .'

She starts to flounder. Everything she says leads to humiliating revelations. Unnerved, she goes onto the attack.

'Yes, you should have told me! I seem to be the only one who doesn't know. Even the waiter knows!'

Too strong. Tone it down.

'I'm sorry. I'm overreacting. It's just that you've put me in the wrong. I've been judging you unfairly. But why have you let me? You know I was shocked by Marcia, but you never told me what was going on. You let me think you were cheating on your wife. I don't get it. All you had to do was say, "It's over with my wife, I'm single again." But you never said a word. You let me go on thinking you were a selfish shit.'

'I am a selfish shit.'

'Yes, but, but.' She waves her soup spoon in the air. 'This changes everything.'

'How does it change everything?'

'Oh God. You know.' She's getting into the mess again. 'So what went wrong? With you and your wife, I mean.'

'You'd have to ask Peggy that.'

'What's your version?'

'My version? I think I'd say we had a great affair and a lousy marriage.'

'In other words you screwed around.'

'Not at first.'

He seems to have no more to say.

'That's it?'

'I'm not getting into the blame game. It didn't work out.

We're both old enough to deal with that in a civilised way. So yes, that's it.'

'OK.' There's something here she's not getting. Several things. 'So why not tell me?'

'Perhaps it suited me not to tell you.'

'But why? Did you want me to think the worst of you?'

'Perhaps I wanted to keep you out of reach.'

Alice feels giddy.

'Why?' she hears herself say.

'You belong with my past.'

With the famous Laura.

'And you've cut yourself off from all that?'

'That's the way it's worked out.'

'One long catalogue of failure. Not a great result.'

'I struggle on.'

'Desire being the opposite of death.'

She has no idea what she's saying. Is this a confession? It feels like something else, something perilously close to flirtation. She sees the way he's watching her, and realises he no longer knows how she's going to respond.

To her surprise she feels a wave of tenderness towards him.

'Oh, Nick,' she says. 'What an old fraud you are.'

'Am I?'

'No, that's not fair. How do I know?'

'I don't mind being a fraud. I'd just as soon not be old.'

'You're not that old.'

Alice thinks of Guy, her father, and how he had an affair with a friend of hers, a girl of her own age. At school they used to call girls like that 'daddy-stealers'. It happens.

'I'm old enough to know what I'm doing,' says Nick.

'What are you doing?'

'Not taking advantage of you.'

'Well, fuck you.' She speaks softly so the other diners won't hear. 'There is no way you could take advantage of me. I do what I choose to do, and I don't do what I choose not to do. I run my own life.'

'If you say so.'

They're looking at each other all the time now, and it doesn't really matter any more what they say. Contact has been made.

'You don't believe me, do you?' she says. 'You're still living in a Victorian fantasy-land of seduction and betrayal. The irresistible male. The helpless female, a moth to his flame.'

He gives a slight shake of his head, never taking his eyes off her.

'What do you want me to tell you, Alice?'

Tell me again that I'm beautiful. Tell me you desire me. Give me the pleasure of telling you to go fuck yourself.

'Don't protect me, Nick. I'm grown-up now.'

'Maybe I'm protecting myself.'

'From what? From me?'

'Why not? Maybe it's you who's taking advantage of me.'

'To achieve what, exactly?'

'How do I know? Maybe it's some unfinished business to do with your father.'

Alice flinches, and the intense eye contact is broken. She feels as if he's slapped her. Then she feels outraged. Then she thinks, What if it's true?

Their main courses arrive. Emmanuel announces them.

'For the lady, pork confit with polenta and pear glaze. For

the gentleman, scallops in a chanterelle mushroom sauce, with potato purée and steamed kale. Enjoy.'

They do not enjoy. They look up from their plates and find each other again.

'Don't listen to me,' says Nick. 'I've no right to tell you anything. I've screwed up my own life. I don't want to be any part of screwing up yours.'

'That's agreed, then.'

Still they don't start eating. Just looking into each other's eyes, and knowing what's coming, and waiting for it to be too late to stop.

Suddenly she doesn't want to be in this restaurant. She wants to be back in his house, the house that belongs to the wife who is an ex-wife, who is no longer a barrier.

'Have you ever ordered a meal in a restaurant,' she says, 'and left without eating it?'

'No,' he says.

'Is it a wicked thing to do?'

'Not if you pay.'

'I'm not going to be able to eat this.'

'I'll ask for the check.'

This is how they know it's going to happen, by speaking of something else. They have moved beyond the point at which she can tell him to go fuck himself.

How did I end up here?

But of course it's been coming for days. And why not? There's no one left to deceive. A brief adventure that hurts no one.

I've none to tell me to but thee.

Outside in the parking lot he gives her a hand up into the

cab of his stupid truck. He keeps hold of her hand. She turns to look at him, standing there in the cold night.

'Don't do this, Alice,' he says.

'I do what I want,' she says. 'You do what you want. That's how it works in the world of grown-ups.'

'I don't want to do this.'

'So don't do it.'

He gets in and starts the engine. The heater roars. They drive out onto Pleasant Street, the road that leads to the cemetery.

'Don't say I didn't warn you,' he says.

After so much talk there are no words when they re-enter the house on Triangle Street. He takes her hand and they climb the wide stairs together like children going to bed. They kiss briefly in the doorway to his bedroom. She goes in first. Their silence is a secret agreement: what they're doing requires no justification, and will leave little trace. They're alone in the big house, but he still closes the bedroom door.

14

In the months that followed the consummation of their love, Mabel and Austin met almost every day. When they could not meet they wrote to each other. They had their special times, at ten in the morning, and at five in the afternoon, when they went walking together. When Mabel was away, they thought of each other at these times. They created their own private prayer, which they spoke in unison when together.

'For my beloved is mine and I am his. What can we want beside? Nothing!'

For a time the lovers were not troubled by their partners. Sue Dickinson, still in mourning for her dead child, kept mostly to her house. David Todd struck up a friendship with a Bostonian cousin of Mabel's called Caro Andrews, a handsome young woman who was bored by her rich husband. A house became available for rent, off Triangle Street, behind the Dickinson houses. The Todds were able to set up their own establishment at last, and bring their daughter Millicent, now three years old, to live with them on a permanent basis. To

Millicent Austin was the family friend, a little frightening in his silences, but almost as familiar to her as her father.

In their quiet walks together down summer lanes, Austin and Mabel never tired of exploring the miracle that was their love.

'Do you ever wish,' Mabel said, 'that we'd known each other when we were growing up? We could have played together as children.'

'I would have loved you even then,' said Austin.

'The grown-ups would have said, "Look at those two! They're inseparable!"'

'So we would have been.'

'But I like it better as it is,' said Mabel. 'There's something magical about meeting someone when you're fully grown, and knowing you've met your destiny.'

'Magical,' said Austin, 'and almost more than I can comprehend. I think I must be in dreamland, I'm afraid to wake. It's too much, the happiness overwhelms me, but I am awake. You are here beside me. The sweetest, richest dreams of my boyhood, and youth, and manhood, have all come true.'

His low fervent voice thrilled her as they walked.

'Dear Austin. My own dearest man.'

'When I look round the pews in church and see the good people of Amherst sitting so comfortably together, all those husbands and wives, I ask myself, Can they feel as we feel?'

'What?' said Mabel. 'The Bartletts and the Bigelows and the Hitchcocks and the Hills? I don't think so! The surprise is that they've managed to procreate at all.'

'And yet we have found each other! What have I done to deserve such a reward?'

'Oh, nothing!' cried Mabel. 'Nothing at all! Except live a life of exemplary goodness, and give unstintingly of your time and energy, and grow year by year in wisdom and kindness, and so become the most respected man of your age.'

'Is that why God has given you to me?'

'I believe,' said Mabel, 'that God created us for each other. I believe that I know God's love through your love. All I ask is that I may be worthy of it.'

They lived in these months in a state of mutual exultation. Their preference for each other was apparent to everyone in the town, but David Todd made it clear that he regarded the friendship as innocent, and welcomed Austin Dickinson as his own friend. This more than anything silenced the malice of gossips. Why shouldn't Mr Dickinson put on his stylish coat and his wide-brimmed hat and take Mrs Todd out driving in his carriage? Before Mrs Todd had ever come to Amherst, Mrs Tuckerman had been a favourite, and had been taken on similar drives. Gentlemen were allowed to admire pretty young ladies. In this way a secret of sorts was kept.

Now that the Todds had a house of their own they had no more need of the Homestead for their secret liaisons. Vinnie complained to Austin that he neglected his sisters.

'Emily is not at all well, Austin. Her back hurts her, and she hardly sleeps at all. She thinks you no longer care for us.'

This last was an invention of Vinnie's, but it had the desired effect. Austin called on Emily. He found her tired, but eager for news.

'Tell me about Mrs Todd. I hear she's a published author. Does she still brighten your life?'

Austin needed no further prompting.

'Mabel is . . . Mabel is . . . what is she not? She's everything to me! I want all the world to know! Instead we must hide and creep about and pretend. I can't bear it, Em.'

'And Mrs Todd, can she bear it?'

'She's an angel. She spreads her beautiful wings and rises above the pettiness and spite.'

'Will you take her a poem from me?'

Austin carried the poem proudly to Mabel, and she received it with reverence. Here was further proof that her love for Austin was blessed by the Myth; and better still, that she was among the very few who were permitted to see her poems.

The poem began:

> *My River runs to thee —*
> *Blue Sea! Wilt welcome me?*

And ended:

> *Say — Sea — Take Me!*

Austin called it charming, supposing it to be a nature poem. Mabel knew better.

'It's about love,' she said. She trembled as she read it. 'She must have loved to write like this.'

'If she has,' said Austin, 'I'm not aware that she's ever been loved in return. There was John Graves, when she was young, and later there was George Gould. But nothing came of it in either case.'

'You think nothing comes of love if it doesn't lead to marriage.'

'Hardly,' said Austin. But then he became confused. He wanted to affirm the primacy of his unmarried love for Mabel, but at the same time he wished with all his heart that the world could know her as his wife.

In October 1884, when the Todds were established in the Lessey house, Mabel's parents came from Washington on an extended visit. Mabel invited her Amherst friends to a house-warming. She served chicken salad and cake, and decorated the house in her own original way, with golden leaves and yellow daisies and vines. Over seventy people came. The party was judged a brilliant success.

Shortly after this, Mabel's mother, Mrs Loomis, heard the rumours about her daughter and Mr Dickinson.

'Mabel,' she said, 'I do hope you're taking care to preserve your reputation. A reputation once lost can't be regained.'

'I have no idea what you're talking about, Mama.'

'I'm talking about Mr Dickinson.'

'Mr Dickinson is a good friend to me, and to David. Why should he not be?'

'No, Mabel, that won't do. People are saying that you go driving with him in by-roads, and that he comes into your house by back ways, and that he stays with you late, after your husband has retired.'

'That's enough, Mama! What are you accusing me of?'

'My darling, I know there's no impropriety here. But there is the appearance of impropriety. You must be more careful of what you are seen to do, or people will start to believe you do much more.'

'People! Who are these people? They're small-minded fools with no better way to fill their time!'

'I'm only telling you what I hear, Mabel. Think of Millicent. Do you want to expose her to this kind of gossip?'

'I do think of Millicent! And David! I'm a good mother, and a good wife! Am I not to be allowed a friend?'

She burst into tears.

Alone with Austin, finding comfort in his arms, she told him of the accusations her mother had made. Austin proved to be a pillar of strength.

'Is there anything in our love of which you're ashamed?'

'Nothing!'

'Then what have we to fear? Our life together is as white and unspotted as the fresh-driven snow.'

'Yes! Yes!'

'We love one another. There may be others who don't understand our love – who hold to the letter which killeth and not to the Spirit which giveth life – but that is the cross we must bear in this world. We know that we would give up our life for our love if necessary. There is no life for me without you.'

'No life for me without you,' Mabel repeated.

Then they said their prayer together.

'For my beloved is mine and I am his. What can we want beside? Nothing!'

For all the brave front they put on for each other, both knew they must be more careful in future. From now on they met less frequently, and took care when together in public to make no great show of seeking each other out. Their liaisons at the Homestead continued, known only to Vinnie and Emily.

As Sue emerged from mourning, her hatred of Mabel came out into the open. When Mabel began singing in the quartette of the First Congregational Church choir, Sue stopped attending the weekly service. When Mabel was invited by the students of the college to be the Matron of their annual dance, Sue forbad Mattie to go. She gave no reason for her actions, but nor did she conceal her motives. When Mabel walked into a room, Sue walked out.

Mabel begged Austin to do something to control his wife, but he was powerless. All they could do, he said, was wait for Sue to come to terms with reality. In the meantime a deep bitterness began to form within Mabel. She could see no end to the snubs and the slights. Amherst, she felt, was turning against her. Everywhere she went she believed she saw spying eyes and heard whispering tongues. When Caro Andrews came up with a plan to go on a trip to Europe, and proposed taking Mabel with her, Mabel talked it over with both David and Austin, and gratefully accepted. She needed a break from small-town life.

She sailed from Boston on the *Pavonia*, for Queenstown, Ireland. She was to be away for three months. Austin found her absence unbearably painful. He poured out his love and longing in letters that chased Mabel from Dublin to London and Paris.

Another of these most perfect of fine days – and you not here. What are days, for now! I don't want any of them – they are a burden – there's no life or meaning in them. They are as blank as this paper untouched by pen, ready to be filled – may hold everything or nothing. There's nothing *for* them to hold but you, my darling, my beloved. I would rather they were all blotted out till you are back. I see David as it happens in the day time, and go over every evening for a while, as regularly as before you walked off, that morning of the fourth. We talk some – each, I think, feels nearer to you through the other than in any other way.

Austin and David became close over this time of Mabel's absence. They shared Mabel in memory just as they had shared her in person. David told Austin how he had first met Mabel, before he even knew her name.

'She was standing with her father outside the Nautical Almanac Office in Washington, wearing an old blue waterproof. It was raining. I think I loved her from that moment.'

It was a precious memory to David, and in describing it he offered it to Austin, so it could become his memory too.

David spoke of Mabel's father, and how she revered him.

'I loved her for that.'

That led them to talk of their own fathers.

'Ah, you should have met my father,' said Austin. 'He was almost a god to us. I don't believe I ever saw him smile. I certainly never dared to touch him. Not until he was dead, that is. I kissed his cheek as he lay in the coffin.'

'And now you and I are both fathers.'

'Am I a father?' said Austin, shaking his head sadly. 'Now that Gib is gone, I feel as if I have no place in my own home. Ned and Mattie are Sue's children, not mine.'

'Do you ever think,' said David, 'how your life might have taken a different course, had you chosen one road and not another, had you opened one door and not another?'

'Every day,' said Austin. 'The old dream of what might have been.'

'You'll laugh at me,' said David, 'but when I was a boy I had a great passion for church organs. We worshipped in the Plymouth Church in Brooklyn, and they had a Hook & Hastings organ there. I was allowed to pump the bellows.'

Austin looked wonderingly at his friend, touched by the eagerness in his eyes.

'Church organs!'

'I couldn't tell you why. The grand sound, of course. But it was the mechanism that fascinated me. I have a natural bent towards engineering, I think. You've heard of Thomas Alva Edison? He invited me to join him in his workshop. I must've been just twenty years old. I was very tempted. But I had just discovered astronomy, and in the end I took that path.'

'My path was always laid out before me,' said Austin. 'I had a notion before I was married that I might go west, and make a career in Chicago. But my father offered me a partnership in his law practice, and built Sue and me a house next to his, and so I stayed. My father was very taken with Sue. I think it was her he wanted to keep by him more than me.'

He shook his head as he remembered.

'I look back on my life and I wonder at myself. How can I have known so little?'

'But you were happy with Sue in the beginning, surely?'

'In the beginning, perhaps. But somewhere in my heart I knew we were wrong for each other. I was young, and she was pretty, and lively, and even Emily was in love with her then. All my family loved her. Who was I to disagree?'

He lowered his voice.

'Sue never accustomed herself to a wife's duties, if you understand me. Never. I remember once she called it low practices. That side of our marriage – well, it's hardly been a marriage.'

'My dear fellow!'

'You can imagine what Mabel means to me.'

'More than imagine. I know for myself.'

'Of course you do.' Then after a pause, 'How extraordinary it is that we two can sit here and say such things.'

'Extraordinary, and yet the most natural thing in the world.'

'A lesser man might feel jealous.'

'Mabel loves me,' said David. 'Nothing has changed. Her love for you takes nothing from me. We've always given each other absolute freedom.'

'And you've never regretted that freedom?'

'Never.'

'To be absolutely clear, you know that Mabel has given me what Sue was unable to give.'

'Of course. She asked my permission.'

'She asked your permission?'

'Mabel and I have no secrets from each other. We never lie to each other.'

'And what she asked – it doesn't disturb you in any way?'

'Perhaps there's something missing in me,' said David. 'I'm well aware that as the husband I should huff and puff over my wife's honour, or my honour, or some such imagined slight. But the truth is my wife is beautiful, and I see no reason why another man shouldn't enjoy her beauty. I'm proud that you love her.'

'Well,' said Austin, 'you're a finer man than I.'

What David did not tell Austin was that he found the idea of Mabel's love affair arousing. Sometimes when alone in his bedroom he conjured up the familiar image of his wife's naked body, and introduced Austin by her side. Then while he stroked himself, he imagined Austin making love with Mabel. In this fantasy the picture of Austin was hazy, he could hardly say if he was dressed or not. The entire focus of his attention was on Mabel, gladly receiving another man's love. He could see her face, her cheeks flushed and her lips parted. He could hear her rapid breaths, and her panting voice saying, 'Love me! Love me!' At the height of her passion he heard her habitual cry, a high wordless note, and as he did so he too would reach his climax.

Mabel's long trip drew to an end at last. Austin's eager impatience rose to a fever pitch.

> I have been reading lately of some of the famous loves of history – but find no parallel to yours and mine. Antony and Cleopatra. Abelard and Heloise. Chateaubriand and Madame Recamier. And others. Heloise loved as well as you. What other! – and what man, as I love you! What a fool Abelard was! And Antony. Madly in love with Cleopatra – but with the opportunity before him, marrying Octavia instead, for political policy. I love you darling – all I am I am yours – for time – and for Eternity . Soon my arms shall be tightly around you. We shall not speak, we shall be too full – we shall be each others and we shall know that we are beyond all possible power to separate. Forever and forever. . .

Mabel arranged her two reunions with husband and lover by letters from Paris, taking both into her confidence. She asked

Austin not to come to the Cunard wharf when the ship docked, but to meet her in her Boston hotel, the Parker House, the next day. This was for the sake of appearances. It would also give her one night with David, to whom she wrote:

David dear – *dear*, DEAR, how I will kiss you and caress you when I once more get you within reach! How you shall *feel* all that I think now about you from afar.

All went according to plan. Mabel's ship docked early on the Sunday morning of September 13 1885. David met her, and spent that night with her at the Parker House. Then as David took a train back to Amherst, Austin passed in the opposite direction, arriving in Boston at 9:40 a.m. on Monday. The lovers were blissfully reunited.

At home once more in Amherst the Todds began to look about them for a permanent house of their own. They had moved from the Lessey house to the Lincoln house, but this too was on a short lease. Austin suggested that he make available a strip of land on the far side of the Dickinson Meadow, across Main Street from the Homestead. There Mabel and David could build a home.

One evening when Mabel and David were alone together, drawing up plans for the house they would build, David said, 'Of course, this will be Austin's house as well.'

'You mean because we are to build on his land.'

'No, my darling. I do not mean that.'

'He can't leave his family, dearest.'

'He has left his family. His spirit lives with us. And when we have our new house, his body will follow.'

184

Mabel kissed him in her gratitude.

'Best of husbands! How can I ever repay you?'

'I think we three could be happy together,' said David. 'While you were away, Austin was very kind to me.'

'I know you've become good friends. That makes me so happy.'

'I would like us to be closer still.'

Then Mabel saw the look in his eyes and she understood him.

'You would like to share our love.'

'You know I adore you,' said David. 'You know I love to look on you. Why should I not see more?'

'Would you like that, my darling? Would you like to see me in another man's arms?'

'Does that shock you?'

'No,' said Mabel, tilting her pretty head on one side. 'I think I like the idea, though I'm sure it's wrong of me.'

'Why wrong? To be loved by one man and admired by another.'

'And that would give you pleasure?'

'More than I can say.'

'Well, then. I shall speak to Austin. I can't answer for him. But we've come so close, we three. Why not closer?'

Mabel found she was enchanted by the proposal. She understood and rejoiced in the desire both men felt for her. To have both desiring her in the same place at the same time . . .

She twined herself round David, nuzzling her face against his.

'Am I a creature without morals, darling?' she murmured. 'Sometimes I'm terribly afraid that I must be. A decent woman would be shocked. But somehow I'm not shocked at all.'

'These decent people,' said David, 'who knows what they get up to behind closed doors?'

'I'm afraid all they do behind their closed doors is gossip about their neighbours. Really we should throw open our doors and let all the town watch! Then they'd have something to talk about!'

Over the weeks that followed, Austin visited Mabel in the Lincoln house most Sunday evenings. There, as he recorded in his diary using a special symbol, he and Mabel made love. On ten of these Sunday evenings, as the diary also recorded, the lovemaking took place 'with a witness'.

In the winter of 1886 Emily Dickinson's illness became acute, and in mid-May she died. She had been ailing for over two years, but her death nevertheless came as a shock. She was fifty-five years old.

Her funeral service took place in the library at the Homestead. Colonel Higginson, a leading man of letters, and one of the few to whom Emily had sent samples of her poems, read out a verse over the coffin: not by Emily herself, but by her namesake Emily Brontë.

> *No coward soul is mine,*
> *No trembler in the world's storm-troubled sphere:*
> *I see Heaven's glories shine,*
> *And faith shines equal, arming me from fear . . .*

Mabel, one of the mourners at the back of the library, listened in irritation. Emily's faith did not armour her from fear, she thought. Why tell lies over her coffin? A single line from her own poems contained more truth than this pious prating.

There followed a simple religious service. Then the coffin was carried out of the back door and across the meadow to the West Cemetery.

Vinnie, now alone in the Homestead, ventured into the room where Emily had lived and died. The room was neat and tidy, just as Emily had left it, with little to show for the life that had so recently found there a sanctuary and a port of embarkation. From here Emily had set sail on the journeys of the mind that she had recorded as her impetuous dash-filled poems. The little desk where she wrote was in its place. But where were the poems?

Vinnie had no idea what she was looking for. It was possible her sister had destroyed her writings as she completed them, keeping only the very few that satisfied her critical eye. She had left no directions, and no instructions. So Vinnie looked where she could.

The two top drawers of the chest contained folded clothing. The bottom drawer was harder to open, because it was heavier, and packed tight. But open it Vinnie did, and so discovered an astonishing hoard. Emily had written far, far more poems than anyone had ever guessed. They were packed in little bundles, each bundle tied with string, in their hundreds.

Vinnie took the poems out, and laid them on the floor, and was overwhelmed. Here before her lay her beloved sister's legacy. Vinnie was convinced of Emily's genius, though she was quite unable to say in what that genius lay. All she knew, as she gazed on the piles of papers, was that someone with more confidence than herself must undertake the task of getting the poems published.

She turned first to Colonel Higginson. Higginson found Emily's handwriting hard to read. He wasn't at all sure the eccentric poems would ever find a publisher. They were clumsily constructed, at times almost illiterate, and disfigured by ugly dashes. Moreover, he was extremely busy. The upshot was that he would look through the poems, but only if someone else made fair copies first, and organised them into some manageable order.

Vinnie then carried a box of the poems over to Sue. Sue understood that for Vinnie this was a sacred mission, but she herself had long lost her early admiration for Emily. She suggested that perhaps a modest private publication could be arranged. Having agreed to go this far, she then did nothing. Vinnie became increasingly agitated, and finally cornered Sue on the matter.

'My dear Vinnie,' said Sue. 'There's an immense amount of work to do here, I can make very little sense of half of the lines. We would have to pay quite large sums to print the poems. And you must see that all we could do then is give them away to our friends. This isn't the kind of thing the public cares for at all.'

'So you mean to do nothing?' said Vinnie.

'I know you feel you owe this to Emily's memory,' said Sue. 'But did Emily really want them to be published? I don't think so. If she had wanted it, she would surely have said so while she was living. And you know, her poems will remain with us, in the family. She won't be forgotten.'

Vinnie took the box of poems back. Sue's lack of faith in Emily served to make Vinnie all the more determined. But to whom could she now turn? Austin, much as he had loved his sister, had never believed in her talents as a poet.

That left Mabel. Mabel was sure of herself in ways that Vinnie could never be. She had professed an interest in Emily, and an admiration for the few poems she'd read. And she was herself a published author. So Vinnie carried her box of poems over to the Lincoln house.

'I don't like to trouble you, Mrs Todd,' she said, laying the box on the parlour table. 'You were always so kind about poor Emily's poems. She spoke of you often, you know? I believe she felt your sympathy.'

Mabel took out the bundles of papers, and was amazed by the quantity.

'There are so many!'

'There are far more, I can assure you.'

Mabel took one poem at random and began to read.

'Vinnie, this is a marvel!'

'I don't know what to do with them,' said Vinnie. 'Sue tells me no one could care for them but those who knew and loved her.'

'Sue's a fool,' said Mabel.

'Perhaps if you could look through them, and advise me?'

'Oh, Vinnie! It would be an honour!'

Here was the Myth herself, reaching out to her from beyond the grave, saying: I choose you.

That first box contained nearly seven hundred poems. There were as many again, Vinnie told her, waiting in Emily's room at the Homestead. Some of the poems were unfinished, many had alternative words scribbled on the margins. The task of transcribing and sorting them would be enormous.

Mabel was overwhelmed, daunted, but above all, proud. Then as she began to read the poems, she fell in love. Here, on these scraps of paper, in words coiled tight as springs, was everything she felt in her own inmost heart.

> *I many times thought Peace had come*
> *When Peace was far away –*
> *As Wrecked Men – deem they sight the land –*
> *At Centre of the Sea –*
>
> *And struggle slacker – but to prove*
> *As hopelessly as I –*
> *How many the fictitious shores –*
> *Before the Harbor be –*

The poems astounded her. Everything she had ever experienced was here, as if Emily had been watching her: her eager embrace of life, her passionate pursuit of love, the pain of living in the world, the coming ache of loneliness.

> *Had I not seen the Sun*
> *I could have borne the shade*
> *But Light a newer Wilderness*
> *My Wilderness has made –*

15

Move down the street, towards a house where the windows glow. It's that time of the evening, when day is not yet done but lamps are lit indoors. Through one window a young woman can be seen seated at a table, intently at work, a pen in her hand. She looks beautiful in the amber light.

Open the gate. Pass up the path to the front door. The door opens, though no one has opened it. Slip silently into the room where the young woman sits, now with her back to the door.

Come closer. Lean over her. See the papers she is working on. They are covered with handwriting. She is puzzling out words.

My handwriting, my words.

Are they really so hard to read? The letters are carefully formed, often separated one from the next. I always did like words to have air to breathe.

Her pen moves over the paper. Her handwriting, my words. I have elected her.

She believes herself to be alone. My voice, when I speak, remains unheard. But I speak to her.

'I've none to tell me to but thee
So when thou failest, nobody . . .'

16

Alice lies at one end of the big bed, naked, partly covered by a rumpled sheet, turning the pages of her copy of the *Complete Poems of Emily Dickinson*. Nick lies at the other end, his body at an angle so that his feet push against her legs, tickling her. He too is searching in his own copy of the poems. Not so long ago they made love, and then they dozed a little. Now they're arguing.

'Not arguing,' says Nick. 'We're having a literary critical dispute.'

Alice reaches one hand round and strokes his leg, feeling up his calf. She's giddy with physical love. His body intoxicates her. She wants never to leave this bed, this closeness, this heat.

'Here we are,' he says. 'Exhibit One. Don't be fooled by the way it starts. The end line is the clincher.'

Their argument is about Emily Dickinson and sex. How much did she know? Nick says it was all in her head. Alice says she felt it in her body.

Nick reads aloud.

He was weak and I was strong – then –
So He let me lead him in –
I was weak and He was strong then –
So I let him lead me – Home –

'I have to tell you,' looking up from the page, 'this is most likely not about a lover at all. The He is most likely Jesus.'

'Why can't it be both?' says Alice.

Nick continues.

Day knocked – and we must part –
Neither – was strongest – now –
He strove – and I strove too –

'For God's sake,' says Alice, 'he's fucking her! They've been together all night and he's fucked her brains out!'

'I said to wait for the last line.'

Back to the reading –

He strove – and I strove too –
We didn't do it – tho'!

'There!' Nick triumphant. 'No ambiguity there. They didn't do it.'

'We don't know what *it* is.'

'Whatever it is, they didn't do it!'

'Well, it sounded like sex to me.' Her roaming hand reaches up his thigh. He twists round in the bed so he can give her a kiss on the mouth.

'My turn,' she says, going back to her book. 'Emily Dickinson gets down and dirty, Exhibit Two.'

She reads aloud.

> *My River runs to thee –*
> *Blue Sea! Wilt welcome me?*
> *My River waits reply –*
> *Oh Sea – look graciously –*
> *I'll fetch thee Brooks*
> *From spotted nooks –*
> *Say – Sea – Take Me!*

'Don't tell me that isn't sex.'

'Spotted nooks? What's that?'

Her hand moves up his thigh to his groin.

'What flows from here into the eternal all-embracing feminine sea?'

'The sea is feminine? The river is masculine? Exactly what gender is this poet?'

'Emily's transgender. Haven't you worked that out yet? She plays on both teams. She gets it about domination, and she gets it about submission.'

She flips the pages, locates another poem, reads aloud.

> *Good to hide, and hear 'em hunt!*
> *Better to be found,*
> *If one care to, that is,*
> *The Fox fits the Hound –*

'It's practically S&M. The palpitating prey submits to the hunter. It makes me go all shivery.'

She turns over and lies half on top of him.

'The hunter's taking a break,' he says.

'Oh, Nick.' She caresses his smiling face. 'Why is it so easy with you?'

'I'm just a sex toy for you. You play with me for a while, and then discard me.'

'Are you my sex toy?' Her face nuzzling over the hairs on his chest. 'Can't I be in love with you?'

'By all means. Be my guest.'

'We could have a prayer we recite together.'

'I think I'll pass on the prayer.'

'Oh, Nick.' She pulls her body fully onto his, smiles down at him. 'You're so adorable. I can't think why. It makes no sense. I know it's all going to end in tears. But I don't care.'

'Whose tears?'

'Mine, of course.'

She offers a line from another poem to clinch her argument.

'And if I gain! Oh Gun at Sea!'

'The eternal all-embracing feminine sea,' says Nick.

'A gun! I mean, do I have to spell it out?'

'Of course she had sexual feelings. I'm not denying that. But that doesn't mean she ever had sex.'

'Most likely she didn't,' says Alice. 'But I love her, Nick, I really do. I want to think she felt like me. I want my Emily to be sexy. I want her to know about actual sex.'

'I suppose,' says Nick, 'she might have peeped through the keyhole. Do you think she did?'

'Spied on Austin and Mabel?'

'Some people do like to watch.'

'Like David.'

'Like me.'

Nick slips off the bed and goes to the closet. Alice watches his lanky naked body. He opens the closet door, pushes it all the way back. On the inside of the door is a long mirror.

He returns to the bed and, kneeling beside her, lifts her up onto her knees facing the mirror. Now he has her in his arms, and they can see themselves reflected, naked in the glass. He keeps his gaze on the mirror, strokes her breasts with one hand.

'Part your legs.'

She does as he asks, kneeling on the bed. His hand moves down her body. She watches him watching her.

'You like this?' she says.

'I'd like to make love to you like this,' he says.

'Then we will.'

It's all so easy. She wants to give him her body as his pleasure ground, to play with as he pleases. She wants to stay in this bed, in his arms, for ever and ever.

Later they feel hungry. Nick goes down to the kitchen and returns with a plate of apples and cookies. They eat eagerly, sprawled over the bed. When they've had enough they lie down again, folded in each other's arms.

'Why can't life always be as simple as this?' says Alice.

'Because of time,' says Nick. 'Now can be great. But then along comes later to fuck it up.'

'I don't see why.'

'It's called entropy. Things run down. And then at the end, guess what? We die.'

'Die again, then we'll be free.' She catches the surprised look on his face. 'That's what you said, according to your suicidal friend Marcia. Marcia thinks you're an old soul.'

'It's all Emily Dickinson, really. She's the old soul.'

'I love it that you love Emily too.'

'She knew what was coming,' says Nick. 'She never lied to herself.'

He pulls a book of the poems over. It's Alice's copy. He hunts through the pages for a poem he half remembers.

'Do I lie to myself?' says Alice.

'You tell me.'

'Wanting to be happy isn't lying to yourself. If all we ever thought about was dying, how could we live?'

'Here it is.'

He reads:

> *The heart asks pleasure – first –*
> *And then – Excuse from Pain –*
> *And then – those little Anodynes*
> *That deaden suffering –*
> *And then – to go to sleep –*
> *And then – if it should be*
> *The will of its Inquisitor*
> *The privilege to die –*

'It's not my will,' says Alice. 'I'm not dying for a long time. I'm planning on living.'

'I see you like to underline the good bits.'

He's flipping through her copy of the poems.

'For my screenplay,' she says.

'Where would this come in your screenplay?'

He shows her the page. She's underlined three lines.

Oh God
Why give if thou must take away
The loved?

'Don't you think,' she says, 'Mabel might have felt that way after Austin died?'

'So it's about Mabel? Nothing to do with you.'

'And about me too.'

He takes her in his arms.

'That's what happens,' he says. 'Things get taken away.'

'I can deal with it.'

'Let me tell you. It gets harder.'

He kisses her softly, lovingly.

'I'm scared,' he says.

'Why?'

'You're too young. You know too much.'

'I'm not asking you for anything, Nick.'

'I'm much more of a mess than you know.'

'All right. I believe you. My lookout.'

'I can't help feeling responsible.'

'You're not my father. You're not even my stepfather. Maybe I am working out some daddy complex. So what? You're a lovely man, Nick. In your body and in your mind. Let me enjoy you. Don't spoil it.'

'All right. I'll shut up.'

'I know I was the one going on about sex. But really it's the time after sex I like the best. Lying about on the bed with you, touching and not touching. Being alive and dreamy at the same time. Loving my body because you've loved it. Talking in lazy circles. That's what I want to go on for ever.'

He smiles for her but he's looking sad. She kisses him quickly, many small kisses.

'You're not to worry, Nick. I promise you I can look after myself.'

'All right.'

For the first time since they entered his bedroom together sometime last night he looks at the bedside clock.

'You realise how long we've been here?'

'Too long. Not long enough.'

'Almost fifteen hours.'

They part at last, to their separate bathrooms, to shower and dress. Alice thinks how he said he was more of a mess than she knew. She wonders what went wrong between him and his wife. His weakness for students, presumably. She finds it hard to believe he has some dark secret she has yet to guess. And even if he has, so what?

He makes me happy.

Such a simple statement, but the fact is she hasn't felt this way since the early days with Jack. She feels the urge to tell somebody. But who?

Hey, Mum, I'm having a great time. I'm having an affair with a man who's older than my dad.

My girlfriends wouldn't get it either. Only Chloe, who actually did fuck my dad, and she's not exactly my friend. Or Laura, who's Jack's mum. So it's not simple.

Except it is simple. He makes me happy.

Then it jumps into her mind that the person she wants to

talk to is, of course, Jack. She doesn't stop to ask herself why. She texts him before she can change her mind.

You home? Want to Skype?

Barely a second later his reply has bridged the three thousand miles and five time zones between them.

Online now.

She brushes her hair and buttons her blouse. Then she's at the writing table, her laptop open before her, and the machine is warbling into cyberspace.

She hears Jack before she sees him.

'Alice?'

'I'm here.'

And there he is, blinking out of the screen, his gaze not aligned with hers because the camera is above the image. He looks tired, hesitant, but that may be down to the erratic signal. His face freezes, jerks, comes back to life, as if he's a ghost appearing to her from beyond the grave.

'How's it going?'

'Really well,' she says. 'I've been to Yale. I've seen Mabel's actual diaries.'

'Cool.'

'How's things with you?'

'Exhausting,' he says. 'Can't wait for half-term.'

'How are the sexy girls in hijabs?'

'Oh, God! Did I tell you that?'

He covers his face with his hands in mock shame. Seeing Jack is disconcerting, but also touching. Like being home again.

'Isn't Skype weird?' she says. 'I feel like you're very near.'

'I don't,' he says. 'I feel as if you're in a parallel universe.'

'I think I may be in two parallel universes. I'm in Amherst

now, and I'm spying on Mabel and Austin back in the nine-
teenth century.'

'How's the screenplay coming along?'

'Hardly at all. I keep trying out fragments, but none of it
adds up. What do you think of the idea of telling the story
from the point of view of Emily Dickinson, only without ever
seeing her?'

'Like the camera is Emily Dickinson?'

'Yes, I suppose so.'

'I'd say that's really exciting.'

'Oh, Jack.' His round face beaming, frozen, on her screen.
'It's so good talking to you.'

'I don't suppose,' he says, 'you'd consider putting on a hijab?'

'Turning into a fetish, is it?'

He sighs and nods.

'I do feel a little ashamed of myself. But I don't think it's
exactly a fetish. I think it's about proximity. You know, like
priests fondle altar boys. It's whatever's within reach.'

'Oh, Jack. That's so like you.'

'Do you think I'm wrong?'

'No, I think you're horribly right. Listen . . .' She realises
with a shock that she's going to tell him. That this is what she
called him to say. 'I'm alone in this house with a man twice
my age, and guess what?'

'You aren't!'

'Just a little bit.'

'Alice! He's Mum's old boyfriend! That's practically incest!'

'Think of it as a holiday romance.'

'Bloody hell! That beats me fantasising about girls in scarves.'

'He's getting a divorce, so it isn't really adultery. He thinks I'm using him to work through my father-obsession.'

'I expect you are. Which father?'

'Guy, I suppose. The useless one. But I prefer your idea. It's just proximity.'

'Proximity and opportunity. That covers just about everything.'

How amazing to be able to say it all like this. The only people you can talk to about new lovers are old lovers.

'Do you think I'm mad?'

'Depends what you want out of it. I got the impression from Mum that he was pretty flaky.'

'He talks about your mum a lot. She's the one who got away.'

'Christ, Alice, just think! If she hadn't, he'd be my dad. You'd be doing it with my dad!'

He clasps his head in his hands and rocks it from side to side, as if trying to pull it off.

'But she didn't and he isn't,' says Alice. 'And you know what? Being so much older makes no difference at all. He's as screwed-up as you or me. More so, maybe.'

'Well, babe.' He puts on a bad American accent. 'I do not know what to say to you.'

'Why are you talking like that?'

'To indicate the withdrawal of my primary self from this conversation.'

'Oh, please, Jack. Can I have the primary self back?'

'I am only flesh and blood, Alice.'

But his accent has reverted.

'Look into the camera,' she says. 'I want to see you looking at me.'

He does as she asks. Those gentle brown eyes, so incapable of deceit.

'Now I'll look at you.'

She stares at the tiny hole in the top of the screen's frame, trying to imagine that Jack is there. Odd that they can't look at each other at the same time.

'OK,' he says. 'I'm better now.'

They resume their misaligned exchange.

'I blame Mabel Todd,' he says. 'She's stuffed your head with heavy breathing. Oh, I get it.' He smacks his head. 'This is research. You're Mabel, Nick's Austin.'

'Don't think I haven't thought it.'

'What about your plan to tell the story from the point of view of Emily Dickinson? Maybe you should stop all the sweaty stuff and become a celibate recluse.'

She smiles as she listens. Just hearing him grounds her, gives her perspective on the heady events of the last two days. The sweaty stuff.

'I'll do my best,' she says. 'But there is something to be said for bad behaviour.'

'No,' he says. 'No. I'm being so strong-willed. I'm being so good. If I elope with a doe-eyed Bangladeshi it'll all be your fault.'

'You do know that they only make up their faces where they can be seen? Take off the scarf and all the edges will be raw.'

'How on earth do you know that?'

'I've got a make-up marketing account.'

He gazes solemnly at her chin.

'That is probably the single most useful thing you've ever said to me.'

'I do love talking to you, Jack.'

'Even though nothing I ever say's useful to you.'

'Yes, it is.' She's nodding at the screen, wanting him to believe her. 'I've remembered what you said about endings. It just isn't so easy actually finding one.'

'For Mabel's story?'

'Yes.'

'There'll be an ending sitting there somewhere,' he says. 'But it may not belong to the story you're telling.'

'So what am I supposed to do?'

'Switch the story. Use the ending you've got. I'm telling you, that's what's important. Work backwards from the ending, and wherever that takes you, that's your story.'

'Yes, but . . .'

What he says begs so many questions she doesn't know where to begin. His flickering features betray impatience. Or maybe her confession has bothered him more than he's saying.

'Or you could just ignore me.'

'No, I'm really trying hard here.'

'Sorry, I'm tired. That's the trouble with Skype. It's free, so we can't say, Oh, God, this call's costing a fortune, we'd better hang up. So we have to go on for ever.'

Alice looks at the time. Five hours later for him than for her.

'Long day?'

'I'm on my knees.'

'You go, darling. Go to your bed.'

'To a can of Stella and *Game of Thrones*.'

'Can I call you again?'

'Anytime, doll.'

That's the dodgy American accent back. His primary self has checked out.

'I'm switching you off now. Bye!'

The screen goes black.

She gets up to go to the bathroom. As she stands, staring into the mirror, she remembers and looks away, as if caught in some shameful act.

Did I really call Jack 'darling'?

17

The new cottage being built for the Todds at the bottom of the Dickinson meadow started construction in the fall of 1886. By the turn of the year the shell of the house was in place, and part of the plumbing and heating had been installed. The kitchen in the basement was usable, as was the top floor, which was to be Mabel's studio. Then with very little warning the owners of the house they were renting decided not to renew the lease, and the family was obliged to move in to the unfinished house. They named it The Dell.

They camped out through that bitter winter. Millicent caught a throat and ear infection. David suffered an attack of kidney stones. Mabel worked. She oversaw the builders, directed the setting out of trees, and painted oil friezes round the upper walls of the entrance hall and the parlours. And every day, whenever she had a spare moment, she continued the long task of copying out Emily's poems, and then typing them on a Hammond typewriter, borrowed from a friend. David helped when he could, acting as a second pair of eyes, checking Mabel's guesses at the words that were harder to read. Even Millicent was pressed into occasional service, forming and reforming the little bundles of papers. The great work went on in the third floor attic room, where Mabel had pinned to the wall a copy of the daguerreotype of Emily Dickinson, taken in 1847 when she was a student at Mount Holyoke College. Beneath this image of the serene and beautiful sixteen-year-old, the only likeness that Mabel had been able to obtain, Emily's poems and their transcripts slowly spread across the floor.

Austin visited daily. By now Mabel considered herself married to him as well as to David. She kept a gold wedding ring that Austin had given her, but she did not wear it in public. Austin kept a soft indoor hat at The Dell, and was as much or more at home there than at The Evergreens. But in the world beyond its walls, they continued to behave to each other as virtual strangers.

Mabel found her double life increasingly hard to bear. The great love which seemed to her to be so right and good had settled into a pattern of secrecy and shame, and she could see no sign that anything would ever change. She felt betrayed by the world, and by God.

She wrote to Austin:

As for God, I feel utterly deserted by Him. I have tried so hard during all these years to trust Him, and to wait patiently. Yet He gives no sign. I am pitifully helpless in His hands, and dare not even reproach Him. The heavens are dumb. He has shown us the possibility of a life as happy and as pure and as noble as heaven itself – and then He lets us go. He sits silently up in the great spaces and watches us suffer – if indeed He cares enough even to notice the pain – and we pray and entreat in vain. Only I shall always be glad that He did show us each other, even if I die for it, which I think not at all unlikely. A sensitive nature cannot hold on forever against such odds. We have each other – but we have each other against the bigoted spite of the rest of the world. And we cannot make it otherwise. There seems no real help but in death.

In her growing despair, Mabel took refuge in the strange poems she was puzzling out in her attic room. Emily's perceptions of the world were sharp-edged, bitter, often profoundly sad. Mabel found this comforting. At the same time, as she untangled the densely packed lines, her admiration for Emily's poems grew. Here was a fellow spirit with the power to utter truths that no one else would admit, but that Mabel was learning for herself. She felt herself to be Emily's first, her only, reader. In the poems she found her own story, of her struggle to declare her love, and of her attempt to brave the unkindness of the town. The poet offered her no consoling redemption; which was a consolation in itself.

> *I took my Power in my Hand –*
> *And went against the World –*
> *'Twas not so much as David – had –*
> *But I – was twice as bold –*
>
> *I aimed my Pebble - but Myself*
> *Was all the one that fell –*
> *Was it Goliath – was too large –*
> *Or was myself – too small?*

Emily gave her the words to express her love for Austin, a love that the world would only allow her to enjoy in snatched moments.

So sets its Sun in Thee
What Day be dark to me —
What Distance — far —
So I the Ships may see
That touch — how seldomly —
Thy Shore?

Every day more convinced of Emily's genius, she worked away at her laborious transcriptions. She purchased a typewriter of her own, that punched out the poems one capital letter at a time. To ease the burden she hired a copyist, but found her quite incapable of deciphering Emily's handwriting. So she continued alone.

As the poems were transcribed, Mabel showed them to Vinnie. Vinnie, devoted to Emily's memory, fierce in her defence, was timid when faced with the task of presenting them to the world.

'Mr Higginson has been kind enough to say he will read the best of them,' she said to Mabel. 'He will approve, will he not?'

'He's a bigger fool than I thought if he doesn't,' said Mabel.

'You truly do think them good?'

'Your sister is a great poet,' said Mabel. 'Greater than Mrs Burnett. Greater than Mrs Jackson.'

'Do you really believe so?' cried Vinnie, her eyes shining. 'You will tell Mr Higginson so?'

When the great task was completed, it was Mabel who carried the stack of transcribed poems to Boston. She lodged in the Beacon Hill house of her cousin Caro Andrews. Here Thomas Wentworth Higginson met her, at Vinnie's request, and read through several of the poems.

His response was not favourable.

'Of course I see that there's some kind of genius buried here,' he told Mabel. 'But the meaning is so obscure, the form so crude. The public will never accept it.'

'How can you say that?' cried Mabel. She was outraged by the verdict, both for Emily and for herself. 'You think the poems crude because she writes in her own way, and you're not familiar with it. But I assure you they are not crude, and not obscure, any more than William Blake is crude and obscure.'

'My dear Mrs Todd—'

'Permit me to read you one or two of my favourites aloud. Do me that kindness before you make up your mind.'

'Very well,' he said with a sigh.

Mabel picked out some poems from the sheaf, and rose to her feet to read. She was a good speaker, and she understood the poems well, and she chose carefully.

Tell all the Truth but tell it slant —
Success in Circuit lies
Too bright for our infirm Delight
The Truth's superb surprise

As Lightning to the Children eased
With explanation kind
The Truth must dazzle gradually
Or every man be blind —

Higginson listened and inclined his head, understanding why she had begun with this poem.

'So I am the blind man. You must dazzle me gradually, Mrs Todd.'

Next she read him a poem to flatter his literary bent.

> *There is no Frigate like a Book*
> *To take us Lands away*
> *Nor any Coursers like a Page*
> *Of prancing Poetry –*
> *This Traverse may the poorest take*
> *Without oppress of Toll –*
> *How frugal is the Chariot*
> *That bears the Human soul.*

'Now surely, Mr Higginson, there's nothing obscure here.'

'No, no. I grant you, when I hear the lines aloud the effect is very different.'

'Then hear just one more. Even a gentleman of your distinction will have experienced times of suffering, I daresay. Miss Dickinson understands suffering better than any poet I know.'

> *After great pain, a formal feeling comes –*
> *The Nerves sits ceremonious, like Tombs –*

'Have you ever experienced such a sensation, Mr Higginson?'

The man of letters once more silently inclined his head.

'Listen to this and tell me the public will never accept it.'

This is the Hour of Lead –
Remembered, if outlived,
As Freezing persons recollect the Snow –
First Chill – then Stupor – then the letting go –

Higginson remained silent for a moment longer. Then he nodded his head again.

'I surrender,' he said. 'You amaze me. I feel as if I hadn't read these poems at all before.'

'And there are so many more! We've only just begun!'

He waved a hand in front of his face.

'Too many. I'm a busy man, Mrs Todd.'

'Then let me pick out the best for you.'

'I think that would be a good way to proceed. Divide them up for me, if you will, into the best, and the next best, and the rest. Not too many of the best, please. Be rigorous. Then come back to me, and I'll see what I can do.'

'You'll take them to a publisher?'

'I'm a reader at Houghton Mifflin. They're a good firm. They respect my opinion.'

Mabel returned to Amherst and worked steadily for twelve days on the task of classifying the poems. In the end she selected six hundred and thirty-four poems, divided into Categories A, B and C. She had pored over these poems for so long now, transcribing them with her own hand, typing them letter by letter, that she felt almost as if she had composed them herself. The completed package was then sent off to Higginson in Boston, and Mabel and Vinnie settled down to wait.

★

The sudden cessation of activity threw Mabel back on the frustrations of her situation. She wrote miserably to Austin:

> The first leisure shows me unpityingly the horror of my life, which goes on without the slightest interest from the Almighty, a life absolutely deserted by Him and left to swing for itself in space, unhelped and uncared for. Prayers are no more than so much extra breath wasted, or as Emily says, no more than if a bird stamped its foot on the air.

Higginson moved with agonising slowness. He was too busy; then he was too ill; then it was Christmas. In the New Year, 1890, he settled to the task at last, and picked out two hundred of the poems, and gave them titles of his own invention to help the reading public understand them: 'Almost', 'In a Library', 'Love's Baptism', 'Troubled About Many Things', 'The First Lesson', and so forth. He also divided them into four sections, headed *Life*, *Love*, *Nature*, and *Time and Eternity*. Mabel was horrified by the titles, but felt she couldn't afford to antagonise her co-editor, as he now classed himself.

Higginson took the collection to Houghton Mifflin. There he suffered the embarrassment of outright rejection. The poems were far too queer, he was told, and many of the rhymes simply didn't work. Humiliated, Higginson told Mabel he had been wrong to give her hope. The poems were not publishable.

Mabel refused to give up. They must approach another publisher. What about Roberts Brothers, also in Boston? Higginson was not prepared for a second humiliation.

'Then I will take the poems myself,' said Mabel.

She called on Thomas Niles of Roberts Brothers. Niles was no more encouraging than the directors of Houghton Mifflin.

'In my personal opinion,' he told her, 'Miss Dickinson's verses are devoid of true poetical qualities.'

But by now Mabel was battle-hardened.

'And yet you take time to see me, Mr Niles.'

'I say, in my opinion. I have also asked one of our readers, Mr Arlo Bates, for his appraisal.' He read aloud to Mabel from the report written by his reader. '"These poems have the real stuff, in no unstinted quantities." So there you are. One contra, and one pro.'

'The real stuff, Mr Niles.'

'I can't see it myself. But Arlo Bates is a poet in his own right. Perhaps he sees something I fail to see.'

Mabel understood that victory was within her grasp.

'You could test the water, perhaps?'

'That is what I've been considering. A small edition. A small number of the poems. No more than fifty or so.'

'Two hundred and fifty, Mr Niles.'

'No, no. A hundred at the most. And I would have to ask the family of the author to contribute to the making of the plates.'

'Agreed.'

Vinnie paid for the plates. Higginson consented to write a preface. Mabel offered the flower painting she had given Emily, to be used as a cover design. Higginson's preface was designed to prepare readers for the clumsiness of the poems, and to hint that the co-editor was far from convinced himself.

This selection from her poems is published to meet the desire of her personal friends, and especially of her surviving sister. It is believed that the thoughtful reader will find in these pages a quality more suggestive of the poetry of William Blake than anything to be elsewhere found – flashes of wholly original and profound insight into nature and life; words and phrases exhibiting an extraordinary vividness of descriptive and imaginative power, yet often set in a seemingly whimsical or even rugged frame . . . The main quality of these poems is that of extraordinary grasp and insight, uttered with an uneven vigour sometimes exasperating, seemingly wayward, but really unsought and inevitable.

The little volume of one hundred and fifteen poems finally appeared on November 12 1890: *Poems by Emily Dickinson, Edited by two of her friends, Mabel Loomis Todd and T. W. Higginson*. The first reviews were puzzled and guarded. What had gone wrong with her rhythms? Why could she not rhyme? Austin remained sceptical, secretly regarding the publication as a vanity project of Vinnie's.

Mabel alone never wavered. She was Emily's first and greatest champion. She fought back against all attempts to soften the poems' bite, convinced of the truth and the power of Emily's perceptions. She wrote to Austin about his sister:

It all seemed to her so cheap and thin and hollow as she saw it, with the solemn realities of life staring her in the face, but she wanted none of it. Never made any difference what sort of day it was – every day was a red-letter day. The greatness, mystery and depth of life was so great and overwhelming to her that she could not see how people could go into all this littleness.

This of a woman she had never known, who had become her other self. She and Emily were now arm in arm against the world, battling the uncomprehending littleness.

Then something unexpected happened. The poems began to sell. By the end of November that timid first edition of five hundred was gone. In mid-December Roberts Brothers reprinted, and again at the end of December. Into 1891 edition followed edition, reaching an unprecedented sale by the year's end of almost eleven thousand.

Emily Dickinson had become famous.

18

Alice has thought of Mabel's story from the beginning as a love story. Now she begins to ask herself if this has been a mistake. What if there's no such thing as a love story, only life stories? In a love story you watch with a kind of anticipatory hunger as the lovers meet, you see how they're filled with longing and fear, you tremble with them until the day dawns when they discover, as you've always known they will, that their love is returned. Then comes tragedy, or perhaps marriage, and the story is over. Such things can happen in the real world, it's not entirely wish-fulfilment; but what a little space of time it covers! What of the long years that follow, the knocking about the world together, the struggle to make a career, the raising of children, the growing old? Falling in love becomes a memory, a snapshot, slips into the past. But the hunger never dies. The greedy self clamours just as loudly for a narrative of recognition and fulfilment. Are we to be forever falling in love? Are there no other stories to be told?

There are so many journeys in a life. Each new road leads

to a destination that becomes, in turn, a new beginning. No final arrival, no resting place. We are born wanderers.

So what's the big deal about love?

Alice sits at her laptop, failing to draft a treatment for her screenplay, interrogating her own shameful dreams.

Why do I feel there's only one true achievement in life? Why am I waiting for a man who loves me as I am, and promises to stay with me for the rest of my life? Everywhere I go I look for him. Until I find him I believe my life will not have begun.

Am I so seduced by cheap music? Can't I see the stage sets, the make-up, the shoddy artifice, the false promises of a culture that wants only my unending dissatisfaction? The fairy story is with us still, but in new guises: images in a commercial break, pictures on a Facebook wall, characters on a phone screen. We all know how the trick is done, but still it gets us every time. They feed us lies, and we suck them up, and ask for more.

Did love bring Mabel Todd happiness? For a time, yes. And then for a longer time, no.

Am I in love with Nick Crocker?

The very question makes her laugh. How could that be possible? This is a game, a passing fancy, in a few days she'll be gone. For now she indulges him, and indulges in him, and why not? He's adorable and funny and wise and a little lost in a way that touches her more than she cares to admit. His body pleases hers so easily, he knows what he wants, which turns out to be what she wants. This is a gift to be gratefully received, is it not?

So a passionate interlude, not a love story.

'How would you describe it?' she asks him. 'Whatever it is we're doing together.'

'Playing,' he says.

She likes that. Like children absorbed in a world of their own creation, pretending to be doctors and nurses, or mummies and daddies. Children aren't stupid. They know playtime comes to an end, and then there's supper, and bath, and being put to bed.

'What game are we playing?' she says.

He smiles at her, with that expression on his face that makes her feel he's really looking at her.

'I don't know, Alice. Let's not think about it too much.'

'I can't help myself,' she says. 'I can't switch the thinking off.'

They're in a national forest, walking down a trail on one side of Chesterfield Gorge. All round them the blaze of foliage in the fall. Slender trunks of ash and hemlock, bars against the sky. Underfoot a carpet of bronze leaves. To their right, beyond a chain-link fence, rock walls drop down to a tumbling river.

A sign declares it to be a National Wild and Scenic River.

'Nature tamed for our pleasure,' says Nick. 'Safe in its cage.'

'I don't care,' says Alice. 'I think it's beautiful. Don't you love the sound of the river?'

She takes his hand and he swings her arm with his as they walk between the trees. The trail rounds a bend. They come to a stop and kiss.

'Have you ever made love in a National Park?' he says.

'No,' says Alice. 'Isn't it against the law?'

'As it happens,' says Nick, 'this is something I've looked up. According to National Parks Regulations, the section on Disorderly Conduct prohibits fighting, addressing offensive remarks, and making unreasonably loud noise. Nothing at all about making love.'

'You seriously have looked it up.'

'Yes.'

'Have you done it?'

'Yes.'

'Weren't you scared someone would come along and see you at it?'

'No.'

'I don't believe you.'

'Want to find out?'

'No way!' She backs away from him, as if he's going to ravish her there and then. 'There is no way I'm doing it in public, in the middle of the day, in a forest, in October! Are you crazy? I'd get scratches all over my bum!'

'OK,' he says, smiling at her consternation.

'You didn't really mean it?'

'Yes,' he says. 'But that's OK.'

They walk on. She finds she's shivering, with shock or excitement or both.

'There are limits,' she says.

'If you say so.'

'Don't tell me if I'd said yes you'd have just dropped your jeans and got down to it.'

'I don't need to drop my jeans,' he says. 'Just undo a few buttons.'

'Well, I do. If I was going to. Which I'm not.'

'Yes,' he says. 'You'd have to pull your jeans down to below your knees. And your knickers.'

'That's enough. I get the picture.'

The trail winds on before them, following the bends of the river gorge. After a while they meet a pair of middle-aged women hikers, in serious boots, walking with Leki sticks. They nod and exchange greetings as they pass.

'There,' says Alice. 'They'd have seen us.'

'What if they had?' says Nick.

'I'd have died!'

He seems to be genuinely puzzled by this.

'But why? You don't know them. You don't care what they think about you. And anyway, how'd you know they wouldn't have liked it? A lot of people rather like sex.'

'If you don't understand,' says Alice, 'I can't explain. It's just . . . it's just private.'

Despite her protestations she finds the idea lodges in her mind. She imagines it, in detail: his jacket thrown onto the carpet of leaves, her tight jeans tugged down her thighs, his buttons undone one by one. The trees, half undressed like herself, rising tall on either side. The rush and roar of the river.

Maybe one day, she thinks. When I'm braver.

As they drive back she says, 'I've no objection to doing it the normal way, in a bed.'

What she means is: I'm excited now. I want you to fuck me.

'The normal way?'

'OK. The comfortable way.'

'You know what I think we should do?' he says. 'I think we should have a party. A celebration.'

'For who?'

'For you and me. Can you dance?'

'Of course I can dance.'

'No, I mean real dancing. Not just making it up as you go along.'

'What, like ballroom dancing?'

'Yes. Like waltzing.'

'No one can do that any more.'

'I can.'

This is so much not her picture of Nick that she bursts out laughing.

'Are you serious? You can waltz?'

'Yes.'

'Why?'

'Because it's romantic. Because it's beautiful.'

'Oh, Nick. You never stop surprising me. Sex in the woods. Ballroom dancing.'

'I could teach you.'

'Really?'

'Then I could dance with you.'

'What, now?'

'Yes. Now.'

'OK,' she says. 'I'll give it a go.'

But what about the fuck?

So the day that began in a forest changes scene to a ballroom. Nick's house, or Nick's soon-to-be ex-wife's house, has a pair of linked rooms easily big enough for a ball. Nick pushes back the furniture and rolls up the rugs. He puts a CD of *Best Loved Waltzes* on the music system, and he takes Alice in his arms, and he teaches her to dance. They're still in their jeans, the jeans they didn't drop in the forest, but now her body is pressed tight against his. Nick teaches her almost entirely without words, using slight pressure on her body to indicate to her how and where to move, and making the lead steps with short clear movements himself. After some initial stumbling she finds she's picking up the basic pattern, letting him nudge her a step back, a step to the side, round, all in time to the beat of the music.

'There,' he says. 'That's the turn. Not hard, is it?'

They dance on. He holds her strongly in his arms, virtually carrying her through the unexpected rotations. The more they do it, the more her body responds.

'Don't think about the steps,' he says. 'Your body knows better than your brain.'

Somewhere a phone rings. They ignore it. The dance absorbs them entirely.

'What's the music?' Alice says, realising she knows the tune.

'Right now? This is the waltz from *The Godfather.*'

One track ends, another begins. One dance ends, another begins.

'You know this?' He's sailing her round the room.

'Of course,' she says. 'It's "Edelweiss". From *The Sound of Music.*'

'I thought you might be too young for it.'

'Everyone knows *The Sound of Music.* All girls do, anyway. Oh, Nick. You do keep on surprising me.'

'Tonight we'll dance to the real thing. Léhar. Strauss.'

'Why? What's happening tonight?'

'We're going to have a real ball.'

He's her leader. She rests in his arms and moves as he wants her to move. Her body knows better than her brain.

'Just tell me what to do and I'll do it,' she says.

On his instructions she goes up to her room and showers and changes into the only smart frock she has brought with her, a tight-fitting black jersey dress. She takes trouble over her hair and face. This is a big date. She's invited to a ball.

Still children at play, but why not?

When she comes downstairs she finds he has transformed the big rooms into a wonderland. The drapes are closed, and candles glow in candelabras on side tables and window sills, on the covered piano, on the two mantelpieces. Nick himself has changed. He wears a dinner jacket, with a dress shirt and a black bow tie. He stands there in the candlelight looking impossibly handsome, watching her descend the wide stairs, smiling with admiration.

'How beautiful you are,' he says, holding out his hand.

He draws her into his arms and kisses her.

'I like this game,' she says.

'This isn't a game,' he says. 'This is our very own ball.'

He turns to a side table, and there she sees a bottle of champagne and two glasses. He fills the glasses and hands one to her.

'Honestly, Nick,' she says. 'Don't you think your routine needs updating?'

She sees a shadow cross his face, and realises she's hurt him. This is not what she expected.

'Sorry,' she says. 'It's only because I'm having a little trouble with my self-image here. I have to keep telling myself it's a game in case I find out I like it too much.'

'I want you to like it,' he says. 'I want this to be one of the most wonderful evenings of your life.'

'But why, Nick?'

'No reason.'

He raises his glass to hers.

'To a magical night of love,' he says.

'What an old romantic you are!'

'Stop it, Alice. Just let me lead.'

'Yes, Nick.' He's holding her eyes so intently. Why not surrender? God knows, she wants to. 'To a magical night of love.'

They clink glasses and drink.

'Do we get to eat, in our magical night?'

'No,' he says. 'Just champagne, and music.'

He starts the music. He's turned the volume up since the afternoon, and the sound of the orchestra fills the room. He puts away her glass, and his own. He takes her in his arms. The slow majestic chords of the 'Emperor Waltz' sweep them away down the candlelit spaces, and all at once Alice feels as if she's flying. There's no effort involved, all she has to do is surrender to his controlling arms. When the change comes, and the orchestra bursts into a more urgent rhythm, she finds herself spinning as she dances, half falling, losing the beat, finding it again, laughing, holding tight, feeling his arms for ever hurtling her onwards. Now back comes the slower tune, and they float together gracefully, smiling into each other's eyes, sharing the joke that they've never done this before, and yet here they are, moving together as if they were born to dance.

When the waltz finishes Nick pours them each a second glass of champagne.

'You really mean it,' she says. 'Just champagne and music.'

'How d'you like it so far?'

'I love it.'

Her eyes shining like a girl of sixteen at her first ball. Which this is, when she thinks about it.

'I should be wearing a long floaty white dress.'

'I should be wearing tails.'

'This really is fun, Nick. Thank you.'

More music, more dancing, this time to Léhar's 'Gold and

Silver Waltz'. Alice feels herself glowing, with the champagne and the spinning dance and the sensation of Nick's gaze on her.

Even if I'm not really beautiful, he makes me feel beautiful.

All at once she's flooded with gratitude. The feeling is so overwhelming you could almost call it love.

Round and round they go, up and down the long rooms in the soft glow of the candles, and the real world recedes into the far distance.

It's only a kind of dream. It means nothing. Enjoy it while it lasts.

'Are you seducing me, Nick?'

'Yes,' he says.

'You don't have to. I'll do anything you ask.'

'I ask you to be happy.'

'I'm happy.'

More champagne. More music. 'The Merry Widow'. 'Tales from the Vienna Woods'. Then at last the 'Blue Danube', and Nick sets a wild pace, turning, spinning, reversing, skipping, leaving her gasping for breath as she follows wherever he goes. By now she trusts him completely, so that it feels to her as if he alone is causing her to fly about the room. And so with the last great chords of the waltz, as they spin to a standstill, she falls helplessly into his arms, flushed and panting, and waits to be kissed.

'Is it over?'

A voice small as a child's. That's what it does to you: you're ready to hand yourself over on a plate.

'Yes. It's over now.'

'But our magical night isn't over?'

'Almost,' he says.

He leads her to one of the deep couches he pushed against the wall, and they sink down among the soft cushions.

'I want you to kiss me, Nick.'

He kisses her. She holds him close, needing to feel all of him.

'I'm not in love with you, Nick.'

'Of course you aren't.'

'But you are lovely. Thank you for my magical night.'

'My magical night too.'

'I'm not at all hungry.'

'Me neither.'

'Will we sleep together tonight?'

'If that's what you'd like.'

'Yes,' she says. 'I'd like that.'

She snuggles into him. She thinks what a nice smell he has. Her body can still feel his body pressed to hers, spinning round the dance floor.

'Will we do it again?' she says. 'Now you've taught me.'

'I don't think so,' he says.

Why not? Is he going away? It comes to her then that he's planned this whole evening, the candles and the champagne and the dancing, for a purpose. It's a valediction.

'Are you going away?'

'Yes,' he says.

'When?'

'Soon.'

Now she knows her instinct is right.

'You're leaving tomorrow, aren't you?'

'That's the plan.'

That's the plan. So all along there's been a plan. She feels the dread gathering in her stomach. She shuts her eyes, and has a short sharp tussle with herself.

Get a grip. He's not your boyfriend. You're not in love with him. He's free to go when he likes, where he likes.

'So what's this plan?'

'I suppose it comes under the general heading of moving on.'

'You're leaving this house?'

'This is Peggy's house. She's been very tolerant. But I should go.'

'Where will you go?'

He doesn't answer that. So she's not to know. Not to know and not to follow.

Hold on tight. This is not a tragedy. You've had some fun. It was never meant to last.

'Will you be OK?' she says.

That touches him, her concern for him. He strokes her cheek.

'Yes. I'll be OK.'

'I think there's a bit of you that could be quite sad,' she says.

'You're right there.'

But you're not sad with me. We have fun together. We have magical nights.

'Will I see you again?' she says.

'No. I don't think so.'

'You might be in England one day. I might come back here.'

Nothing from Nick. She tries to stop the feeling but it's there. A little hurt, a little angry.

'If we're never to see each other again, what was the point of tonight?'

'Oh, Alice. Don't say that.'

'I'm not saying anything. I'm only asking.'

'Can't we just have a good time together, without it being some kind of down payment on something more?'

'Yes,' she says. 'Yes, we can.'

She feels ashamed, she hadn't meant to sound needy. But then she thinks, It's not being needy. If you have a good time with someone, it's natural to want to do it again. It doesn't mean you're in love or anything.

'I'm just saying we had fun,' she says. 'That's all.'

'I wanted to see if I could make someone happy,' he says. 'At least for one night.'

'You can,' she says. 'You did.'

Someone was happy. Someone loved it more than she had allowed for. Someone is now wanting it not to end.

'Nick, if you're going away, does that mean I should leave too?'

'No, not at all,' he says. 'I've spoken to Peggy. The room's yours as long as you want it.'

'So I'd be in the house alone?'

'Actually, I think Peggy's planning on coming back any day now. Maybe tomorrow.'

This is all so strange. He speaks in a matter-of-fact voice, as if it's the most natural thing in the world, but she's never met Peggy, and Peggy was his wife, and she is or was his lover, however briefly.

'There's something else you should know,' he says. 'Tonight's meant a lot to me. You've been wonderful. Everything I could have wished for. Thank you.'

'Thank you too, Nick.'

Then for no reason at all she starts to cry. She stops herself as soon as she realises it's happening, and snuffles a bit, and dabs away the tears.

'Too much champagne,' she says. 'I'm falling apart.'

'Let's go up.'

She sleeps with him that night in the big bed in the master bedroom. They make love without words, holding each other close, and for the moment it's as if they're dancing again. Then they sleep.

In the morning she wakes to find herself alone. She gets up and goes downstairs. The yard door is open, the screen door propped back with a duffel bag. Nick is carrying stuff out to his truck.

She stands shivering in the cold breeze, watching him load his life into the truck. Then he's done and he comes and gives her a goodbye kiss.

'As easy as that?' she says. 'Load up. Move on.'

'As easy as that.'

'You take care of yourself, Nick Crocker.'

'You too.'

He climbs into the cab and drives off. As easy as that.

Alice shuts the door, goes into the kitchen and brews herself a pot of coffee. When the coffee starts to trickle into the jug she starts to cry. There's no one to see her so she doesn't try to stop herself. She cries and cries.

Fuck you, Nick. How come it turns out I'm in love with you after all?

19

As interest in the poems of Emily Dickinson grew, Mabel Todd, their editor, began to receive requests to give talks. Her first lecture was at the Springfield Women's Club. She began with an account of Emily's life as she understood it, then spoke of her struggle to get the poems published, and concluded by reading some of the poems aloud. She was gratified to discover that she was a natural speaker. The rapt attention of an audience brought out the best in her. It was both a performance and a presentation of her real self. All agreed that the evening was a great success.

At her next talk, to the College Alumni Club of Boston, Austin was in the audience. He looked on with pride as she enthralled her listeners, among whom were several newspaper critics.

'Now all the world will love you,' he told her afterwards.

'So long as you love me,' she replied, 'that's enough for me.'

But the acclaim did make a difference. Life in Amherst was

made harder for her every day by Sue's increasingly open hostility. Mabel begged Austin to confront his wife on the issue.

'I'm sure she believes that if she can make me miserable enough you'll give me up and go back to her.'

'She's a fool if she thinks any such thing.'

'Have you spoken to her? Have you told her in plain words that you love me in a way that you can never love her?'

'For pity's sake, Mabel! How can any man say such a thing to the woman who's the mother of his children?'

'Then how is she to know?'

To Mabel it seemed so clear. For as long as Sue had hopes of regaining her husband's love, she would do all in her power to destroy her rival.

'My dearest darling, don't you see? You must talk to her. You must make her accept it's all over between you.'

'Well, well. I'll see what can be done.'

Austin did talk to his wife, though perhaps not with the frankness Mabel hoped for. He addressed her with angry pride, as her husband and lord and master. He meant to make it plain that it was not for her to question his conduct.

'I expect you, as my wife, to be civil to anyone I choose to call my friend.'

Sue responded humbly, glad of the chance to air the matter at last.

'I think Mrs Todd is rather more than a friend,' she said.

'And if she is, that is my concern.'

'And you, Austin, are my concern,' said Sue. 'I'm not entirely blind. I can see that this woman has bewitched you. I can see how much you admire her. You're such a good and upright man,

Austin. I pray that she doesn't take advantage of that goodness.'

'I can assure you,' he said coldly, 'that Mrs Todd is as good and as upright as you or I.'

'You are my husband,' said Sue. 'You are the one and only man in my life. All the love a woman has for a man I have for you alone. Mrs Todd has a husband too. Does she not love him? And if she does, what portion of her heart is left for you?'

'That is for Mrs Todd to say.'

He turned away, displeased.

'No, Austin, don't go. Please understand. I'm so afraid you're going to be hurt by her. Don't you see? Women like her don't love, they want only to be loved. By you, by her husband, by all the world.'

'I have nothing more to say on the subject.'

He reported this conversation back to Mabel with great indignation.

'David indeed! She seemed to think your feelings towards him were to be spoken of in the same breath as your love for me! What could I say? It made me want to take out your letters and read her passages aloud, and say to her, "That is love! That is devotion! That is the true sacred flame that can burn between a man and a woman!"'

'But you didn't, I presume.'

'What we are to each other,' cried Austin, in full flow, 'the height and the depth of it, the totality of it, how can there be any room left for any other love? But merely because in the eyes of the world he has the name of your husband, and because you continue to show him a proper respect, she presumes on feelings in you, and manipulations, and double dealings, and I don't know what!'

'Would it make your wife happier if I were to separate myself from David?'

'No! It would terrify her!'

'Then I don't see what I'm to do.'

Austin took her in his arms and kissed her.

'Love me as you do,' he said. 'Love me for ever, as I love you. There's nothing else either of us need do. This is everything.'

So she kissed him, and said no more.

Powerless to alter the status quo, Mabel and Austin dreamed of escaping it together. Whenever they were able to steal time alone, they drove in Austin's carriage round the neighbouring hills, in search of the ideal plot of land where they could build a secret home. They dressed up this fantasy with every kind of detail. Their love nest was to be on a hilltop, commanding immense views of the landscape, so that they could watch the sun and the rain sweep from valley to valley. It would have open porches on all four sides, where they could sit and listen to the crickets. Austin would have a room for his work and his books; Mabel would have a room where she could sit undisturbed and write her lectures. There would be a cosy living room, with two comfortable chairs before the fireplace. There would be a curving staircase, and at the top a light pretty bedroom, and a bed that they would share.

They talked about their house as if the building of it could begin any day, and waited only on the finding of the perfect spot.

'I shall decorate the walls with stencils,' Mabel said. 'With patterns of trees, and birds.'

'I'll want a good stable,' said Austin. 'Tom and Dick must come with us.'

They considered plots in the Leverett hills, and by Mount Holyoke, and across the river in Whately and Deerfield. It was a way of believing that there was a future waiting for them, in which all the obstacles to their love had fallen away. Sometimes, for Mabel in particular, the image of their house on the hill was so clear in her mind that it was almost as if it already existed. But it was no more than a dream. In reality, their times together were stolen, and all too brief.

In compensation, Mabel's new career as a lecturer blossomed. Her talks on Emily Dickinson, given in private houses and public places, were turning her into a minor celebrity. She was invited to lunches and dinners, and began contributing book reviews to periodicals. Letters to Austin reported success after success.

Should have liked to have seen you in your cloud of glory Wednesday night,

Austin wrote to her,

and tomorrow night you dazzle them again. Well that is all right, but hadn't you rather be out in the woods with me?

As Mabel's life expanded, Austin's began to decline. He was not well. He was plagued by a persistent cough, which his doctor diagnosed as a problem of the palate. A small operation left him in agony, unable to swallow. Sue nursed him at home in The Evergreens, feeding him milk punch. Mabel found herself shut out, unable to see him or even get a letter to him.

Frantic with worry, she got her news from Vinnie, and by waylaying Dr Cooper on the streets of Amherst. She wrote notes and entrusted them to Vinnie, who smuggled them in to Austin on his sick bed. While the news remained uncertain she stayed in Amherst, waiting on the bulletins, unable to read or work. Then as word came that Austin was improving, Mabel found Amherst unbearable again. She could not endure that Sue saw him, nursed him, comforted him, while she herself, his true love, had all doors closed against her. She left for Boston, plunging herself into a round of lectures, starting with the New England Women's Club.

Austin recovered. Mabel returned to Amherst. They met as they had done in the early days of their love, in the dining room of the Homestead, where Vinnie now lived alone. They sat side by side together on the black horsehair sofa, holding hands, murmuring aloud their old prayer.

'For my beloved is mine, and I am his. What can we want beside? Nothing!'

Mabel was shocked and frightened to see how weak he had grown.

'If you need to return to your bed, my darling, you must do it.'

'But how am I to see you?'

'It doesn't matter if we don't see each other for a while. All that matters is that you get well again. If that means I must leave you to *her* care, then I do it gladly. Let her nurse you back to health, and to me.'

Austin returned to his sickroom. He was tired, but he found it hard to sleep. He had no appetite, and suffered from frequent bouts of nausea. A new doctor, Dr Bigelow, described his condition as 'nervous exhaustion'. Austin found it increasingly hard even to write the notes he was sending to Mabel.

Mabel for her part wrote him daily letters in which she poured out her anxiety and love, but Vinnie no longer came to collect them, feeling unable to take the letters into the sick-room. Mabel kept writing anyway, telling herself that Austin would read them when he was well again.

In sympathy with his suffering, paralysed by powerlessness, she found herself also unable to sleep or eat.

David kept Mabel company, and joined in her prayers for Austin, and did his best to persuade her to look after herself. It was mid-August now, and a warm sun shone out of a deep blue sky, seemingly indifferent to the slow crisis unfolding in The Evergreens. David urged Mabel to go out in the fresh air, but she would not, choosing instead the protection of darkened rooms. She could not bear to walk the summer lanes. The woods and hills belonged to Austin, she had loved nature with him and through him. Without him the world was empty and cold.

Then the weather changed. Rain clouds rolled across the Connecticut Valley. The grey skies dressed the world in the sombre colours of her thoughts. As the rain passed, Mabel ventured out at last, on her own, and walked a little way up the Leverett road. She cried as she walked, but the wind dried her tears and she became calmer. To the east, in the distance, she could see rain falling over the hills.

'God save my beloved,' she prayed. 'God, make him well again.'

Then she spoke aloud Emily's lines, which she knew by heart.

'Oh God, why give, if thou must take away the loved?'

After praying she walked on quietly. Then she felt the warmth of the sun, and turning, found the clouds had parted to the west. Over the Pelham Hills rain was still falling. There was a shimmer in the sky, and a rainbow formed, clear and bright and beautiful. She gazed at it in wonder. Surely this was God's answer to her prayer! The rainbow seemed to speak to her, telling her God was merciful, there was hope yet, God smiled on their love.

No longer crying, she hurried home and said to David, 'He will get better. I'm sure of it.'

The next day Dr Cooper reported a distinct and surprising change in Austin's condition. His pulse was stronger. Hope was returning.

Mabel wrote in her long unsent letter:

10th August 1895, Saturday morning: My darling, my darling, I wonder if the time seems long to you since you held me in your arms, and if you would not like to have me come in now and kiss you, and take your dear hand in mine. I have solemnly promised God that when you are well again, and I feel your beloved arms around me again, and I know I have you safe, that from that hour I will live up to the best and highest there is in me, and make you happy as I never did before. Only God has a faint conception of how I love you – nothing human can compass such knowledge – unless you know. If you had died it would have been the utter end of my life.

Very slowly, but surely, oh my heart's beloved, you are getting back, and you will be in life again. How simple for me to come in and see you, and kiss you and love you into health! And yet

China is nearer in possibility. But my darling, get well and come back to me, and I will try not to repine at any circumstance. I belong utterly to you.

Tuesday morning, 13th August: Do you hear the crickets, *our* crickets, my beloved, at twilight? And when you hear them do you think of me? I sat on the east piazza last evening, listening to them, and again in front of the house, until it seemed to me you must be with me. Do you hear them, sweetheart?

Wednesday 14th August: Good morning, my dearest love! My heart has been with you all night, and will be all day. For my beloved is mine and I am his. What can we want beside? Nothing!

On August 16 1895, Mabel accompanied David to a centenary celebration in nearby New Salem. As they returned in their carriage at the end of the day they passed the gate of The Evergreens, and saw Vinnie coming out, head bowed. Mabel stopped the carriage to enquire after Austin. As soon as Vinnie looked up, and Mabel saw her white face, she knew the worst.

'He's gone,' said Vinnie.

Mabel felt her breathing stop. She was quite unable to speak. Vinnie hurried away along the high pavement. David ordered the carriage to drive on. He took Mabel's hand.

'I'm so sorry, puss.'

'I feel nothing,' said Mabel. 'Nothing at all.'

They arrived at The Dell. Mabel entered the hall, and saw

there Austin's hat on its hook. A convulsive shudder passed through her. Then at last the tears came. David held her in his arms and let her cry.

'Why is Mama crying?' asked Millicent.

'Her best friend has died,' said David. 'And my best friend too.'

Now that she had begun to grieve, Mabel was unable to stop. Her grief choked her, at times she could hardly breathe. Nothing David could say or do was of any comfort. She was inconsolable.

Millicent, left to her own devices, wrote in her diary:

This has been one of the saddest days that I ever passed in my life. Mama has been crying all day, and Papa has cried some and has looked so sad that I have been perfectly bewildered.

The funeral was set for Monday, August 19. Until then Austin's body lay in an open casket in the library of The Evergreens. Mabel knew that she was forbidden to enter the house, but in her anguish she appealed to Ned, who had loved her once. Ned took pity on her. He left the French doors to the library unlocked while the family was at dinner, and so allowed her a moment alone with Austin to say goodbye.

That evening Mabel wrote in her diary:

My Austin has left his dear beloved body and gone – I do not know where, but away, out of sight. I kissed his blessed cold cheek today and held his tender hand. The dear body, every inch of which I know and love so utterly, was there, and I said goodbye to it, but all the time I seemed singularly conscious that my own Austin himself was out in the sweet summer sunshine, more light-hearted and blithe and strong and hopeful than he has ever been before since he was a boy . . .

The town shut down for Austin's funeral. The service took place at The Evergreens. The coffin was interred in a grave in Wildwood Cemetery, his own creation. A great crowd followed the hearse, but the Todds were not among them. Mabel stayed home, reading and rereading Austin's letters to her, weeping ceaselessly.

To the scandal of the town she put on full mourning, with a black veil over her face, and Austin's ring on her finger beneath black gloves. In this way she announced to the world what she knew in her heart, that she was Austin's true widow. She longed to die.

I feel my eyes closing to Earth – and opening – to Austin. I want Austin – I agonise for him – I call for him, I reach to him. If only I could die this night!

The reality of his absence is so crushing that I start up from force of habit thinking I hear his dear knock – and his beloved garden across the street is so empty that it makes my physical heart actually ache to look over there. The dear old hat and coat he wore when he was browsing about among his shrubs and trees seem actually before me . . .

I try to be busy but I cry and cry and cry. My heart is dead and I want my body to be.

Apart from the letters of her dead lover, her only other recourse was to the poems of his sister Emily. Austin's death drew Mabel even closer to Emily. Here was one who by some sympathetic magic had known what it was to feel as she felt now.

> Pain — has an element of Blank —
> It cannot recollect
> When it begun — or if there were
> A time when it was not —
>
> It has no Future — but itself —
> Its Infinite contain —
> Its Past — enlightened to perceive
> New Periods — of Pain.

As for God, to whom Mabel had prayed, and who had given her false promise with a rainbow on the Leverett road, Emily had his measure:

> God is indeed a jealous God —
> He cannot bear to see
> That we had rather not with Him
> But with each other play.

20

Left alone in the house on Triangle Street, Alice sits in the kitchen drinking coffee, eating cookies, and thinking of Nick. She tells herself to get up and go to her room and work on her screenplay, or to go out into the town, or simply to move at all: but she remains, as if paralysed, at the kitchen table. To her horror she is gripped by a sensation she's never felt before, as if she's nursing an injury that's left a deep wound, only in place of physical pain there's this aching emptiness, this universe of regret.

I want Nick. I want him back. Bring him back to me.

Like an infant deprived of the breast: knowing only the intensity of her need, crying for the return of what has been lost.

She doesn't cry out loud. Instead her mind tortures her with memories that bring him before her, that return him to her so that she can lose him again and be hurt again. Fragments of things he said come back to her. Piecing them together she understands what she never understood at the time, and punishes herself for her stupidity. Again and again – she sees it now

– he was telling her how much life has hurt him, but she saw only what she wanted to see, his intelligence, his beauty. 'We all live our lives in hiding,' he said. In hiding from what? She never asked.

Forgive me, Nick. I had my eyes closed. I wasn't looking. All I cared about were my own needs. You told me I was beautiful. You told me you wanted to make me happy. What did I ever give you in return?

Now that he's gone she cries to have him back, cries inside herself, without tears. She wants to hold him in her arms again and kiss him, soothing his pain. She wants to be in the forest with him again, and this time when he asks for her love she'll give it, she'll lie down with him on the leaf-soft ground, she'll hold him closer than close.

Love me, Nick. Make love to me. Be happy with me. Find your joy in me. You're not alone.

'Who cried?' he said, when she told him about breaking up with Jack.

Why didn't I understand? Of course someone always cries. He knows that because he's one who's cried. That's what he was telling me.

I cried, Nick. I cried when you left me. I'm crying now.

Alice jumps up from the table, and clatters the crockery about in the sink, and is angry with herself.

This is ridiculous. This is shameful. A man twice my age, a man old enough to be my father, a man I've only known a few days. What nonsense is this?

Then into her mind comes the memory of the mirror in his bedroom, and the reflected image of herself naked in his arms, and it stops her breath. She gasps with the pain of it.

Hold me in your arms again. I've never loved like that before.

Oh God, why give if thou must take away the loved?

Who else is there in all the world who knows Emily Dickinson's poems as well as he does?

> *You left me – Sire – two Legacies –*
> *A Legacy of Love*
> *A Heavenly Father would suffice*
> *Had He the offer of –*
>
> *You left me Boundaries of Pain –*
> *Capacious as the Sea –*
> *Between Eternity and Time –*
> *Your Consciousness – and Me –*

She calls to him, calling him back. Look, Nick. Listen. Here's Emily again, putting into words what I can't say for myself. We each of us make ourselves an Emily in our own image. You told me that.

God help me, it's the understanding that devastates. You understood me. No one else does. Now that I've found it's possible, how am I to do without it? How am I to do without you?

> *A Door just opened on a street –*
> *I – lost – was passing by –*
> *An instant's Width of Warmth disclosed –*
> *And Wealth – and Company.*

The Door as instant shut — and I —
I — lost — was passing by —
Lost doubly — but by contrast — most —
Informing — misery —

His words keep coming back to her, mingled with the poems. Now, hearing him again, she wants to rip time apart, go back to the living breathing moment, play it again. Only this time she'll hear him truly, and give him true answer. For example: he told her her screenplay was about two lonely people who start loving for the wrong reasons, but their love turns into the real thing.

Is that what you want, Nick? Do you think it might happen with you and me? I want it to happen. Shall we try?

She remembers how he said the staff would clear up their dinner, and how she heard him later washing up all by himself. What was wrong with me? Why didn't I go down and help?

Because I thought I was the one in need, and he had all the power. He the older man, the irresistible one. I never thought to ask myself what fears haunted him in the night. In the day too, up in his glass-walled tower.

Forgive me, Nick. Come back to me and let me make amends. You told me but I didn't hear you. You said, 'I've none to tell me to but thee.' I'm listening now.

She is listening. There's a car pulling up outside. Her heart bounds. Is he back?

She hurries through the back door, through the screen door, to the yard outside. A Mercedes convertible stands in the drive. A tall elegant woman is getting out. Slim black trousers, silver-grey top, dark hair cut in a perfect bob. A pale face, not attempting to look young, but beautiful.

'Hello,' she says, turning, reaching out a soft leather bag. 'You must be Alice.'

'Yes, I am,' says Alice stupidly.

She feels badly dressed, ugly, ashamed. This is the kind of woman Nick could love.

'I'm Peggy. Nick's told me all about you.'

She smiles and shakes Alice's hand. Alice meets her eyes and realises this beautiful woman is looking at her with undisguised curiosity.

'I hope you don't mind me still being here,' she says.

'Not one bit,' says Peggy. 'Is Nick in?'

'He's gone. I thought you knew.'

She follows Peggy into the house.

'Nick's been going to go for weeks,' Peggy says. 'So he's actually done it, has he?'

She doesn't seem surprised, or in any way bothered. She parks her bag in the room Nick had called her office, pulls an iPad out onto the desk, plugs it in to charge.

'He left early this morning,' says Alice. 'He loaded up all his stuff and drove off.'

'Did he say where?'

'No.'

'Most likely he's gone to his cabin in Vermont.'

Peggy turns her full attention back to Alice.

'So you're the girl from England. You're working on some Dickinson project, right?'

'I'm supposed to be,' says Alice.

'You want a coffee? I've just driven from Boston and I need coffee.'

They go into the kitchen. For all her clattering at the sink Alice has not cleared up properly. She sees Peggy taking this in.

'I'm sorry,' she says. 'I didn't know you were coming today.'

'No problem,' says Peggy.

With a brisk movements she restores order, sets a pot of coffee to percolate, smoothes her cheeks with her hands, sits down at the table.

Then she gives this wordless interrogative look. She just stares at Alice, head cocked a little to one side, seeming to say: So?

Alice feels an absurd urge to confess everything. Peggy looks so smart and so kind, it's hard not to believe she knows it all already. But Alice controls the impulse.

'I really appreciate being able to stay here,' she says.

'Nick told me you have mutual friends back in England.'

'Yes, that's right.'

'And when do you go home?'

'Friday.'

'I'm just here for a couple of nights. I have a dinner in town. Then I'm off on my travels again. So you'll have the house to yourself.'

'It's really good of you,' says Alice. 'It's such an amazing house.'

'Yes, it is,' says Peggy. 'It's very special. It was built by my great-grandfather. But I don't use it enough, to tell you the truth. And now that Nick's gone, if he really has gone, I can't see myself keeping it.'

'You think he might come back?'

'I don't know.' Again that searching look. 'You probably know better than me.'

'He said he was moving on.'

She can't help herself, her voice gives her away. Just the smallest catch in her throat.

'Moving on?' says Peggy drily. 'Yes, that's Nick.'

Peggy's phone rings and she takes the call, cup of coffee in hand, to her office. Alice hears her there, making further calls, her voice brisk and decisive. It's past noon by now, and Alice is just beginning to realise she's hungry when Peggy reappears.

'Got any plans for lunch?'

They walk up the road to the Lord Jeff Inn.

'It's not so bad,' says Peggy. 'You can hear yourself talk there.'

They sit at a corner table in the hotel restaurant. They talk about Mabel and Austin. Peggy knows all about the affair.

'So who's going to play Mabel?' she says.

'Oh, it'll probably never get that far,' says Alice.

'Has to be someone very sexy, don't you agree? I mean, she really threw poor old Austin a loop.'

'I think maybe he was ready to be thrown,' says Alice.

'I guess he was. He didn't get much action with Sue, as far as we can tell.'

'I don't think it was just about sex,' says Alice tentatively. 'He seems to have had an awful lot of emotion penned up inside him, waiting to break out.'

'And boy! Did it break out!'

'How much do you think Emily knew?' says Alice.

'Please!' Peggy lifts her elegant hands, disclaiming expertise. 'I'm no scholar. I read the book about the affair, and I've forgotten half of that. All I can remember is they both kept up this great wail about how their love was holy and blessed and God was up in heaven rooting for them.'

Alice laughs.

'There is rather a lot of that.'

'But you buy it, right? I guess you have to if you're making a movie out of it.'

'I believe they loved each other, yes. But people love each other for all sorts of reasons.'

'You don't think they, oh, I don't know, worked it up? How could they stay so hot for each other for so long?'

'It's because they weren't ever able to settle into any kind of regular routine,' says Alice. 'Their love was always forbidden, always secret, always stolen. That's where the heat came from.'

'Lucky them,' says Peggy. 'We don't have any secrets any more. Nothing's hot.'

'I've been trying not to think that.'

'Oh, I'm most likely wrong. I'm fifty years old, and by the time you get to my age you learn to settle for less, I guess. I've seen too many passions cool. Nick being only the most recent.'

'How is it with you and Nick? Or would you rather not talk about it?'

'No, I'm fine talking about it. How is it with me and Nick?' She wrinkles her brow and smiles at Alice.

'I'll tell you, but first I have to ask you to tell me. How is it with *you* and Nick?'

'Me?'

Alice blushes a deep red, which says it all.

'Believe me, sweetheart,' says Peggy, 'I know Nick well enough. He's a very attractive man, and he's free to do as he pleases. I just hope he hasn't left too much of a mess behind him.'

'No, no, not at all,' says Alice. 'I mean, there's nothing, nothing at all. That is . . . oh God, I feel such a fool. I'm so embarrassed.'

She can feel tears pricking at her eyes.

'Hey, hey!' says Peggy. 'No need for that. I'm not accusing you of anything. I just don't want him hurting you, is all.'

'No, he hasn't hurt me. He's been lovely.'

Her face tells the story she can't bring herself to tell.

'But you've gone and fallen for him,' says Peggy.

'Just a little,' says Alice. 'Just the smallest bit. It'll pass. I'm not usually such a fool.'

'No more of a fool than me. I fell for him.'

'Yes, I suppose you did.'

'I was crazy about him,' says Peggy. 'He's a beautiful man. He's sensitive, he's sexy, and he can actually read. What more could a girl ask? OK, so he's not faithful, he can't help himself in that department, but that's like inheriting money, you know? It's no good keeping it all for yourself. You have to share.'

Alice watches her as she speaks and thinks how beautiful she is. No wonder Nick loved her.

'You really didn't mind?'

'Yes, I minded. Of course I minded. But I could handle it. Why wouldn't he want to fool around with twenty-year-olds? I'd do it myself, only I don't get the offers.'

'So what made you break up?'

'You really want to know?'

'Yes,' says Alice. 'If it's not too private.'

'Oh, I don't mind telling you as far as that goes. But I don't want to rain on anyone's parade. I don't own Nick any more. I've no call to go round telling other people what's wrong with him.'

'Even so. I'd like to know.'

There's almost no one else in the hotel's dining room. Peggy has a Caesar salad and Alice has a bowl of soup, and they sit on at their table long after they've finished eating, and Peggy tells the story of her marriage.

'At first I thought it was the money that was the problem,' she says. 'It usually is money that's the problem. Nick never made much, and then his course was cancelled, or not renewed, or whatever. I said to him that money shouldn't be an issue because I had plenty, and what was I supposed to do with it? I'll say this for Nick, he's never really wanted stuff himself, smart clothes, fast cars, all of that. He's some kind of ascetic, I guess. So it wasn't the money, and it wasn't the affairs. It was something else that began to get to me.'

She's gazing across the table, but for once her eyes are unseeing, her thoughts elsewhere.

'I remember,' she said, 'sitting at dinner with him, at home, I guess, the house on Triangle Street. He was across the table from me, the way you are now. He wasn't speaking. And suddenly I got this really strong sensation that a door had closed in him. So I said, "Nick, what is it?" And he said, "What's what?" And I said, "You're shutting me out." And he said, "I'm not shutting you out." And I said, "I feel like I can only get so far with you and no further." And he said, "How much further do you have to go?" And I said, "All the way." And he said, "No one goes all the way. There are parts that are unreachable."'

She shrugs, and spreads her hands in the air.

'That's what he believes. He really does. He believes every-one's alone.'

'Maybe he's right,' says Alice.

'Maybe he is, but it began to get to me. You know he's kind of antisocial? Maybe you don't. He doesn't like parties, he won't go to them. I have to attend a lot of functions, one, two a week. He just wouldn't do it. We had a few rows over that. Does that sound petty to you?'

'No,' says Alice.

'It got worse. He became more and more like a recluse. You know he loves Emily Dickinson? Have you worked out why?'

'Why?'

'He wants to be her. He identifies with her. He wants to be the myth, and never be seen, and have everyone talk about him. The only trouble is, he's not a genius, and he doesn't write poetry.'

She puts her hand to her mouth and shoots Alice a guilty look.

'I'm being bitchy, aren't I? You have to stop me.'

'I don't want to stop you,' says Alice.

Everything Peggy is telling her about Nick she's checking against her own experience of him. Some of it connects. Not all.

'I get what you say about him wanting to be a recluse. But I haven't picked up that he thinks he's a genius, or wants to be a myth.'

'So maybe I'm wrong. All I can tell you is there's some deep damage there, and he's not letting anyone in for a look. He's a wounded beast, and he creeps off to his lair to hide.'

Alice thinks of how Nick said to her, 'We all live our lives in hiding.'

That connects.

'In the end I realised, or I thought I realised, Nick doesn't want to live in the world. He's more than antisocial, he's anti-life. I'm not anti-life. I didn't want to be sucked down into his lair. I didn't want a solitary life. It may be shallow, but I like to be among people. I like parties. I like doing things to make the world just that bit better than it might otherwise be. Nick thought all my charities were basically a form of therapy for me. He never believed anything I did was worth the time or money beyond the feeling of worth it gave me. That's because he doesn't believe you can make the world any better. He's a pessimist. He thinks our task is to accept and endure. So we had rows about that, big rows. I said he was ducking his responsibilities, he said I was kidding myself I made any difference. It went down from there. Then one day I said, "Are you coming to this dinner?" I was Chair of the Governors, I had to make a speech, this was a big night for me. And he said no. He said, "That's your life, not mine." So that was it. That's when I knew it was over.'

'How did he take that?'

'I think he was relieved.'

'And after that,' says Alice, 'you stopped having rows and got along just fine?'

'Of course. Sweet as pie.'

Alice thinks about Jack. How well they've got along since they broke up.

Peggy says, 'Does any of that make sense to you?'

'Yes,' says Alice. 'What you're telling me is Nick doesn't know how to love. Or can't handle it. Or won't.'

'You got it.'

'That's a bummer.'

'Not for me,' says Peggy. 'I'm out the other side. But you – you've gone and fallen for the jerk, haven't you?'

Alice nods. She's no longer blushing, no longer ashamed. They've both been in the same war zone.

'Not what I had planned, I can tell you,' she says.

'You've only had a few days. You'll get over it.'

'Of course I will,' says Alice, 'but you know what scares me? I'm scared I'll go through the rest of my life thinking that he was the one that got away. That he was the real thing. That nothing else comes close.'

'Trust me,' says Peggy, 'the guy's a disaster.'

She gazes across the table at Alice with concern and sympathy in her eyes.

'You said he's most likely gone to his cabin in Vermont,' says Alice.

'That's my guess.'

'Could you tell me where it is?'

'So you can pay him a visit?'

'Maybe just one.'

'Isn't that like the alcoholic who says, "Just one more drink"?'

'I can't leave it like this,' says Alice. 'He really will turn into a myth.'

'Keep away,' says Peggy. 'I don't want to be the one who drives you over the cliff.'

'I'm driving myself,' says Alice. 'You can't make my mistakes for me. I have to make them for myself.'

A long intent look. Then Peggy takes a pen out of her bag and a little notebook, and writes directions.

'There's no address. You go up I91 into Vermont, turn west onto Route 25, then north onto Kimball Hill Road. Five or six miles, and look out for his truck. It'll take you three hours, maybe less. You have his cell? His phone'll be off, but you can try.' She adds the number. 'He's not going to like it. The beast does not like being tracked to its lair.'

'The beast is going to have to deal with it,' says Alice. 'If you start something, you have to finish it.'

But for all her brave words, Alice is afraid. If she goes chasing after Nick, what can she expect from him? They've said their goodbyes. He owes her nothing. What is there left to say?

I'm hurting, Nick. Please make the hurting go away.

She leaves the house, walks up the road to the cemetery, wanting time to think. She sits on the grass by the railings round Emily's grave, as if being so close will transmit to her some of the poet's resilience. But the grass is damp and the grave is silent.

She phones Jack. She's tapped his name before she can stop to consider the cost. When he picks up, she hears the buzz of voices in the background.

'Where are you?'

'Alice?' She can hear him moving away from the noise. 'I'm in the pub.'

'Can you talk?'

'Yes. Are you OK?'

'Not really. Nick's buggered off. I'm feeling a bit blue. I need your advice.'

'Try me.'

'Should I go after him?'

'What for?'

'I don't know. I just feel terrible. Like it hasn't properly ended.'

'Oh. That.'

'Sorry.'

'Oh, Alice. You do sound low. What a bummer.'

She hears someone calling to him, a shrill woman's voice. 'Jack! Come back!' She hears Jack say, 'Won't be a mo.'

'Who was that?'

'One of my colleagues.'

'I should let you go.'

'So where's he buggered off to?'

'Somewhere in Vermont. A cabin in the woods.'

'All by himself?'

'As far as I know.'

'And you want to show up at his cabin and say what, exactly?'

'I know. It's stupid and pointless.'

'No, it isn't. It's Act Three. You want your final act.'

'Something like that.' She realises as she speaks that it's exactly like that. She doesn't want any particular outcome, just a proper sense that things have run their course. 'But this is real life, Jack. It's not a story.'

'Stories are real life. If they're any good.'

'So you think I should go?'

'Go, girl. Do it. Act Three, a Cabin in the Woods.'

She feels herself smiling.

'You're kind of brilliant, Jack. How do you always know the right thing to say?'

'We'll see about that. Let me know how it goes.'

'I'll be home soon. Will you be down in Sussex at all?'

'Half-term. See you then.'

Again the distant cry: 'Jack! Jack, come back!'

Over there in England he says, 'Coming!' And to Alice in New England, 'I'd better go.'

Alone that evening in her borrowed room Alice does what she swore she would never do. She goes onto Facebook and stalks Jack. She finds a picture he's posted of a crowd of teachers at the opening of his school. Standing right behind him, one hand touching his shoulder, there's a young woman with a mass of curly brown hair. She's smiling too much.

21

A thick mist lies over the interstate all the way into Vermont, through Brattleboro and Bellows Falls. As Alice follows the route north into this featureless white world, her courage ebbs away and she tells herself she's a fool. What does she expect Nick to say? How can there be any other outcome but humiliation? But just past Hanover the mist clears, and she finds herself dazzled by colour: reds and purples and oranges splashed with abandon as in a child's painting, against a backdrop of tawny yellow and dark umber. This is the famous New England fall, in the second week of October; no relation to the tasteful modulations of an English autumn. Her spirits rise. Her speed increases. What does it matter how Nick responds? This is for her. What right has he to sidle away into myth?

Face the music, Nick. Finish the dance.

Just before Bradford she takes the junction at Route 25, and drives north-west up the Waits River Road. The blazing woods fall away, and she follows the river through straw-coloured farmland. Slow out of the little town of West Topsham, hunting for the right turn into the hills. Back into the trees, the road climbing, the forest closing in: and there it is, Kimball Hill Road.

These are remote parts. Hard for anyone raised in a crowded little island to credit how empty America can be. Mile follows mile with no visible habitation. Tracks lead off into the trees, there may be dwellings up there, who can tell? The people who choose to live in these woods are not neighbourly types.

She's down to twenty miles an hour, crawling along the road, afraid to miss her destination. She passes a cabin set back from the road, but it's closed up, there's no vehicle pulled alongside. A mile or two on and there's another cabin, this time with smoke leaking out of the cinder-block chimney. She's driven by when she looks in the mirror and sees the red Dodge truck parked on the far side.

A cabin of weathered planks, roofed in shingle, sitting on an apron of dirt up a rise from the road. Behind it, like embracing arms, the woods stand guard. It's small, surely no more than a single room, with a rain butt to the side of the narrow door. No light shows in the windows.

Alice reverses and turns off the road. She half expects the door to open, but there's no sign of life. She gets out of her car and looks more closely at the red truck. It's Nick's, no question. Why hasn't he heard her arrival? With her engine switched off the silence is startling. Perhaps he's asleep.

She hesitates before the cabin door. Now that she's here her presence feels clumsier than she had intended. But what can she say? I happened to be passing by?

Nothing to be done. She's not going back now.

Her knock on the door is unanswered. She looks in at the

window. A table strewn with books, some chairs, a kerosene lamp. No one home.

She tries the door, and it opens. Inside the cabin is suddenly warm, making her realise she's grown cold. A black-iron wood-burning stove is alight, glowing red through its scorched window. She stands close to it, warming her hands, looking round.

Just the one room. A basic kitchen at one end, an open gas ring for cooking, a sink. A long table in the middle, with his books spread round the lamp. Shelves on the timber walls. More books. A bed at the far end, covered with a thick rug woven in orange and black. Through the windows nothing but trees.

No fridge. No TV. No electricity of any kind, as far as she can see. No bathroom. He must wash in the sink. There must be an outhouse of some sort, for a lavatory. Or does he squat in the woods?

The undignified image makes her laugh, breaking the solemnity of this first encounter. The cabin's simplicity daunts her. Is it really possible to live this way?

She checks the books open on the table. *Don Quixote*, which he was reading when she first saw him in Rao's Coffee House, the bookmark now almost at the end. She hadn't stopped to think back then, but there's a clue here. Don Quixote is a fantasist, isn't he? A romantic. One who invents his life to make it more significant than it actually is. Not that she's ever read any more than the first chapters.

That's what we do with love. Create a story to overlay the passing events of our lives so that a pattern emerges. What was random develops meaning.

Love as story-telling.

Austin Dickinson as Don Quixote, Mabel his Dulcinea, the peasant girl he has willed into playing the role of princess of his dreams. So where do the windmills come in? All the great unfeeling world outside the dream, all of reality that denies the dream, there stand the giants against which he must forever set his lance.

So is Nick just another more recent incarnation? The fantasist who finds that real life disappoints him, and so retreats into a story?

On the table beside the book there's a tin tobacco box, worn by much handling. Alice has never seen Nick smoking. A secret vice? She picks up the box and it rattles. She opens it. It's full of small cream-coloured oval pills. So Nick pops pills: another surprise. To get high? To get to sleep at night?

She tries calling his cell, but an automated voice tells her his number is unavailable. She goes outside and calls his name out loud, feeling foolish, scanning the surrounding trees. No one answers. She thinks of leaving a note, but decides against it.

So this is how it ends.

On the drive back she feels increasingly angry with him. It's taken more courage than she's admitted to herself to make this journey. Last night she slept badly, agitated by thoughts of seeing him again. And now – nothing. No resolution. He seems able to switch her on and off as he finds convenient, but she can't switch off.

As she turns at last into the yard of the house on Triangle Street, she sees that Peggy's car is gone. A man is standing by the back door, peering through the screen: a small bald man in leather jacket and jeans. When he turns, hearing Alice's car pull up, she sees the handlebar moustache and recognises Nick's friend Luis Silva.

As she gets out of the car and locates her door key, he hurries to her side.

'I'm trying to raise Nick,' he says. 'He's not answering his phone.'

'He's left,' says Alice. 'He's moved on.'

Silva looks startled.

'Is that what he said? Moved on?'

'He's gone to his cabin in Vermont.'

'Oh.'

This information seems to trouble him. He doesn't ask Alice what she's doing here. It seems only polite to explain.

'He's been letting me stay in the guest room. Peggy was here, but it looks like she's out right now.'

'Did Nick see Peggy before he went?'

'No.'

It strikes Alice then for the first time that Nick left on the morning of Peggy's return. Had he known when she would be coming home?

'Had you arranged to meet Nick?' she says.

'Not exactly arranged.'

But something's clearly not right.

'You want to come in for a coffee?'

He checks his watch.

'Maybe for a moment.'

He follows Alice into the house. Peggy has left a note on the kitchen table.

How was the beast? Back late. Peggy.

Silva reads the note, and makes the connections.

'The beast? You've been to see Nick?'

'Yes,' says Alice, putting on the coffee. 'He wasn't there.'

'He didn't answer the door?'

'The door wasn't locked. I went in. All his stuff was there, but no sign of him. I guess he was out walking in the woods.'

'Fuck,' he says. He sits himself down at the kitchen table and puts his chin in his hands. 'He was your lover, I suppose.'

'I really don't see—' But catching the expression on his face, she stops. 'What's the matter?'

'Nothing. I hope I'm wrong.'

'About Nick?'

'He's such a fucking fatalist. Sorry.'

'Don't mind me. I know he's a fucking fatalist. What is it you're afraid of?'

'I'm afraid he'll play his Get Out of Jail Free card.'

Alice brings the coffee to the table, with a carton of semi-skimmed milk from the fridge.

'Black? White? Sugar?'

'Just black. Thank you so much.'

'What does that mean?'

Silva sips at his coffee. The rising steam from the mug glistens on his moustache.

'Nick's a lovely man,' he says, 'and a much-loved man. But he's also a fucking idiot. He doesn't believe in his own right to happiness. Perhaps there's no such right. Whatever. Nick has to take it one step further. He believes in the inevitability of loss.'

'Loss of what?'

'Loss of hope. Loss of love. Loss of meaning. Nick believes we start out with a surplus of vital energy, which is youth, and it's this energy that gives us the illusion of hope and meaning. Then the energy runs out, and the illusion fades. At some point we discover there is no hope or meaning. Life continues, but without joy. And so the time comes, according to Nick, when the wise man chooses to call it a day.'

Alice feels herself go cold.

'You mean, commit suicide?'

'Get out of jail free.'

'Seriously?'

'Sure. He told me many times that he was only able to bear the indignities of life because he had his exit route all prepared.'

Die again. Then you'll be free.

'How?'

'He has pills. He's collected them over the years. He's shown me.'

'In an old tobacco tin?'

'Yes.'

Alice's heart is now pounding. Fragments of the last few days come bursting to the surface of her mind, bearing frightening new meanings.

When we become bored, we begin to die.

I'm not going anywhere.

I wanted to see if I could make someone happy.

'I saw his pills,' she says to Silva. 'They're on the table in his cabin.'

'Did it look like he'd taken some?'

'I don't think so. Anyway, he wasn't there.'

'He'd have gone off into the woods. There's a spot he loves there, he told me. The top of some hill, with a big view.'

Alice shudders.

'Do you really think he'd do it?'

'Yes, I do.'

'How can we stop him?'

'Stop him?' says Silva sharply. 'Why? I have no right to stop him. Nor do you. Life is not a duty.'

'Isn't it?' says Alice, feeling stupid.

'If he's made the decision, there'll be letters in the mail. He promised me. I'll get a letter.'

But will I? thinks Alice.

Silva rises.

'There's nothing to be done,' he says. 'We each have our own lives to live.' His eyes fall on Peggy's note on the table. 'Nick is not the beast. He's an honest man. There are few enough left. If he really has played his last card, I shall miss him.'

So he goes. Alice is left in turmoil. Her first instinct is to get back into the car and drive back to the cabin. But what if she's too late? Does she want to be the one to find him? That's Peggy's right, surely. Or Peggy's duty.

Life is not a duty.

Is that true? Does Nick owe it to her, or to anyone, to go on living?

She searches for a phone number for Peggy, but finds nothing. And even if she were to find it, what would she say? It may all be a fuss over nothing.

Except it is exactly that: a fuss over nothing. Kill yourself and you put yourself on the side of the nothing. She feels the anger rising. Of course Nick has a duty to live. We all have a duty to live. We're something, not nothing. He's physically fit and healthy, he's part of the human race. He's not in jail. Death is not freedom, it's annihilation.

She wants to tell him so, to his face. Call him a coward. Call him a deserter. And if he still insists on his right to surrender this most precious gift, then . . . then . . .

He can write me a fucking letter too.

Suddenly she knows she's going to go back. The morning's long over. Her return journey will be in darkness, which she hates. But it can't be helped.

She plays the radio as she drives, searching through gospel preachers and country music until she finds a station that plays oldies. She fills the car with the sounds of the Andrews Sisters and the Beatles, as she retraces the road to Vermont.

We're in a chain, Nick. We all help each other. We pass it on. If you give up, it makes it harder for the rest of us.

Now that she knows the route it seems to pass faster. She's on the road that climbs between trees long before she expects it. Then she's rounding a bend and there it is, the cabin with the smoking chimney. The red Dodge truck.

He can't still be wandering the woods. It'll be dark soon. He must be in the cabin. Alive or dead?

It seems ridiculous to ask so melodramatic a question, but she saw the pills with her own eyes. His Get Out of Jail Free card. If he has the pills out, he must be thinking of taking them. Maybe he has taken them. What does she do then?

She tries to think clearly. Have a plan. Be prepared.

Drive to the nearest town, find someone to report to, the police presumably. There'll be an investigation. It could mean she misses her flight home.

Getting out of the car, she feels scared. Not of Nick's suicide, but of the dead body. She's never seen anyone dead before.

She goes first to the cabin window, and looks in. And there

he is, sitting at the table, large as life. He looks up and sees her. He frowns. He's up, and the cabin door opens.

'What the hell are you doing here?'

At once the terrors melt away, and she feels foolish.

He's wearing a padded jacket and hiking boots. A line of stubble darkens his jaw. His voice is hard, angry.

She says, 'I wanted to see you.'

Her own voice is timid, appeasing, like a child.

'You've seen me. Now leave me alone.'

He goes back into the cabin, slamming the door hard behind him.

Now she's angry again. After her fears for his life, after her long drive, she deserves better. She bangs on the cabin door. She opens the door and marches in. He's bending over the wood-burning stove, taking logs from the stack by the chimney to feed the dull burn within. He straightens up and turns to her, his face flushed.

'Now what?'

'I've had a long drive,' she says. 'The least you could do is offer me some coffee.'

'Coffee?' He seems surprised by the proposition. 'Then you'll go?'

'Yes.'

She sits herself down at the table. The old tobacco tin is still there, beside his book. He moves about the cabin, knocking into chairs. His body is saying, I want to barge you out of my way. I want to tread on you. He goes to the sink and runs water from the tap into an iron kettle. It sounds like pissing.

He makes the coffee with a filter cone and a jug. It strikes her that this is not the backwoods style. Somewhere he must have a stash of paper filters.

'What's so funny?'

'Nothing. You. Living here like Davy Crockett. Reading Cervantes.'

'There's no milk,' he says. 'You want milk, you get back in the car and drive to Topsham.'

'Black is good.'

He brings the mugs of coffee over to the table. Lights the lamp with a cigarette lighter he pulls out of one pocket. She drinks the hot bitter liquid and is strengthened. She thinks, I won't be bullied. Let him be the first to speak.

He drinks his coffee in silence. Then –

'I suppose Peggy told you.'

'Yes.'

'She should have known better.'

'She told me not to come.'

'So why did you come?'

'Unfinished business.'

With each moment that passes she's losing her initial embarrassment. She can see it now, in the way he won't look at her, in the restlessness of his hands. He's not angry, he's frightened.

'Nothing ever gets finished,' he says.

'Do you have some kind of lavatory here?'

'Outside.'

She goes out into the twilight. There's a small privy behind the cabin, with a wooden seat over a bucket. Beside the seat is an orange tub full of sawdust. No toilet paper.

'I can't use that,' she says, returning. 'There's no paper.'

'It's in a box. To stop the mice shredding it.'

'I thought maybe you used the sawdust.'

'No. The sawdust goes into the bucket when you're done. When the bucket's full you put it outside for a few months, and it turns into manure. There's only me here. It takes a while to fill up.'

'So now I know.'

She sits down at the table facing him. They look at each other properly for the first time, and neither of them speaks. She picks up the tobacco tin.

'Your Get Out of Jail Free card.'

'Who told you that?'

'Your friend with the moustache.'

He takes the tin from her and opens the lid. It's full of pills. 'See? Untouched.'

'But you have the tin out.'

'I like to keep it where I can see it.'

'Might you use it?'

'I might. Not that it's any of your business.'

'Am I that insignificant in your life?'

'Yes,' he says.

'I don't believe you.'

He gives a shrug that says: believe what you want.

'You wanted to see if you could make someone happy,' she says. 'And you did make someone happy. And that someone was me.'

'And now I have to pay for it.'

'Am I asking you for anything?'

'How do I know? You're here. I didn't invite you. You must want something.'

'Well, for a start, I want you not to kill yourself.'

'Why? What use am I to you?'

'You made me happy.'

'And now it's over.'

'Don't you get it, Nick? We're all in this thing. We have to support each other. Why can't you leave me with a sweet memory of a lovely man who made me feel great about myself, even if only for a week?'

'I'm to go on living so you can have a warm feeling?'

'Pretty much.'

'Well, at least you're not telling me it's for my own good.'

'No, it's all entirely selfish. I've only thought of myself from start to finish.'

He has the grace to smile at this.

'What we had was just a bit of fun, Nick.' She's lying but it's necessary. 'I'm really only here because we never said goodbye. Not properly.'

'You're here to say goodbye?'

'You know how it is. Every story has to have a happy ending.'

'What would a happy ending look like?'

'I'm not sure. But there has to be a kiss.'

He smiles at that too. And as he smiles she sees again the frightened child that lives within him. What is it that's made him so afraid?

'When you go home,' he says, 'what will you tell Laura?'

'Does it matter?'

'No, not really. It's just that I'm not all that proud of what I've become. I used to be better.'

'How long ago is it?' she says.

'Thirty years. More.'

'Long time.'

'Long time.'

'I'll tell Laura,' says Alice, 'that we had some good times together.'

Then they're both silent. What's he doing, hiding in the woods? This lovely man with so much to give.

'Your friend with the moustache told me you have a favourite spot in the woods,' she says. 'A hilltop with a view.'

'That's right.'

'How about you show it to me, before it gets too dark.'

'It's a bit of a climb.'

'How long?'

'Fifteen minutes, maybe.'

'Let's do it. Then I'll go.'

She wants to get him outside, into the twilight. Then they can talk without seeing each other's faces.

'You promise you'll go?' he says.

'Are you scared I'll move in with you?'

'It has happened.'

'Not with your plumbing.'

So he puts on an oilcloth trapper hat, and Alice buttons up her coat, and they set off. There's a trail running through the trees behind the cabin, up the flank of the hill. They walk in single file, Nick in front, and for a while they don't talk. It's very dark in the trees.

'So what's the idea, living out here?' says Alice at last. 'Apart from killing yourself, that is.'

'Out here,' he says, 'I have no phone, no internet, no newspapers. I don't even have a mirror in the cabin. I've stripped out all the distractions I can. I bring food with me, enough for a month. Then I settle in and talk to no one. Then after a few days, a week maybe, I start to feel like I'm standing on solid ground again. I've got away from the unreality.'

They're pounding steadily up the trail as he speaks. Alice listens. She wants him to do the talking.

'You're writing this love story. We all want to hear about love. But love isn't the big thing we make of it. It's just another part of the unreality. It's a mug's game. We can't win. We think there's someone out there who can make us happy, someone who'll make us complete, but that's not how it works. We think not getting what we want is the problem, but it's the wanting that's the problem. We want the whole world to feed us. Everything has to be fodder for the great open mouth. And this self we're feeding, it's insatiable. We can't satisfy it. There's no end to its hunger. We end up as slaves, chained to our hunger, doomed to service its bottomless need for ever. There's only one way out of that. You have to break the chain. You have to cut the self loose, let it go. That's when real life begins.'

So there it is: the Gospel according to Nick.

'You know what I feel most of the time?' he says. 'I feel disgust. I feel sick with unreality. I feel sick with self. So I come out here.'

He comes to a stop, breathing heavily. The hill has become steep. Alice says nothing, but she does understand. She thinks she does.

I, just myself, and because it is I. Was Mabel sick with self?

Now the trail opens out, the trees fall away, and they're on the summit. From here a great view reaches in all directions. Dun farmland and tinted forest beneath a dusk sky. They stand getting back their breath, breathing in the distance.

'What is it about views?' says Alice.

'It's a big world. A good view makes us feel small.'

'Why should we want to feel small?'

'Because we are.'

She gazes out over the land towards the faint light on the western horizon.

'Your friend thought this is where you'd come to die.'

'Could be.'

'How would you do it?'

'It's not complicated. You take the pills. You go to sleep.'

'But how exactly? Would you bring a flask of water? Would you sit down?'

'I suppose so.'

'Where?'

Nick looks round. He points to the one pine that stands on the hilltop.

'Back against the tree. Looking west.'

'Go on, then. Sit down.'

He gets what she's doing now. Shoots her a wry look from under the flap of his stupid trapper's hat.

'Where have I heard this line before?'

'Come on. Sit down. Back against the tree.'

He shakes his head, but he does as he's told.

'Now open the tin. Get out your flask. Put the pills in your mouth, two at a time.'

'You've thought about this.'

'Lot of pills to get through. You have to make sure they do the job. Swallow them down.'

He makes some token hand movements, miming taking pills, to show willing.

'Now wait for the drug to take effect. Will it hurt?'

'Shouldn't do.'

'So now you're getting sleepy. This is it, Nick. Sun's gone down, night's coming. All your troubles will soon be over. You're really cutting the self loose now. You'll be free soon. Free for ever.'

He gazes up at her, amused, full of admiration.

'You Dickinsons.'

'Shut your eyes.'

He does as he's told.

She claps her hands. The sound startles birds from the trees. His eyes open.

'That's it,' she says. 'Game over. Life goes on.'

'What do we do now?'

'We go back down the hill.'

He rises to his feet, shaking his head.

'You Dickinsons,' he says again.

He leads the way back into the darkness of the trees. Back down the track. Below she can see the glow of lamplight from the cabin window. Soon they'll get to the cabin, and her car. Soon she'll be driving south, and it'll be over.

I can't come all this way and not say it.

'After you left,' she says, 'I went a little bit crazy. We'd had a good time, and suddenly you were gone, and I couldn't take it. For at least twelve hours I convinced myself I couldn't live without you. Stupid, isn't it?'

'We did have a good time,' he says.

'But I'm not in love with you,' she says. 'It's not love.'

'Of course it's love,' he says.

There's the cabin before them now, smoke climbing from its chimney. There's the car.

She says, 'I want you to promise me something.'

'What's that?'

'If you ever take those pills for real, I want a letter.'

'I wouldn't know where to send it.'

'I'll text you my address.'

She's by the car now. Time to go. Don't string it out.

'So I did make you happy?' he says, wanting to be convinced.

'Yes, Nick.'

'There has to be a kiss.'

He takes her in his arms and they kiss. His stubble scratches her cheek.

'Bye,' he says. 'Again.'

'Bye, Nick.'

All the way back, driving from Vermont into Massachusetts, into the night, she doesn't think of him at all. She doesn't think anything.

22

The road out of Lewes passes under the brow of Mount Caburn, over Glynde Reach, over the railway line from Eastbourne, down to the Edenfield roundabout. Driving herself to Jack's home in her mother's car, Alice slips back in time and she's a child again, on her way down this same road to school. She feels again the scratch of her school kilt on her bare thigh, and the dread in the pit of her stomach. She hears her mother cursing the slow-moving traffic under her breath. She herself wants the journey never to end.

Those pitiful partings.

'In you go, darling. Just one more kiss, then.'

The feel of her mother's arms round her. The terror of the embrace coming to an end. The chill of being on her own.

Dear God, was it really so bad? A small country prep school run by kindly teachers. And yet printed deep in her physical memory is this sensation of stark fear.

She turns off the main road at the roundabout, and the ghosts of school hide their faces. Here, entering the village of Edenfield down the Newhaven road, she meets other memories, inherited memories, passed on by her grandmother, the one who now lives in France. This is the village where her grandmother grew up, in the very house to which she's now driving. Just one of the many cords in the net of time and place that hold Alice so tight: Jack's family home was once her grandmother Pamela's home.

Newly returned from Massachusetts, lovelorn and jet-lagged, Alice is in a fragile condition. Today is Saturday. On Monday morning she'll be back at her desk in Mortimer Street making up for the last two weeks. For two days only she can be her mother's little girl again, and put off the reckoning with adult life.

She turns right at the village shop, down the narrow lane past the line of council houses, past the field where they hold the village fete, and onto the unmade track that leads to River Farm. She parks in the yard by the barn. From inside the barn come banging noises and the occasional grunt.

Jack is not home. He's gone into Lewes on some errand, promising to be back in time for Alice, but he's not back.

Laura, his mother, says, 'It gives us a chance to gossip about Nick Crocker.'

Laura is still beautiful, now in her fifties. She leans against the Aga in the kitchen, waiting for a kettle to boil to make them tea, strands of loose blond hair falling across her face.

'Is he still breaking hearts?' she says.

'All the time,' says Alice.

'Even though he's got a wife.'

'They're getting a divorce.'

'Poor old Nick. So what's he doing these days?'

Alice is on the point of saying, He's been thinking of killing himself. But Nick so wanted Laura to think well of him. It's a small enough parting gift.

So she says, 'He's taken himself off to live in a cabin in the woods.'

'A cabin in the woods.' Laura busies herself making tea. 'Not so romantic when you're over fifty.'

Henry, Jack's father, appears looking red in the face.

'In case anyone calls,' he says, 'I'm in the barn chopping logs for kindling. Oh, hello, Alice.'

'All right, darling,' says Laura.

'But no one will call.'

He goes again.

'I don't know whether to be sorry for him or to say it serves him right,' says Laura. 'Nick, I mean. Not Henry.'

'He says he's trying to cut the self loose.'

'Oh, really. He doesn't sound as if he's changed at all. You know, for years I thought he was a bastard, but secretly I rather admired him for dumping me. Then he showed up here, and I realised he wasn't a bastard at all. Just . . . well, lost.'

'I think he has changed,' says Alice. 'Maybe he has. Actually, I wouldn't know.'

She becomes confused, and realises she's blushing. Laura gives her a quick look.

'Don't tell me he had a go at you.'

Alice says nothing, which is admission enough.

'You have to give him his due,' says Laura. 'He doesn't give up.'

'I'm embarrassed,' says Alice.

'Don't be,' says Laura. 'I've been there.'

She pours them both a cup of tea, and shakes out a packet of caramel chocolate digestives onto a plate, and they sit down at the kitchen table like a couple of teenagers.

'He used to be impossibly attractive,' says Laura.

'He still is,' says Alice.

'Has he looked after himself? I mean, he hasn't got all flabby, has he?'

'No,' says Alice. 'Not at all.'

'He had such a beautiful body. Oh God, I'm talking over thirty years ago now.'

'He's still in good shape.'

'And can he—' She breaks off, laughing. 'Listen to me!'

'He has strings of girlfriends,' says Alice. 'All younger than me.'

'Oh, honestly! When's he going to grow up?'

'You know,' says Alice, 'when I first met him I thought all of that, but I still wanted him to want me. What's wrong with me?'

'We're all the same,' says Laura. 'Henry says it comes down to status. We want the men that other women want.'

'But it's not just that. Please don't tell anyone I said this' – she means don't tell Jack – 'but for a day or two I was really crazy about him. Real full-on passion.'

'Me too,' says Laura. 'For a lot longer.'

'Does Henry mind about Nick?'

'Oh, Henry knows Nick's no threat. Even though I was never passionate about Henry the way I was about Nick. I was fond of Henry, and I felt safe with him. I knew he was in love with me, or thought he was. So there wasn't really any need for me to be in love with him. But guess what? With every year that's gone by I've loved him more.'

Alice thinks of the red-faced balding man chopping wood in the barn, and feels touched.

'But don't you miss the passion?' she says.

'Passion's all about anxiety, isn't it?' says Laura. 'With Nick, I was never sure of him. He never told me he loved me. I never felt worthy of him. I expected him to leave me every day. And one day he did.'

'But it works with Henry?'

'Yes. It works.' She waves a hand round the kitchen. 'We've made a world together. Raised children. Got history. That's strong stuff, Alice.'

They hear a car pulling up in the yard outside.

'That'll be Jack now.'

'You won't tell him, will you?' says Alice.

'Wouldn't dream of it.'

Jack comes in looking cross.

'Sorry, sorry, sorry. I've been in a bloody second-hand book-shop, where no one has a clue where anything is, trying to find a stupid book for a friend.'

'Why don't you just go online?' says Alice.

'I would, but I don't know the title, or the author. I'd know it if I saw it. It has a picture on the front of a boy on a wooden horse blowing a trumpet. The title has Christmas in it.'

'*Christmas with the Savages*,' says Alice.

Jack stares at her.

'That's exactly it. How extraordinary.'

'My mum used to read it to me.'

'I'm going to call Jenny right away. Get her off my back.'

He pulls out a phone, and moves away into the hall. Alice can hear him leaving a voice message.

'Jenny, I found it. Not the book, the title. It's *Christmas with the Savages*. It'll be easy to get online. See you Monday.'

Alice sees Laura looking at her, and gives a shrug of her shoulders.

'Funny the things you remember.'

She doesn't want Laura to see she's put out by Jack's pre-occupation.

'I'd better get back to my emails,' says Laura.

She goes as Jack reappears.

'That's that out of the way,' he says.

Then he just stands there, looking at her. Alice has a sudden sensation that everything between them has changed. It makes no sense, their history remains the same. Then it hits her. She's the one who has changed. Nick has changed her.

'So,' she says.

'So.'

He knows too much and too little. Where do you start?

'Mum's given you tea and biscuits, I see.'

He helps himself to a chocolate caramel digestive. Stands there in front of her eating it, dimly aware as he does so that it's bad manners, but wanting it too much. The biscuit crumbles in his hand.

'Do you have to be such a pig, Jack?'

'No,' he says. But he goes on eating.

'So who's this Jenny?'

'One of the teachers. We got into this thing about books we loved as children.'

'Does she have lots of curly brown hair?'

'Yes.' He looks startled. 'How do you know?'

'Facebook.'

'Oh. Right.'

'So is she a serious prospect?'

'A serious prospect? No, not at all.'

'I don't see why not,' says Alice. 'She looked pretty.'

'Yes, well.' Jack's face manages to finish his biscuit and express ambivalence at the same time. 'Look, how about this walk?' This is the plan they've made, to meet up for a walk on the Downs. 'Caburn or Edenfield?'

'You choose.'

He chooses what he calls the home walk, up Edenfield Hill. As soon as they're on their way the awkwardness between them drops away. They pass the big house and turn up the farm track. Climbing the hillside, walking abreast, they're able to talk at last.

'You really helped me, you know, Jack. What you said about endings.'

'I can't remember what I said.'

'You said to use the ending I've got. I started out thinking I was writing about Mabel and Austin. Now I think it's really about Mabel and Emily.'

'What about the love affair? What about sex in the dining room?'

'The love affair still happens. Only now I'm making Emily be the driving force. Austin was very timid and conventional. I like the idea that it was Emily who pushed him into the affair. Passion by proxy, sort of thing.'

'Listening at the dining room door.'

'Plus – and this is my latest idea – Emily wants to hook Mabel. She's spotted Mabel is the one she needs to champion her poems to the world. Which of course Mabel does.'

Jack's impressed.

'That's clever.'

'At the end I thought I could have Emily visit Mabel, just before Mabel dies. As a kind of ghost. She goes to her to thank her.'

'So all along Emily was seducing Mabel.'

'I have this sense that Emily had a will of iron. I think she was pretty ruthless in the way she made all the people round her serve her genius. Mabel was like her surrogate. She could have sex through Mabel. And Mabel could live on after her, and run her bid for immortality.'

'Which paid off.'

'That's my ending.'

'Well,' said Jack, 'so much for love. Trumped by poetry.'

'There'll be heaps of love. Heaps of sex. But that'll all be a subplot.'

They pass the swing trees, with the low curving branches. From here on the track becomes steeper.

'So how about the other love story?' says Jack.

Alice doesn't pretend not to understand.

'That one doesn't have an ending. It just stops.'

'Did you go to the cabin in the woods?'

'Yes, I went.' She means to leave it at that, but he does that teacher trick of his, leaving a space for her to tumble into. 'I don't know what to say, Jack. I think he's one of those people who only really knows how to be alone. I met his wife. His ex-wife. She says he's like Emily Dickinson, only without the genius. She could be right.'

'So he didn't ask you to share his cabin?'

'He didn't even want me in the door.'

'I'm sorry.'

The way he says it sounds like he means it. He can tell she's been hurt, and he feels sympathy, which is decent of him.

'Thanks, Jack. All my own stupid fault. God knows what I thought I was doing.'

'Having an adventure.'

'Yes. Something like that. You know, I had a really good talk with your mum before you got back. She was great. She said passion comes from anxiety.'

'We all want it, though, don't we?'

They're climbing up onto the brow of the hill, by the concrete triangulation point. A stiff breeze hits them, coming off the distant sea. They follow the top path that leads to Firle Beacon. To the south lies Newhaven, with its jetty reaching out towards France. To the north the green and grey plains of their world.

'You can see our house,' says Jack.

He points it out, in the angle between the main road and the river.

'Our house is somewhere out there too,' says Alice.

It's masked by the mass of Mount Caburn, but it's not so far away. You could walk from there to Jack's house if you were feeling energetic.

Jack points to the strip of faraway playing fields.

'Remember?'

The school they both attended, a decade and more ago. They can just make out the tiny figures of children racing about the cropped grass.

'Feels like another life,' says Alice.

'Down there, in that long field, that's where I saw the farmer kill your gran's dog. Toby Clore made me do that.'

'Whatever happened to Toby Clore?'

'God knows.'

'Did I ever tell you?' says Alice. 'I've got another grand-mother who lived in your house just after the war.'

'In our house?'

'They were called Avenell.'

'I never knew that.'

'And her mother was billeted in the big house in the war.'

Edenfield Place lies directly below them, a cascade of roofs and towers tumbling down to terraces and lawns and a bright lake. These days it's a country house hotel, with a conference centre and a spa.

'The grounds of the hotel, all round the lake, that was an army camp full of Canadians.'

It makes her giddy trying to fit all the parts together: as if she's not one person with one life, but many people, men as well as women, a human chain, all holding hands, going back into the past.

'Look, see Newhaven over there? That's where the troops set sail for Dieppe. Most of them died there, or were captured. My great-grandfather got the Victoria Cross there. And over in that valley is the cottage where the old artist killed himself, the one who painted your sister. My grandmother knew him when he was famous.'

Turning back, she faces the wind again.

'And over there's Seaford beach, where we sat on a bench and looked at the horizon, and said how we liked it because it went on for ever.'

She doesn't say it's where they had their first kiss. But Jack hasn't forgotten.

They set off walking again, their coats billowing in the breeze.

'All this story-making,' she says. 'The stuff you teach your class. What do you call it?'

'Narrative structure.'

'It's got a lot to answer for. We want life to be like stories and it isn't. There's no beginning and no end. We want there to be, and we keep looking, waiting for the story to start. But it started long ago, and we're in it.'

For a while they walk on in silence. They've not talked about how once they were lovers, and how they parted. The hurt and the guilt are past but not forgotten, just more links in the never-ending chain.

'You know, Jack,' she says, 'you wear really boring clothes.'

'Do I?'

'You should let me come shopping with you. I could do you a makeover. You could look great.'

He turns to her and gives her one of his sweet rueful smiles.

'You do realise it would still be me inside?'

'I can live with that,' she says.

23

The camera glides down a sunlit street, past white-painted houses where coral vine and morning glory climb trellised walls. The only sound is the slow wash of the ocean, a block to the south. This is Coconut Grove, Florida, and the year is 1932.

She sits in the shade of a green awning on the porch of a house called Matsuba: a lady in a broad-brimmed straw hat, a book resting in her hands, her eyes closed. The latch of the gate rattles in the still air as it gives way. Footsteps pass down the short path.

The lady in the straw hat opens her eyes. She shows no surprise.

'I've been waiting for you,' she says.

She rises slowly, with difficulty. She's old now.

'Come in,' she says. 'Out of the heat.'

She moves with a limp, slightly dragging her right foot. There's a parlour at the back, a cool white space with windows onto the green glare of a little garden. The old lady lives here alone.

'David's in a nursing home.'

She sits herself in a cane chair, arranges white cushions for her comfort.

'He spends his time devising a system for eternal life. He calls it Vital Engineering.'

A faint smile lights up her lined face. A glimpse of the beauty that once set hearts racing.

'I'm quite sure he'll outlive me,' she says.

She looks up shyly, searching for a face she has only ever seen in a photograph, the likeness of a sixteen-year-old girl. Instead she sees the ghost of a homely middle-aged woman, who bears a passing resemblance to a man she once loved.

'I shall die soon,' she says. 'I've always known we'd meet before the end.'

This is so. This is a visit of duty, and gratitude.

'My dear,' she says, not wanting to be thanked, 'everything I did, I did for love.'

But there have been casualties.

She takes her limp right wrist in her left hand, and lifts it and lets it drop. She has never fully recovered from a stroke over twenty years ago.

I have come to seek forgiveness. I asked for too much love, from too many. She understands me.

'There's nothing to forgive,' she says.

She points with her good left hand to the table before her, where there lies a book of poems.

'Austin left me long ago, but you have never left me. Not for a single day.'

She reaches for the book. Clumsily, she opens it to the fly leaf. Here she has written:

I've none to tell me to but thee

A true reader is a lover. This love story has now run its course.

'Read to me,' she says.

I take up the book and turn the pages, even though their author is long gone. As for this old lady, this vain and charming creature charged with the burden of a poet's immortality, she too will soon be gone. But the words remain. I read to her.

> *This is my letter to the World*
> *That never wrote to Me —*
> *The simple News that Nature told —*
> *With tender Majesty —*
>
> *Her message is committed*
> *To Hands I cannot see —*
> *For love of Her — Sweet countrymen —*
> *Judge tenderly — of Me*

Author's note

I have relied for details of the affair between Mabel Todd and Austin Dickinson on Polly Longsworth's superb *Austin and Mabel: The Amherst Affair and Love Letters of Austin Dickinson and Mabel Loomis Todd*. This is the source of most of my extracts from their letters and journals. I'm indebted to Polly Longsworth for her scholarly work, for her kindness and assistance to me when in Amherst, and for her further assistance in fact-checking my manuscript. I have added material from my own researches in the Todd–Bingham Archive at Yale, and from Mabel Todd's short story 'Footsteps'. For the rest, I have of course turned to my own imagination to recreate the scenes between the lovers.

My story is limited to the love affair, but relations between the Dickinsons and the Todds became complex and acrimonious in later years. Austin's will was disputed and Emily's legacy fought over in claims and counterclaims, in rival editions of the poems and in rival memoirs. A full edition of the poems was only published in 1955, in three authoritative volumes edited by Thomas H. Johnson.

I'm grateful to Jane Wald and the staff of the Emily Dickinson Museum for their kindness to me in Amherst, and for their openness to my project; and to Scott Ardizzone of Jones Group Realtors, Amherst, who first answered my questions about the houses in the town, and then gave me a personal guided tour; and to Libby Klekowski, who showed me round the Hills house at 35 Triangle Street, which has for many years been the home of the Amherst Woman's Club.

The fictional characters in *The Lovers of Amherst* have appeared in my earlier novels. Jack and Alice can be met at the age of eleven in *The Secret Intensity of Everyday Life*. Their tentative romance begins eight years later in *All the Hopeful Lovers*. The story of Alice's grandmother develops in *Motherland* and *Reckless*. Nick Crocker's past love affair with Jack's mother, Laura, and his attempt to rekindle that love, is told in *The Secret Intensity of Everyday Life*. The family tree on pp. 296–7 shows the connections between the characters who recur in the sequence of novels. Attentive readers will find many more seeds which I've planted, waiting for their turn to flower.

This sequence of six novels has been overseen by my matchless agent, Clare Alexander, and by my editor, Jane Wood. Jane's sensitive and thorough notes have guided and enriched the novels, and I'm more grateful for her stewardship than I can say.

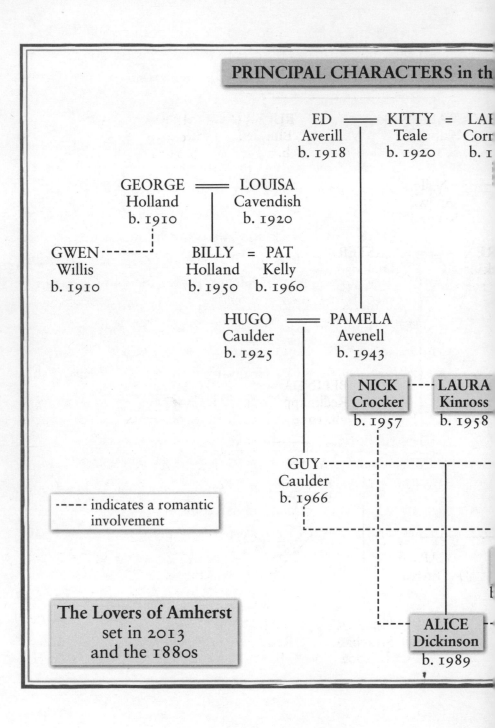

PRINCIPAL CHARACTERS in th

ED === KITTY = LAF
Averill Teale Corr
b. 1918 b. 1920 b. 1

GEORGE === LOUISA
Holland Cavendish
b. 1910 b. 1920

GWEN------- BILLY = PAT
Willis Holland Kelly
b. 1910 b. 1950 b. 1960

HUGO === PAMELA
Caulder Avenell
b. 1925 b. 1943

NICK ----- LAURA
Crocker Kinross
b. 1957 b. 1958

GUY-------
Caulder
b. 1966

----- indicates a romantic
involvement

The Lovers of Amherst
set in 2013
and the 1880s

ALICE
Dickinson
b. 1989

GERALDINE
Blundell
b. 1925

RUPERT = MARY
Blundell   Brennan
b. 1917   b. 1932

Nell
Shaw
b. 1926

REX ═══ ASTER
kinson   Dickinson
1920   b. 1930

HENRY
Broad
b. 1956

BELINDA ═══ TOM
Redknapp   Redknapp
b. 1956   b. 1953

LIZ ═══ ALAN   MEG ------- MATT
Dickinson   Strachan   Strachan   Early
b. 1968   b. 1971   b. 1975   b. 1968

CARRIE
Broad
b. 1991

MAGGIE ----- ANDREW
Dutton   Herrema
b. 1980   b. 1978

CASPAR
Strachan
b. 2002

CHLOE
Redknapp
b. 1989

Bibliography

'Footprints', Mabel Loomis Todd, *Independent,* 1883

Ancestors' Brocades, Millicent Todd Bingham, Harper & Brothers, 1945

Emily Dickinson: A Revelation, Millicent Todd Bingham, Harper & Brothers 1954

The Complete Poems of Emily Dickinson, ed. Thomas H. Johnson, Little, Brown, 1955

Emily Dickinson's Home, Millicent Todd Bingham, Dover Publications, 1967

The Life of Emily Dickinson, Richard B. Sewall, Harvard University Press, 1974

Austin and Mabel: The Amherst Affair and Love Letters of Austin Dickinson and Mabel Loomis Todd, Polly Longsworth, Farrar Straus Giroux, 1984

Emily Dickinson, Cynthia Griffin Wolff, Addison Wesley, 1986

Lives Like Loaded Guns, Lyndall Gordon, Viking, 2010